Miss Whittier Makes a List

Miss Whittier Makes a List

Carla Kelly

PRESS

Seattle, WA

Camel Press
PO Box 70515
Seattle, WA 98127

For more information go to: www.camelpress.com
www.carlakellyauthor.com

First published by Signet, an imprint of Dutton Signet. a division of Penguin Books USA Inc., 1994

Cover design by Sabrina Sun
Cover illustration by Artist

Miss Whittier Makes a List
Copyright © 1994, 2013 by Carla Kelly

ISBN: 978-1-60381-897-1 (Trade Paper)
ISBN: 978-1-60381-898-8 (eBook)

Library of Congress Control Number: 2012953736
Printed in the United States of America

With love to fellow charter members
of the Low Maintenance League:
Marty Abell, Helen Abell,
and Liz Kelly.

I mean to go in harm's way.

—*John Paul Jones*

Books by Carla Kelly

Fiction

Daughter of Fortune

Summer Campaign

Miss Chartley's Guided Tour

Marian's Christmas Wish

Mrs. McVinnie's London Season

Libby's London Merchant

Miss Grimsley's Oxford Career

Miss Billings Treads the Boards

Mrs. Drew Plays Her Hand

Reforming Lord Ragsdale

Miss Whittier Makes a List

The Lady's Companion

With This Ring

Miss Milton Speaks Her Mind

One Good Turn

The Wedding Journey

Here's to the Ladies: Stories of the Frontier Army

Beau Crusoe

Marrying the Captain

The Surgeon's Lady

Marrying the Royal Marine

The Admiral's Penniless Bride

Borrowed Light

Enduring Light

Coming Home for Christmas: The Holiday Stories

Marriage of Mercy

My Loving Vigil Keeping

Non-Fiction

On the Upper Missouri: The Journal of Rudolph Friedrich Kurz (editor)

Louis Dace Letellier: Adventures on the Upper Missouri (editor)

Fort Buford: Sentinel at the Confluence

Chapter One

Not until the third morning out of Boston did Hannah Whittier discover that she cared whether she lived or died. The brig *Molly Claridge* wasn't pitching any less, but as she lay in her berth with her hands folded across her chest, she realized that her stomach was no longer ricocheting about from her big toe to her shoulder and back again. It stayed right in the center of her body, where it belonged, and when she pressed the flat of her hand against her middle, it growled back.

"Thank goodness for that," she said to the ceiling. Or was it the deck above? Her brothers would tease her if they knew she could not remember nautical nomenclature. Her first attempt at dining two nights before had been a disaster of shocking proportions. But how was she to know that the jelly would quiver so, in time with the motion of the ship? That, combined with the greasy smell of pork roast, borne in by the ship's cook and set before her with a flourish, was sufficient to send her stumbling down the companionway and out onto the deck, where she knelt and retched until the bile ran.

There were no more attempts at table. For two days, she wrestled with her stomach in the peace of her tiny stateroom, determined to die without an audience, and most especially not those sailors who had winked at each other as they swabbed up her stomach's complaints from the deck. There was no cause for more humiliation. She would die and let it go at that. The ship's sailmaker could sew her into a canvas bag, and then drop her over the railing, where she would drift slowly down and commune with the fishes.

She smiled about it, now that her stomach was settled, and snuggled with a sigh into her berth, which rocked gently from side to side with the motion of the *Molly Claridge*. Papa had warned her about the motion. "For all that thee is well acquainted with little skiffs, Hannah, thee will be on the ocean, and that is a different matter," he had warned in a series of last-minute admonitions before the *Molly* put to sea.

Hannah had laughed at him then. "I can only be grateful that thee is not here," she said out loud, and then gave the matter further reflection. No one needed to know how disgraceful had been her conduct, not unless she chose to tell them. Hannah flopped comfortably onto her side and doubled the pillow under her head. It was rather like the first day of dame school, when she was six, and her brothers had already graduated to the celestial exaltation of the Lattimer Street School. No one was there to tattle on her. If she chose not to tell Mama the events of the day, Mama had no way of knowing; or Papa, either. "I will let thee think I am a proper sailor," she said, "and Hosea, too, when he greets me in Charleston."

She thought of Hosea, stiff and serious with responsibility when she last saw him on the dock at Nantucket. That was four years ago, when he was newly minted from Harvard, and embarking on the creation of another branch of Whittier Mercantile in Charleston. Mama and Papa had attended his wedding in that far-off city, and returned with tales of the new Mistress Mercy Whittier. "For all that she is a Friend, as we are," Mama had told her, "don't those Charleston Quakers have a flair!"

"Flair. That is what I need," Hannah declared. She leaped out of the berth, bracing herself as the ship rolled, and moved carefully to the little shaving mirror tacked to the wall, no, bulkhead, by the porthole. She peeked in, wondering what the ravages of seasickness had done to her bloom.

"Oh, dear," she whispered, and crept back into the berth. The bloom was quite gone. Her chestnut hair was still much too curly for a Quaker miss, and her brown eyes just as big, but that sprinkling of freckles across the bridge of her nose that she so detested looked quite green, when contrasted with the paleness of her face. "So much for flair," she moaned, and threw the covers over her head.

With the optimism of seventeen, her depression lasted only until she grew too warm under the blanket. She flopped it back, and reflected that a heavy meal and a turn about the deck would put her back in proper trim. "But thee still will not have flair, Hannah Whittier," she said. "That is not a birthright of New England Friends."

She thought again of Hosea's wife, now approaching the final month of her confinement. Hosea had summoned his little sister south to help out when the baby came. "For I know that Hannah will do all things proper, and provide Mistress Whittier with needed succor," he had written. Hosea is so formal these days, she thought, remembering the letter. It must come from writing in ledgers too much. She thought then of Mama's lecture on where babies came from, and was reassured that Hosea surely must have heard it, too. What a relief to know that he was not proper all the time.

She remembered the lengthy postscript to his letter, suggesting to Papa that his only daughter could likely contract an advantageous alliance of her own amongst the Friends of Charleston. He even mentioned the earnest Makepeace Thacker, who owned the town's largest sailmaking establishment, a "man of certain consequence in these parts," as Hosea had written. "He is a widower of some five years, and just the man to provide Hannah with that steadiness thee wishes for as a good match for thy daughter."

"Bother it," Hannah said succinctly, remembering her disappointment when Mama showed her the postscript. Of all the qualities in a husband that she and her friends had giggled about when Mama thought they were sewing samplers or reading improving works, steadiness was not high on the list. "I think it makes Mr. Thacker sound rather like a mule or a family retainer," Charity Wilkins had sniffed. Of course, Charity was engaged to Counsel Winnings, who probably never had a wild thought beyond whether to have white bread or brown with his mutton.

Perhaps Hosea would introduce her to someone more dashing than the redoubtable Makepeace Thacker, she thought, and then rejected the idea. Older brothers could be almost more prickly about such matters than fathers. No, depend upon Hosea to make her acquaintance with every boring, careful, parsimonious, devout, unentangled Friend in Charleston.

She gathered herself into a tighter ball, wondering what it was she wanted. I am seventeen, she thought, and should have settled on a husband by this time. She listened to the water whispering against the hull of the brig, lulled by the sound of it, but far from content. If I expect a husband to drop onto the deck who meets all my requirements, I have windmills in my head, she thought. But what is it I want?

She sat up suddenly and looked about for her journal. She found it on the deck near the door, where the brig's motion must have flung it. Hannah retrieved it and got back into her berth, sitting crosslegged. She turned to her last entry, the one written as seasickness descended. "Oh death, where is thy sting?" she read out loud. "Silly me."

She shook her head over her own folly, and tore out a blank page from the journal. The stub of a pencil was still jammed in the binding. She removed it and held it poised over the paper. "What I wish in a husband," she wrote at the top, and then paused to consider, thinking of all those whispered conversations with her friends, all the giggling and the blushes.

He should be handsome, she thought, and wrote that at the top. If he had blond hair and brown eyes like Adam Winslow, I would not mind, and if his shoulders were broad, that would be sufficient. I do not want him to be too tall. I am short, and I dislike skipping to keep up with people. It is not dignified, and Mama says it is high time I thought about dignity.

She added that to her list, and then paused again. He must be patient and slow to anger, like Papa. Her eyes misted over as she remembered when she was five, and Papa, to the scandal of the neighbors, taught her to swim. "I care not what others think," he told Mama when she objected. "I will not have my daughter at the mercy of the water." Yes, any husband of hers must be a patient teacher, and not liable to shout over inconsequentials. It went onto her list, with one underline.

He should be kind, she thought, dabbing the end of the pencil with her tongue, and writing the word. I must always know where I stand with my husband, and I must never have cause to fear him.

She drew her knees up and rested her chin on them. He should like children, because we will probably have plenty of them about. There would be daughters to train in all the domestic arts, which Mama had so laboriously drilled into her, and sons to follow his profession.

Hannah frowned, looking down at the page. He must have a respectable profession, if our sons are to follow after him. "There will be no whaling captains, or seafaring men of any kind," she murmured. Nantucket was full of children who saw their fathers only every four years or so, when a ship returned, full to the bumpers with sperm oil gleaned in faraway whaling grounds. Her older brother Matthew was a whaler, and Hannah knew the agonies of shyness his children suffered as they became reacquainted with a father they scarcely knew.

She thought about the redoubtable Makepeace Thacker, and his Charleston sailmaking establishment. Perhaps Hosea was right, she admitted to herself. *I insist that my husband stay on land, even if he makes sail, or rope.*

"Devout," she wrote next, feeling a little guilty that it was so far down on her list. She reminded herself that Mama never needed to know about the list anyway. She considered the matter, and then moved it up a notch. *My husband must take his worship seriously, like Papa and my brothers.* And no swearing, she wrote, underlining it twice.

What was left? She read over her list. *He must love me excruciatingly,* she thought, but she did not write it down. Hannah flopped onto her stomach, the list still in front of her. Mama never spoke to her of love, but she saw how Mama's eyes lighted up when Papa came home every night, or most especially when he returned from a buying trip to Boston. Hannah smiled to herself. Mama and Papa would always find an excuse to go upstairs early after those Boston trips. *Yes, he must love me and none other.*

But it was more than that, she realized as she rested her head on her arms and closed her eyes. *He must put my welfare before his. I must be the most important thing in his life.* She opened her eyes and added, "My welfare first." Written on the page, it looked so selfish that she added, "And I will esteem him equally."

She stared at the list and could think of nothing more to add. *I am seventeen,* she thought. *By a year from now, I will probably be married.* She folded the list and placed it back in the journal. *And I will be a long time married, so I had better take a careful look about me.*

But now her stomach was beginning to growl again. Surely it was near noon. For the longest time she had been smelling salt pork and beans cooking somewhere on the *Molly.* Perhaps if she dressed, she would be in time for a meal. She would eat whatever was put before her, and spend the afternoon on deck, watching the waves and looking for dolphins.

She dressed quickly, her mouth watering at the thought of food after days of self-imposed exile from a dining table. Her hair took longer to brush than usual, knotted this way and that as it was from several days of tossing about in misery. This is surely to teach me patience, she thought, as she worked the brush through her curly hair. "This is not Quaker hair," she announced to the little shaving mirror after a quarter hour's effort. She pulled it back and tied it at the nape of her neck—grateful that Mama was not there to bully her into braiding it—and twined it up on her head.

She also reconsidered her bonnet, and left it on the berth. There would be time enough, and to spare, to be proper in Charleston. Besides that, the sun looked so inviting, dancing like diamonds on the tops of the waves as the *Molly* cut a shimmering froth. She wanted to feel the breeze on her face, unhampered by a bonnet.

Hannah picked her way carefully along the narrow companionway, moving slowly to retain her balance, and already marveling at the sound of sailors moving quickly on the deck above. How long did it take to be so surefooted, she wondered, as she concentrated on keeping upright.

The ocean breeze snatched at her hair immediately, and whirled her curls about her face. She turned to face the sun, and took a deep breath, celebrating her release from the murky soup that passed for air below deck. She looked up at the sails bulging with the wind, squinting against the brightness of sail and the deep blue of the sky.

"Thee is among the land of the living, eh?"

She turned around and curtsied to Captain Aaron Winslow. "Oh, yes, sir," she replied, dimpling up nicely. "And I do apologize for my indiscretion at table two days ago." She leaned forward with the familiarity of one addressing an adult friend since childhood. "And don't tell Papa."

Captain Winslow laughed and led her to the railing, where

he rested his elbows, and gazed out at the water. "Now, now, Hannah. Thee knows I cannot tell a lie." He grinned at her. "But what David Whittier doesn't know will not hurt him."

She smiled her gratitude at Captain Winslow, father of her dearest Nantucket friend, and looked at the water. "Where are we now?" she asked. "Are we close to Charleston?"

"We're getting there," he said, and turned back to squint up at the mainsails and bark an order to his first mate, who shouted something that sent two seamen into the riggings. "We're close to Chesapeake Bay. I'll feel better when we're around the Outer Banks."

"Pirates, Captain Winslow?" Hannah teased.

"Very like, Hannah," he replied, his voice serious. "If the *Molly* doesn't mind her manners, she could be overtaken by a British man-o'-war, and I could find half my crew impressed." He looked down into her eyes, and chucked her under the chin. "And then I would be so shorthanded I would have to send thee into the riggings to help us to Charleston!"

"I think that is perfectly beastly of the British," she said indignantly.

He nodded. "Aye, lass. Someone forgot to tell them that we won the War for Independence. I lost two able-bodied seamen to the British on my last coasting voyage."

He was silent then, gazing across the water. He looked back at her after a moment, and noticed the frown on her own face. "But never thee mind, Hannah Whittier! I do not mean to frighten thee. Two days more, and thee will be greeting thy brother Hosea." He tugged at her curls. "And wearing thy bonnet again?"

She blushed. "The sun tempted me, Captain Winslow. Don't...."

"... tell Papa!" he finished and they laughed together.

The noon meal, eaten below deck in the officers' mess, stayed safely in her stomach where it belonged. The pork was too salty for her complete satisfaction, but Captain Winslow assured her that at least the biscuit was not weevily yet.

"I could tell thee of voyages where the weevils turned our biscuit to powder," he said, and then raised his quart mug of tea to his lips.

Hannah began some reply, what, she couldn't remember, even seconds later. As she sat there with her mouth open to speak, the bosun's whistle, urgent and shrill, sounded down the companionway. Captain Winslow slammed his mug of tea to the table and half rose to his feet as a cannon roared.

Her heart in her mouth, Hannah leaped to her feet. Already at the door, Captain Winslow turned back to her, even as he motioned to his first mate to follow. "Stay here, Hannah!" he ordered as he pounded along the companionway, the mate at his heels.

Hannah ran to the porthole and looked out. She could see nothing but ocean, beautiful and blue green. The *Molly* continued as before, serenely cutting through the water. Hannah looked down, expecting to find seawater rushing in from a hole below the waterline. There was nothing. And then she heard men running onto the deck.

Bother this, she thought to herself. She hurried into the companionway and climbed the ladder that led to the deck. She crouched there, not quite on deck, then sucked in her breath and covered her ears with her hands as a cannon roared again.

"Don't think for a minute that I will not board you, you ignorant Yankee."

The voice came from far away, shouted across the water as if through a speaking device. All was silent on deck, and then she heard Captain Winslow's voice, sounding weary beyond his years and with an urgency that she could not mistake. "Back the sails, lads, smartly now."

She ventured further onto the deck and seated herself on the grating of the cargo hatch, her eyes wide with wonder at the sight before her.

A ship bore down on the *Molly Claridge,* a ship with gunports open and cannon pointed at the little brig that was backing to a stop, the sails luffing overhead. As she watched, sailors on the other deck reloaded the deck gun, a carronade pointed directly at the brig. The acrid smell of powder sent a shiver down her back, as a man on the opposite quarterdeck raised his speaking trumpet again, this time directed at his own crew.

"Prepare to board! Ready with the grapples!"

Captain Winslow turned away in disgust, unable to bear the sight, as the sailors on the other vessel swung out with their grappling hooks and dug them into the *Molly's* railing. Hannah tried to make herself small on the grating, but the captain did not order her below. Instead, he came across the deck and sat down beside her.

"Thee does not need to fear," he said to her in a low voice as he watched the ships swing together, and then motioned his own crew down from the riggings. "Think of this as something to tell thy brother when we pull into Charleston,"

"What is happening?" she asked.

"My dear, thee is about to see His Majesty's Royal Navy impress my crew."

Chapter Two

Captain Winslow gave her shoulder a reassuring pat, then stood up and straightened his coat as the captain of the other vessel leaped gracefully onto the deck of the *Molly Claridge*, followed by other sailors and a lieutenant of Marines. She watched in dumbfounded amazement as other Marines in red coats climbed into the riggings of their own vessel and trained their muskets down onto the deck of the *Molly*, which bobbed below them in the water.

The captain strode across the deck, nodded to her, and stood in front of Captain Winslow.

"Captain, I am Captain Sir Daniel Spark and this is His Majesty's frigate *Dissuade*. I am requiring and requesting that you turn over to me all deserters from His Majesty's Royal Navy."

"I have none on board," Winslow growled.

"I think you do," Captain Spark replied, biting off each word as though born to command. "I demand that you summon your crew and have them show me their papers." When Winslow said nothing, he looked over his shoulder at the carronade, which was now reloaded and pointed at point-blank range. "Well now, sir?"

Wearily, Winslow motioned to his men who stood about the deck, talking among themselves in guarded tones, and then glanced up at the Marines in the *Dissuade*'s shrouds. "Line up and show them your papers, lads."

"Good of you to be so obliging," said the captain.

With a growing sense of stupefaction that someone without a by-your-leave could so coolly commandeer a ship of another country, Hannah sat with her hands balled into tight fists and observed this intruder to the *Molly*.

He was tall, impeccably dressed in the white pants, white vest, and blue coat of the Royal Navy, and rendered even more imposing by the high fore-and-aft hat he wore. I wonder how he keeps those trousers so white, she thought, fascinated in spite of herself. Gold epaulets fringed both shoulders, proclaiming him a full captain. His face was mahogany-colored from constant exposure to the sun, with weather wrinkles around his eyes and mouth. He was thinlipped and grim, with a straight nose. From his buckled shoes to his hairline, he was well built, but without an ounce of fat anywhere that she could see. In any other setting, she would have thought him a magnificent specimen.

"Dear me," Hannah whispered under her breath, making herself smaller on the grating where she sat.

She thought she spoke softly, but he turned toward her, raising one eyebrow in a scrutiny that lasted only a brief moment, but which seemed to go on and on. His eyes were the cool blue of ice rimming a deep winter pond, and stood out distinctly in contrast to his tanned face.

He cleared his throat. "If there is something about me you see that does not meet your scrutiny, please let me know." His words were crisp and lively with command.

Hannah blushed and looked away from him, raising her chin proudly and gazing out beyond the rigging to the port bow.

There was a long pause, as though he waited for an answer. Reluctantly, she looked back at him.

"Well!" he asked her, one eyebrow raised.

"I think thee is a perfect beast," she replied as distinctly.

"Oh, does thee?" he replied, his voice heavy with mockery. To her further dismay, the lieutenant of Marines standing beside him laughed out loud.

One glance from the captain's disconcerting blue eyes ended that outburst and turned it into a cough. The captain directed his gaze next at Aaron Winslow, who stood beside his men lined on the deck.

"Sir, Lieutenant Ream here will examine your crew's papers. If anything is out of order, he will seize that party and return him to the Royal Navy, where he belongs."

Winslow made no reply. The Marine made his way down the line of seamen while Captain Spark stood ramrod straight, eyes ahead, taking no notice of Winslow. The Marine read each paper carefully, then stopped before the sailing master. When the man did not hand over his paper, he tapped his chest. "You there," he barked.

The sailing master stepped forward, forcing the Marine to back up. He turned smartly and faced Captain Spark. "Elijah Cogburn, late of the *Temeraire*."

Captain Spark allowed himself a tiny smile. He strode to the sailing master. "I thought I recognized you, Cogburn," he said, his voice mild, but with that hint of sarcasm that Hannah was already beginning to loathe. "We thought you jumped ship."

"I found a better berth, sir," Cogburn replied, eyes straight ahead. "And a better country."

Captain Spark came closer, until Cogburn was forced to take a step backward. "May I remind you—all of you—once an Englishman, always an Englishman!"

The sailing master made no reply. At a small gesture from the captain, two sailors sprang forward and hustled Cogburn to the ship's railing. He looked back at Winslow, the bare pleading evident on his face. "Captain Winslow! Can you do nothing?"

Her heart wrung out, Hannah scrubbed savagely at the tears in her eyes. She knew she should not say anything, but something deep within her compelled her upright. In a moment she was standing beside Captain Spark, who regarded her with faint amusement. She looked up and up to his face, and nearly lost her courage, staring into those unsettling eyes.

"What gives thee the right to do this thing?" she raged, amazed at her own temerity, even as she spoke.

"The right of the Royal Navy, and I might add, a man who has guns and muskets trained on this deck," he replied coolly. He glanced at Captain Winslow. "I suggest you retire this little termagant below deck or I might be tempted to use her for chum and troll for sharks!"

Hannah gasped. "Thee is despicable!"

"I certainly am," he roared back. "Now sit back on your grating before I paddle you!"

She did as he ordered, not doubting for a moment that he would have turned her over his knee. Tears came to her eyes once more as the Marines in the shrouds and the sailors on the opposite deck laughed. She sat as tall as she could, while tears of rage and humiliation streamed down her cheeks.

After a moment, the Marine lieutenant continued his perusal of citizenship papers. He pulled out an Irishman and two Canadians, then saluted to Captain Spark. "That's it, sir," he said, showing him the papers.

Spark read them quickly and nodded. He looked back at another officer still on the deck of the *Dissuade*. "Mr. Lansing, have we need of any others?"

"Two more, sir," Lansing hollered back.

His hands clasped behind his back, the captain walked up and down in front of the remaining Americans. He stopped in front of one sailor, Nantucket born and bred, and nodded to his lieutenant. The Marine grabbed the man and dragged him to the railing as he protested and tried to dig with his bare feet into the deck.

"By God," muttered Captain Winslow, his face white.

Captain Spark continued his stroll of the neck, stopping at last before Winslow's own son. "This one," he said to his lieutenant.

Captain Winslow leaped forward, shouting, as the young man cried out. "By God, sir, that is my own son! And this his first voyage! Has thee no heart?"

"None whatsoever, Captain Winslow. Take him aboard," the captain snapped. "Terms of enlistment are up when this ship docks in Portsmouth, and not one moment before." He tipped his hat to Captain Winslow, who was held back in the iron grip of his bosun.

The impressed seamen were quickly bundled over the side and hauled up onto the other deck. Captain Winslow dropped to his knees and wept, his head in his hands. It was more than Hannah could bear. She jumped up again and ran to the British captain, who waited to reboard his vessel. She grabbed his arms and tried to pull him around.

"Thee cannot do this! Have we no rights?" She tugged his arm, but he was anchored fast to the deck and would not budge.

"You have no rights," he said quietly. "None whatsoever. You belong to an impertinent nation that will soon be a failed experiment. Let go of my arm."

She did as he said and wiped her streaming eyes with her sleeve. "I wish thee to hell, sir," she said, her voice as quiet as his and more fierce.

"Well I won't go, Miss Spitfire," he replied.

To her utter amazement, he grabbed her by the mass of hair on the back of her neck, hauled her close, picked her up, and kissed her. Her feet dangled off the deck and she grabbed onto him to take the pain off her hair, while he kissed her once, and then again more thoroughly. She clung to him, her head on fire, and tried to speak, even as he kissed her a third time, completely in command of the situation. Wild-eyed with fury, she stared at him, noting even in her rage how improbably long his eyelashes were. His eyes were closed, and he seemed to be enjoying himself immensely.

And then it was over. He set her back on the deck and released her hair. "I haven't had that pleasure in two years," he said softly. He stepped aside quickly in case she should strike out. "May I add that you needn't improve upon a fine thing?"

He sprang to the railing, his arm draped gracefully in the rigging to maintain his balance, and then leaped across the space between the ships as his men laughed and cheered.

"Release the grappling hooks," he ordered, and then looked at his first mate, who wiped tears of laughter from his eyes. "Wear the ship, Mr. Lansing, lively now."

As she watched in total humiliation and stunning fury, the sailors on the opposite ship grinned at her and released the grapples from the *Molly's* mutilated railing. The vessels moved apart quickly. Captain Winslow joined her at the railing and put his arm tight about her shoulder. He was shaking, and his face was as gray as a Nantucket winter sky. "Oh, lass," was all he could manage as the ships swung apart and the Marines climbed down from the riggings.

But there was Captain Spark on his quarterdeck again, a speaking trumpet to his mouth. "A word, Captain Winslow."

In pointed disgust, Winslow turned his broad back on the British officer.

"I advise you to douse your running lights tonight," called Captain Sir Daniel Spark. "The French are out and seem not to be asking questions before they open fire."

Winslow said nothing. At a word from his bosun, the remaining sailors fell to the ropes to continue their course toward Charleston.

"It's good advice," Spark called out, his voice much farther away now. "Good day, Miss Quaker. I hope we meet again."

"Impertinent bastard Englishman," Winslow said, his voice

drained of all emotion. He hugged Hannah close. "What am I ever going to tell my wife? She did not want Adam to go on this voyage."

Dinner that night was eaten in silence. Winslow toyed with his mutton and biscuit, then set his fork down, defeated. He bowed his head over his plate in silence until Hannah touched his arm. With an effort he looked at her, and pushed the plate away. "We'll be in Charleston tomorrow night, Hannah," he said, speaking for the first time, his eyes staring down again. "And then I do not know what to do."

"Captain, surely Adam will be all right, once that abominable ship docks in England," Hannah said.

"If he gets there alive. Thee does not know what happens on a British warship. I do not suppose there is a harder service anywhere."

The other ship's officers at the table nodded in agreement. "Why do ye think so many jump ship?" asked one of them of no one in particular. "Adam's a tender lad, and those jailbirds on the gun deck are a rough lot."

Hannah shook her head and put her finger to her lips, and the man was silent. The captain finally raised his eyes to the others. He rose as the bosun on deck whistled for the night watch.

"Are you going to douse the running lights like that wretched captain said?" one of them asked.

"No," was Captain Winslow's brief reply. He trudged from the cabin, and in another moment, they heard his footsteps on the deck above.

The other officers ate quickly then, talking among themselves, but always coming back to Adam and the other American crew member, captive now on a British vessel bound for England. When Hannah could stomach no more of their whispered conversation, she left the table and retreated to her own quarters. The bed looked better to her than it had in three days, even with the covers still rumpled from her tardy rising.

She wanted to crawl into the berth and pull the blanket over her head, and not emerge until they docked in Charleston and Hosea opened his arms to her.

Her own eyes dull, her heart sick, she removed her clothes and just left them in a pile on the deck. Too tired to look for her nightgown, she crawled into the berth in her chemise. Her head still ached where Captain Spark had grabbed her hair and pulled so tight. She massaged the spot, and then touched her lips, which felt bruised and swollen from their encounter with Captain Spark. A glance in the mirror earlier had told her they were nothing of the kind. He had not kissed her to hurt her, she had to admit, as she lay there in the dark and let the ship rock her toward slumber. Under other circumstances, she might have enjoyed it.

It galled her and threw her into the depths of humiliation to realize that her first kiss ever would come like that. She had hoped it would come from the man she loved, and not some captain of the Royal Navy too long away from a woman, any woman. She blushed in the dark, reliving the shame all over again. *I wonder if I will ever kiss another man and not remember that degradation,* Hannah considered.

It was a disturbing thought. She lay in her berth, hands behind her head, and allowed the gentle motion of the *Molly* to soothe her jangled nerves. As her eyes began to close, she thought of her list of all those qualities she required in a husband. "Well, Hannah Whittier," she spoke out loud, her voice drowsy, "there is one man thee can cross from any list. Captain Sir Daniel Spark is the last man on earth thee would ever marry." She closed her eyes and let the ship rock her to sleep.

Why she woke, hours later, Hannah could not tell, not then or ever. The *Molly* was making fair progress under a full moon, running smooth and swift toward Charleston. She was familiar by now with the creaks and groans of the well-weathered timbers, and the hum of the wind in the riggings.

Suddenly it was as though all sounds were suspended, and then superseded by an enormous roar of cannon.

The percussion tumbled her onto the deck, and she lay there, trying to collect her wits, as the *Molly* leaped like a wounded animal, and then shuddered to one side. Even as she lay there, doubled into a little ball with her hands over her ears, Hannah heard the shrieks of the wounded, and the crunch and groan of settling timbers.

She could not move. She gritted her teeth and waited for another explosion. When it came, she braced herself and closed her eyes tight, as if to keep out the horror. This time she heard the mainmast crash through the deck. The brig heeled sharply to one side as the sails and rigging from the mast dragged in the water and threatened to pull the *Molly* under. The deck slanted, and she slid hard against the berth she had left so unceremoniously only seconds before.

Hannah wailed in terror and tried to crawl toward the companionway. The force of the explosion had blown the door off its hinges. She could make out its vague silhouette, half in and half out of the companionway. She stared at the door stupidly for a moment, thinking how useless it was, lying there like that. She rose up on her knees and discovered they were wet.

In growing panic, she patted the planks. They were all wet with cold water that seemed to bubble up out of the hold itself. Dear God, she thought, her mind suddenly crowded with memories and thoughts long-forgotten, but rushing back now in a most peculiar review. Was this how it felt to die?

And then the thoughts were gone, leaving her almost exhausted. Her trunk floated by. I must get out of here, she told herself as she struggled to gain her footing on the deck, which continued to rise at an absurd angle. As she paused, someone grabbed her under the armpits and hauled her into the companionway.

"Hannah, is thee all right?"

It was Captain Winslow. She felt the wool of his soggy uniform against her bare skin.

She nodded, then realized that he could not see her in the dark. "Yes," she gasped. "Only let me find a dress, or something besides this chemise!"

"No time," he said, his voice sharp.

The companionway lay at crazy angles, with floating rope and boxes. The hanging lamp tilted weirdly, its flame extinguished. She shrieked as a rat ran across her bare shoulders, its feet digging into her flesh, and then mad with fear, leaped with a splash into the steadily rising water.

Somehow Captain Winslow pulled her toward the gangway. The steps were gone. As they stood there in water waist deep, someone above her grabbed her long hair and tugged at her. She raised her arms and he pulled her onto what remained of the deck.

In another moment, Captain Winslow stood beside her. Before she could gather her wits about her to speak, he picked her up again and half ran, half staggered to the ship's railing. She pushed against his chest in a sudden surge of fright as he lifted her over the railing.

"Oh, please, no!" she shrieked.

"Hannah, thee has no choice," he said. "When thee hits the water, swim away fast!"

She tried to clutch at his buttons, but he pulled her hands away and threw her into the water. She reached out for him, even as she sank below the water's surface. The water was colder even than the water on the sinking ship. Her hair streaming above her, Hannah sank down into the darkness. When her panicking brain told her that she must surely touch bottom, she began to rise. Her lungs desperate for air, she kicked with her feet to hurry the return to the water's surface, which seemed to boil above her.

When she reached the surface, she took a huge gulp of air, and looked around. By the light of the full moon, she could clearly see the *Molly* on her side, her keel oddly out of the water. Sailors were leaping off the wreck and into the water. She started to swim toward them, then stopped.

Bearing down on the *Molly* was another ship, much larger, with gunports open on two decks, the cannon pointed down at a steep angle. Her heart almost stopped beating as the ship opened fire again, blowing the swimmers apart. She took a deep breath, ducked below the water's surface, and swam away.

When she dared to look back, the *Molly* was gone. Like a wolf circling a wounded deer, the larger ship wore around the wreckage that popped to the surface. Through ears still ringing with the percussion of cannon, she heard the mate calling orders in French to the seamen in the rigging. Soon the sails were set on a new course, and the ship slowly tacked away, its aft lantern light winking red in a silent sea.

Her mind a curious blank, for all the crowded sensations that filled it, Hannah started toward the wreckage, then stopped, treading water. She could not bring herself to go closer and risk the further terror of dead men's bodies. And what of sharks? The water was boiling suspiciously, evidence of some force at work. She closed her eyes and held still, waiting for a tug on her legs that would drag her under. When it did not come, she swam slowly away, in what direction she had no idea. The sky was filled with stars, but their direction was a mystery and revealed nothing to her of the compass points.

She drifted on her side, fixing her mind resolutely against what swam below the surface, making as little movement as possible. And then she saw it up ahead.

She stopped, too numb to do anything but watch, as a dark form about ten feet long bore down on her. It was futile to swim below it, for it would only turn and come back at its leisure. Then, silent and swiftly running, it was right upon her; she closed her eyes and put up her hands in pitiful defense.

She grasped wood, almost fainted with relief, then hung on more tightly than a barnacle, feeling the object like a blind woman. It was a grate from the *Molly Claridge*, maybe the one she had sat on only yesterday and observed the insolence of the Royal Navy.

As she hauled herself onto the grating, she remembered Captain Spark's words about dousing the running lights. "Well, the French got us," she said out loud as her teeth chattered in the freshening breeze. "I hope thee is happy, Captain Sir Daniel Spark."

Considering that it was summer, she was colder than she had ever been before. She shivered until her stomach ached. Her long hair hung sopping down her back, and she wore no more protection than her chemise. Goosebumps marched up and down her shoulders, back, and legs as she drew herself together as tightly as she could and willed the dawn to come.

Chapter Three

If this is death, then I have not been very good, Hannah thought to herself. She lay with her eyes tightly closed against the spectacle of a daunting eternity that must stretch before her. She was hot, so hot, boiling from too close contact with hell's fires, surely. Nothing else could possibly account for the heat and pain that was rendering her immobile. Her wickedness must have thrust her straight down to Hades.

Thee has not lived a blameless life, she told herself as she lay there in a crypt that was rocking gently from side to side. But surely the Almighty was more forgiving than this? Was it possible that the sin of wishing a captain of the Royal Navy to the devil had earned her a place in Beelzebub's kingdom, too? The heat was almost more than she could bear, and rendered more unrelenting by the knowledge that it would be her own burden for eternity. The thought made her groan out loud.

"There now, didn't I tell you that she was coming round?"

The words registered slowly in her brain. Somehow, it came as no surprise to her that the devil, or at least one of his minions, would have such a pronounced British accent. It seemed fitting that she would be tormented through eternity by someone who sounded distressingly like Captain Sir Daniel Spark. She thought it thoroughly unkind of the Lord.

But there was this matter of the pain that throbbed through her body. Still keeping her eyes resolutely closed against her first view of hell, she tried to move her legs, and groaned again. Her skin felt too tight for her body, as though it had been stretched across a drum, and then heated almost past bearing. All that was missing was for some demon to pound on her.

Then she felt a hand resting lightly on her wrist. She flinched and drew it away, yelping in pain. She lay there another moment, gathering her courage, then opened her eyes.

Her first sight of hell was a compass tacked to the deck directly over her head. How odd that Satan should require direction, she thought. She stared as the needle jiggled lazily in the compass box. "East by northeast," she said out loud.

Satan chuckled. "Aye, miss. At least your eyes work."

There was that disconcerting voice again. Steeling herself, she turned her head slightly to the right, and then opened her eyes wider.

Captain Sir Daniel Spark sat beside the berth she lay in, watching her with a half smile on his face. The man standing next to him reached for her wrist again, holding his fingers in practiced efficiency against her pulse. As she watched in dumbfounded silence, he raised her wrist, and she saw how sunburned she was. So much for the fires of hell.

She was dressed in a man's shirt and nothing more. There was no sheet over her legs, bare from the knees down. She closed her eyes in embarrassment, unable to look at the two men so close beside her in the cabin.

The man holding her wrist let it down at her side. "You are too sunburned to be wearing anything, but we weighed that against the proprieties, Miss ... Miss ...."

"Hannah Whittier," she said, barely moving her lips.

"Charmed," said the man. "And I am Andrew Lease, ship's

surgeon." He cleared his throat. "I believe you have already met the captain."

She opened her eyes again and turned her gaze on the man seated beside her. "Oh, yes."

Although he was not dressed in the full uniform she remembered, but in white canvas trousers and a well-darned shirt, she could never have mistaken Daniel Spark. He perched on the edge of his chair, back straight, as one unaccustomed to the luxury of sitting down often. Again she was impressed by that tightly contained air he possessed, rather like a watch on the edge of being wound too much. His dark hair, which she had not noticed yesterday because of his hat, was curly like her own, and a needed relief to the seriousness of his face, now that his half smile had retreated to wherever it was those things went.

But was it only yesterday she had last seen him? She tried to raise herself up on one elbow and gasped with the pain. She sank down as a series of shivers racked her body, and gritted her teeth against this unexpected additional torment.

"A natural reaction to shock, my dear," said the surgeon, his voice kind, his eyes full of sympathy.

"Is it possible to feel so cold and hot at the same time?" she managed, even as her teeth chattered.

The captain rose and placed a sheet lightly across her. "There, now," he said. "Is that better?"

It was. She nodded. In another moment, her convulsions passed, and she was merely hot again.

"How long ..." Even words seemed to take a vast effort. She felt drained and wrung out like laundry on a line.

"We don't know, Miss Whittier," the captain said. "We fished you off that grating this morning."

She lay there in silence, vaguely remembering a day spent on the grating, staring out at the empty sea as saltwater washed over her reddening skin. She remembered a night of terror, with sharks or dolphins rubbing against the grating as she sat in the middle, her fingers digging like claws into the lattice. She tried to push her memory farther, but all she could call to mind was lying down finally in resignation and staring up at the stars.

"It was at least a day," she said, "and then another night." She turned her head on the pillow to look at the captain. "I was so afraid."

He nodded. "Shipwreck's not a pleasant event, Miss Whittier." She heard not an ounce of sympathy in his voice, but there was something of understanding, as though he had been shipwrecked before himself.

She thought then of the others. "Did thee find anyone else?" she asked.

Spark shook his head. "We sailed through some debris. That was all."

She closed her eyes again, feeling hot tears behind her eyelids, appalled at how quickly living, breathing men with wives and children could be reduced to a few barrels and cracker boxes bobbing on a deserted ocean. "I think it was the French," she said, when she could speak. She yearned to cry for the *Molly Claridge*, but her body was too dry for tears.

"I am sure it was," Captain Spark said. "And until your President Madison realizes that neutral ships are safe from neither side, others will suffer the same fate."

There was nothing to say to his harsh observation, so she was silent, thinking of Hosea, looking for her day after day and pacing up and down on the Charleston docks. She could imagine the letter he would be writing to Papa. She reached out gingerly and touched Captain Spark's sleeve. "Sir, can we not put in to Charleston? Surely we are not far."

He pointed to the compass over her head. "East by northeast, Miss Whittier," he reminded her. "We are bound for England, as I seem to recall mentioning to you a couple of days ago. And you, apparently, are our guest."

She thought of Papa and Mama in mourning for their

youngest child. "And thee is a perfect beast," she said.

To her surprise, his lips twitched. He nodded to the surgeon. "What do you say, Andrew? Should I pitch this ungrateful shark chum overboard? Here she is, in my berth, and wearing my shirt ..." He shook his head.

"Thee wouldn't," she began.

"No, I wouldn't," he agreed, unruffled by her vehemence, which sounded exhausted and puny to her ears. He rose, stooping to avoid striking his head on the deck above. "A gentleman would at least wait until the lady was healed. Then I'll set you adrift in a boat with a compass and some ship's biscuit, you wretched baggage!"

The surgeon turned his head away, but Hannah could see his shoulders shaking.

"Dreadful man!" she exclaimed, and hauled herself into a sitting position. She groaned and rubbed her hip, wondering at this new pain. "What *is* that?"

The captain paused at the door, his hand on the knob. "You have a bruise of enormous proportions on your bum," he said, his face breaking into the smile he had obviously been struggling against. "I suggest you lie down, Miss Whittier. I only very seldom prey on the infirm, but I would be happy to make an exception in your case, if you continue biting the hand that fished you from the briny deep. As you were, Andrew. Have a little countenance."

He closed the door quietly behind him and she sank back onto the mattress. "I am mortified," she said out loud, her eyes boring into the compass, which continued its maddening east northeast course. If she could have closed her eyes and willed herself dead, she would have.

The surgeon, his face perfectly composed now, shook his head. "No need to be embarrassed, my dear, no need at all. The only ones who saw you were the entire crew, assembled for a reading of the Articles of War and one of Captain Spark's inimitable sermons. It is the Sabbath, after all. That can't number over one hundred and ninety. We lost some crew to the French recently, so I may be off in my calculations."

He looked at the horror that spread across her face, and took her hand again, sitting beside her in the chair the captain had vacated. "What I am trying to say, Miss Whittier, is that it's better to be alive on a crowded deck, even if a bit sparsely clad, than burned black, swollen beyond recognition, and drifting away."

"But ...." she began.

"I can guarantee that not one man on this ship saw anything he's never seen before, with the possible exception of that young one ... Adam Winslow? Is that his name? Now sit up again. I want to spread some more of this salve on your back. Captain Spark ordered me to have you shipshape and Bristol fashion as soon as possible, so he can have his cabin back."

She considered the matter, decided the surgeon was right, and sat up again, her back to him as she primly raised the shirttails and leaned forward.

"Excellent, my dear! I knew you were a reasonable female," the surgeon murmured as he dabbed on the salve, spreading it across her back with gentle fingers. He paused when she flinched, and then continued, his touch light.

Hannah closed her eyes in relief, as the salve sank into her tormented skin. Suddenly she was more thirsty than she had ever been in her life. As the surgeon gently rubbed the ointment into her raw flesh, she thought of the pond at Isaiah Qualm's gristmill at home, where the wheel turned and turned, tossing the water into a fine spray when the wind was blowing. She longed to be there, turning around and around herself in that spray, her mouth open.

"Please, sir, I am so thirsty," she said finally, when he finished.

"In a moment, my dear," he replied. He wiped his hands on his surgeon's apron, then poured her a cup of water from a battered silver carafe. "Drink it slowly. The water's only been in the casks for a month, so it's practically fresh."

She did as he said, relishing the coolness down her throat, and overlooking the taste of wood well tempered with mold.

"I am going to leave this pitcher beside the berth. Drink as much as you can," he said. He returned to a small table and spooned another dollop of ointment into the jar he held. "When I leave, I want you to smear this on the rest of your body. If you need help, I'll help, but I think you would rather do this yourself."

She took the ointment from him, avoiding his eyes, but managing a little smile. "I suppose you will tell me that you've already done that, so I needn't feel embarrassed."

"I wasn't going to say that, but I could." He grinned and tugged at her hair, which was neatly braided. "Don't be a ninnyhammer, Miss Whittier! I am, after all, a surgeon."

"Yes, but on board a ship with nothing but men about," she grumbled as she began gingerly to apply the salve to her poor knees. "I hardly think it is the same."

He watched her a moment in silence, until she looked up, a question in her eyes. "I have not always been a surgeon in the company of men," he said, his voice quiet.

She thought for a moment that he would say something else, but he did not. "Everywhere, mind you," he reminded her. "I can always make up more salve."

Hannah nodded, her eyes on her legs again. She dribbled a line of salve from her ankle bone to her knee. "Sir, do you think the captain will allow me to speak to Adam Winslow?" she asked. "I should tell him of his father."

"I am sure he will allow that, but it can wait, Hannah Whittier." He opened the door. "Bad news can always wait."

He closed the door behind him. When she heard his footsteps receding down the companionway, she raised Captain Spark's shirt for a good look at her hip. The captain was right, she admitted. It was a bruise of enormous proportions, probably a result of her tumble onto the deck of the *Molly Claridge* at the first broadside from the French.

Hannah unbuttoned the shirt, choosing not to think who had buttoned her into it, and stared down at her body. She had been wearing only a chemise when Captain Winslow threw her into the ocean, and she could see the contrast of white on her breasts and stomach, where she had not been burned by the sun. She touched her stomach, thankful that there was one part of her anatomy that did not hurt. "I will be a wretched specimen when I start to peel," she said out loud as she gritted her teeth and slathered on the ointment.

When she was finished, Hannah could not bring herself to put on the shirt again. She tugged the sheet up to her chin and lay down again, pulling her long braid away from the ointment and draping it across the pillow. She regarded it for a moment, wondering who had braided her hair so neatly. She remembered the tangle it had been in after her days of seasickness, and her own perfunctory attempt at reducing chaos to order. Someone more patient than I, she thought, remembering the gentleness of the surgeon's fingers. He had told her his name, but she could not remember it.

She lay as still as she could, shivering now and then as her body protested its cavalier treatment She took another drink, spilling most of it on the pillow, but not minding the cool wetness on her shoulders. She thought of Adam, and dreaded telling him of his father. "And now we are both impressed," she murmured and looked up at the compass again.

When she woke, it was morning again. The sun streamed through the porthole as she lay quietly, wondering how painful it would be to move. "Thee is not dying, Hannah Whittier," she said out loud finally, and sat up.

While the pain still made the hairs rise on her back, she knew she could endure it. She draped the captain's shirt around her bare shoulders and tugged the sheet to her waist. Feeling old and rheumatoid, she managed to pour herself another drink of water from the carafe that must have been refilled during the night. The jar of ointment had been replenished as well.

Thoughtfully, she began to apply it to her arms as she looked around the room.

It was a sleeping cabin, spare and lacking in any creature comforts beyond the berth and a truly comfortable pillow. There was a chair of uncompromising proportions, and a small writing desk with a pull-down lid. A battered sea chest with SPARK painted in black letters adorned the opposite bulkhead from where she sat. Above it was the only incongruous item in the room, a cross-stitched sampler which read, "England expects every man to do his duty" in flowing script. The threads looked as battered as the trunk below and reminded her of similar efforts at home in the parlor on Orange Street. She wondered who thought enough of Captain Sir Daniel Spark to create such a sampler. Surely no woman would ever get close enough to the captain to produce female offspring. It must be a sister. Her own experience with samplers reminded her that samplers were always a good present for brothers, who generally deserved nothing better.

She crawled carefully from the berth, wondering at the sharp pain in her feet. She hung on to the berth and lifted one foot to stare in frank amazement at her sole. It was sunburned, too. She lowered her foot and perched back on the berth, deeply aware what one more day adrift on that grating would have done to her. It appears I should be more grateful, she thought as she pulled her arms into the shirt and buttoned it.

The door to the compartment beyond was open, and she went in, walking gingerly on the black-and-white-painted canvas that covered the deck beneath. The cabin, which stretched across the vessel's stem, was better decorated than the sleeping compartment, with several comfortable chairs, a table spread with charts, and a rather elegant lamp overhead. It could have been a room in a typical manor, with the exception of the two cannons, secured into their trucks with ring bolts that adorned opposite bulkheads. They faced closed gun ports.

How odd, she thought as she sat down carefully in one of the chairs, favoring her bruised hip. She looked closer at the walls dividing the two rooms. They were fastened to the bulkheads with another series of bolts that could easily be thrown to remove them when the warship went into action.

"Not exactly your country home, eh?"

She looked around, careful not to move too fast, to see the ship's surgeon standing in the doorway, a nightshirt draped over his arm.

"No, sir," she replied, embarrassed to be discovered out of her berth and where she did not belong. With an effort, she pulled her knees closer together and crossed her ankles, which made her suck in her breath.

"My dear Miss Whittier, please do not hold with formalities," he said, coming closer. "You'll only do your ankles a disservice, in their present condition."

She uncrossed them and took the nightshirt he held out to her. It was soft from much wear.

"I know I should not be here."

He merely shrugged. "It is no concern of mine. I do not think you are out to steal Captain Spark's silverware. For one, I am glad to see you moving about. Nothing distresses me more than a moribund patient."

She smiled in spite of her discomfort. He came closer, pulled her braid over her breast, and peered down her back before she could protest.

"Hmmm," he said, sounding like her doctor at home. "Hmmm, I was most worried about your back and shoulders, but you appear to be progressing on schedule. Now, stand up and let me see the backs of your knees. Oh, dear. I suggest you apply my salve liberally there and spend this day on your stomach, Miss Whittier."

She made a face. "That bad?"

He nodded, but his voice was full of good cheer. "Nothing's worse than skin that never gets sunburned. As it is, you'll probably come through this intact, but with a nice suntan."

He smiled at the look of concern on her face. "And cheer up! Think of this as an adventure. Here you thought you were only going to see Charleston!"

"Thee doesn't need to remind me," she said and returned to the sleeping compartment. The surgeon remained where he was in the great cabin.

"Miss Whittier, put on that nightshirt and lie on your stomach. I will apply salve to the back of your knees."

She did as he said and climbed back into the berth, thankful to be wearing something that allowed more coverage. Thee is a dunce, Hannah, she thought as she settled herself as modestly as possible. This man, and Captain Spark, too, have already seen all thee possesses. At this point, it is fruitless to blush.

She suffered in silence while the ship's surgeon daubed ointment on her legs, and then her shoulders. She opened her eyes when he finished.

"I should thank thee for untangling my hair and braiding it, sir, but I have forgotten thy name."

He set down the jar of salve and poured her a large drink of water from the carafe. "It is Andrew Lease, Miss Whittier, and you do not have to credit me for that daunting task. You looked like a wild woman when you came on board. It was Captain Spark's work."

She took the cup from him and drank, wondering at a man with such patience, especially one who was an ogre in a naval uniform.

"I would have cut it all off, myself," Lease was saying as he poured her another drink. "Captain Spark allowed as he understood curly hair, and also that he was deep enough in your disfavor without approving such a thing."

She drained the cup again and watched as he refilled it. "I am surprised," she said at last.

"My dear, life is full of surprises, only a few of them pleasant." he replied. When she finished the cup, he filled it again and set it down on the table when she shook her head in protest. "I'll send in Trisk, Captain Spark's orderly, with some gruel, which you will consume in its entirety. Should you require a chamber pot, it is under this berth. I do not think you will need one yet, though. You are still wondrous parched."

With that, he nodded and left the sleeping compartment. She shook her head in surprise, and forgot to be embarrassed. What a strange circumstance I have stumbled into, she thought as she closed her eyes and returned to sleep.

She woke to a scratching at the door, which opened to admit a small man bearing what looked like a basin of porridge. He didn't even bat an eye at her situation, but set the basin down on the berth beside her.

"Captain Spark sends this with his compliments. You are to eat it all, ma'am, or he says he will do something dreadful." He spoke with a pronounced Cockney twang and wore a pigtail as long as her own.

She gasped at his words, but picked up the spoon he proffered and began to eat. The orderly left the room without another word. She stayed where she was on her stomach, with the pillow tucked under her breasts and the porridge in front of her. It tasted better than her favorite dinner at home.

She ate it all, resisting the urge to run her finger around the rim of the bowl. She put the empty bowl and spoon on the night table, next to the carafe and someone's reading spectacles and was composing herself for a return to sleep when there was another knock on the door.

"Hannah?" she heard through the door.

"Oh, come in, Adam, come in!" she exclaimed after a glance around to make sure that Captain Spark's nightshirt hadn't hiked up.

Adam Winslow let himself into the compartment. As he closed the door, she could see a glimpse of scarlet coat with white piping. "I like that!" she exclaimed indignantly. "Does he have a guard on thee?"

"Oh, no, Hannah," Adam replied, crossing the room to stand

beside her. "The guard is on thee."

"Well, I suppose I should be grateful," she said after a long pause. She motioned for him to draw up the chair, and he sat, resting his arm along the wooden edge of the berth.

"Thee looks a sight," he said finally, with the familiarity of an old friend. "I am reminded of lobsters."

She sighed. "The ship's surgeon says I am progressing on schedule, whatever that means." She reached for Adam's hand. "Adam, I do not know how to tell thee ...."

He shook his head. "Thee does not have to. Captain Spark already told me that thee was the only survivor." His eyes misted over and he looked away. "Poor Papa."

Hannah was silent as Adam struggled within himself. Thee is only sixteen, she thought, a year younger than me. And now thee is the head of the Winslow household. Hosea is probably beside himself, and we can do nothing to assuage the sorrows of either of our families.

"Well, this voyage will not last forever," Adam said finally. He released her hand. "I must hurry topside. The bosun said I was to take only a minute."

"Is ... is thy situation horrible?" she asked as he turned to the door.

He shook his head. "I am well enough, Hannah. They are rough men, but we have seen sailors before."

Hannah sighed. "And they have seen me," she said, reddening further despite her vow to remain unembarrassed by her precipitate arrival on board the *Dissuade*. "Mr. Lease said I came sailing into everyone's view during Captain Spark's sermon yesterday."

He smiled then. "Did he? Ah, yes." He sat down again beside her. "We were assembled on the main deck. Captain Spark had just finished reading the Articles of War and had announced his sermon when he stopped, ran to the railing, called for a blanket, and climbed down the chains with a grappling hook as thee floated past. Thee was relatively covered and slung over his shoulder like a meal sack as he climbed back onto the deck."

He laughed at her expression. "I only knew it was thee by that tangle of hair." He was sober then. "And I knew what it meant, to see thee floating past on the *Molly's* grating."

He couldn't say anything else. He looked at her for a long moment, then opened the door. Hannah raised her head from the pillow.

"Adam, we must think of something to get us off this wretched vessel," she said as he disappeared into the companionway and was replaced, to her acute discomfort by Captain Spark.

"I still think we should chum you for sharks, Miss Whittier," he said, his face perfectly wooden. "And I will kindly thank you not to incite my crew to mutiny!"

"Thy crew!" she fired back, wishing with all her heart that she could leap up and pummel him, instead of continue to lie on her stomach. Thee snatched him from the *Molly Claridge's* deck." she stormed. "It is most undemocratic of thee!"

He was obviously going to say something else, but her last charge brought him up short. "Miss Whittier, the *Dissuade* is not a democracy," he managed at last, a faint smile on his face. "And you are a dreadful baggage."

She thought it was a smile, but it was gone before she could make sure. With a nod in her direction, he closed the door with a decisive click, leaving her to writhe in further discomfort entirely of her own making, and heartily wish Captain Spark to the devil again.

Chapter Four

She did not see Captain Spark for another three days, during which time she mulled over her many sins—chief among them hasty words—lay on her stomach, and suffered the ship's surgeon to slather those parts with ointment that she could not reach. When she begged for something besides gruel at mealtime, he was implacable.

"But I am tired of it," she argued on the evening of the fourth day of her tenure on board His Majesty's *Dissuade*. "Is there nothing else?"

"Not for you. Miss Whittier," he said firmly as he capped the ointment and covered her with a sheet again. "Ship's fare is entirely too salty, and you are still dehydrated." He gave her one of his gallows smiles. "I assure you that before we get to England, you will be equally sick of salted beef and weevily biscuit. Hush now."

With a sigh, Hannah flopped her chin back down on the pillow. "And now I suppose thee will leave me to my own ruminations," she said.

"I should," he replied, pouring her another large cup of water and standing there until she finally took it and drank.

"Except that they are probably most unprofitable these days, and I would not have you think ill of all of us. Miss Whittier, do you play draughts? Checkers to you, I suppose."

She brightened up immediately. "Mama doesn't think I know how, but my brothers taught me," she said.

"Well, I would hardly like to be party to your total dissipation," he began, a twinkle in his eyes. "Perhaps I can find an improving book, like *Coastal Shoals and Lee Shores of Mediterranean Spain*," he said. "I know Daniel has a copy."

"Oh no," she said hurriedly. "Checkers, if thee pleases."

It was hard to think of the captain as having a first name that anyone ever used, she thought as the surgeon tapped on the door separating the sleeping cabin from the great room and was invited in by His Majesty. He was gone a long while; she closed her eyes and resigned herself to another evening spent in isolation. Soon she began to worry about her parents, and Hosea, who was probably beside himself by now, wondering what had become of the *Molly Claridge*.

She rested her chin on her hands. When news reached Mama and Papa on Orange Street, there would be a memorial service. It will be a sad one for her family, she thought, and also for the Winslows, mourning both a husband and son. There would be a long, long prayer, the kind that made her squirm, and then a melancholy pilgrimage to the dock, where Mama would drop a handful of flowers into the water and sob on Papa's broad chest. Her own chin quivered. How much they will miss me.

"My God, Miss Whittier, such a mournful expression," came a familiar voice at the cabin door.

She opened her eyes to see the captain himself standing there, leaning against the door frame, conforming himself gracefully to the roll of the ship. He was dressed in white canvas trousers and a white shirt and his shoes were off.

"I am contemplating the memorial service my parents will have in the Friends Meetinghouse, when they hear the sad news from my brother," she replied, tugging the sheet up a little higher on her flaming shoulders in an attempt to dignify her situation.

"I cannot fathom anyone missing you," he said frankly. "You're certainly a lot of trouble to me. Tell me, will they hold a similar meeting of thanksgiving when you finally return?"

"Probably not," she replied, her voice formal.

"I shouldn't wonder at that," he murmured and went back into the great cabin. In another moment she heard the rustle of charts, and then the surgeon reappeared.

"He is so rude," she whispered as Andrew Lease set the checkerboard down in front of her and pulled his chair up close.

"The captain?" Lease asked, placing the pieces on the board. "He's supposed to be. Now, mind yourself, if you plan to win."

She won two games out of four as the ship slid silently through the water, taking her farther and farther from home. During the final game, she heard the scraping of a fiddle on deck, and the sound of men dancing. Down below in the hold was the rhythmic clanking of the pumps, and faintly, the lowing of a cow.

"This is a strange place," she said as she watched the surgeon put the checkers back in their cloth bag.

"You'll get used to it," he said.

She couldn't keep her eyes open. The fiddle was soothing. "How long before we get to England?" she asked, settling herself more comfortably in the berth.

Lease laughed. "You probably plagued your parents on every trip you took, didn't you? Long enough, Miss Whittier. Time for you to learn to appreciate the HMS *Dissuade*. Maybe even Captain Spark."

"Never," she said, her voice drowsy. "He is completely undemocratic and a dreadful beast." She paused to let that sink in as her eyes closed. "And I am equally sure he can have nothing kind to say about me."

The surgeon chuckled. He put the back of his hand to her

forehead, nodded approvingly, and settled the sheet about her shoulders. He blew out the lamp. "He did mention that he wanted his bed back, and without you in it."

"Dreadful man," she repeated as she wiggled into a comfortable position and surrendered to sleep.

She felt human in the morning, for the first time since her rescue from the sea. Hannah sat up in the berth and pulled on the captain's nightshirt, wincing only slightly as it came in contact with her tender shoulders. Her arms were beginning to itch and peel. She tugged idly at the skin on her forearm, marveling how it sheeted off and left a handsome tan behind.

Mama will be chagrined, she thought. Soon I will be browner than an Indian. She leaned against the bulkhead, holding her breath against the anticipated pain, and letting it out in relief when there was none. I could almost like this, she thought as she settled into the gentle rolling motion of the ship as it rose on each swell, then shimmied into a little spiral as it fell into the trough of the wave. She knew instinctively there was a sure hand at the helm.

When Captain Spark knocked on the door from the great cabin, she felt decidedly charitable. "Come in, please," she said.

The captain, still in stockinged feet, stuck his head in. "I need a shirt," he said, observing her. "Well, you are sitting up. Does this mean I will be getting my cabin back soon?"

"As soon as thee can find me another space, sir," she replied. "And some clothes."

"Done, Miss Whittier," he replied as he opened his sea chest and rummaged about for another shirt. "I'll put my first mate on it right away." He found a shirt and closed the chest. "All we need to do is dispossess a midshipman and purloin a shirt and trousers from a small crew member. I trust you are not too particular." He paused in front of her. "By God, you're going to be peeling for a week, at least." He touched the end of her nose. "I did that once, and looked about as silly as you do. At least there is no one here you have to impress. I'm afraid it would be quite impossible. Cheers, Miss Whittier."

She blinked her eyes in surprise as he closed the door to the cabin. "What an odd man," she said out loud. That was more words than he had said to her before. She was still marveling at his loquaciousness when his orderly entered with the eternal basin of gruel and coffee.

She wrinkled her nose at the coffee. "I do not know how anyone manages to drink this," she said as the little man placed the tray on her lap. "Does thee boil it for hours?"

He stared at her in surprise. "Of course, miss. Is there any other way?"

She sighed and took a sip. The orderly shook his head and left the cabin. Before she gave up on the coffee, there was another knock. It was the ship's surgeon, with white trousers and a black-and-white checked shirt draped over his arm.

"Daniel informs me it is moving day," he said after a perfunctory tug on her nightshirt and a professional scrutiny of her shoulders. "The cabin boy died of the bloody flux in the Caribbean, so we have his clothes for you."

Her eyes opened wide. "Thee does not think they are contaminated?"

He chuckled. "No! You may find the smallclothes a bit perplexing, but then, not many slop chests have clothes for the female form on His Majesty's warships."

She blushed and accepted the garments. The surgeon smiled and returned to the door.

"When you're dressed, come into the companionway, and I'll escort you to your new quarters," he said.

Hannah climbed out of the berth and tugged on the smallclothes, refusing to be embarrassed by them. The shirt, heavy cotton worn soft from many washings, was a loose fit, which pleased her enormously. As she buttoned the shirt, she was grateful for once for her own slim form. Wearing that loose shirt, there would be nothing remotely enticing about her figure. As small as they were, the trousers were a little long, but fitted her nicely across the hips. She pulled them up, tied the drawstring at the waist, and tucked the shirt into the pants. It was a simple matter to roll up the trouser legs.

She stood barefoot on the deck, enjoying the feel of wood under her bare feet, and relishing the relief of no stockings. A person could be almost comfortable in this rigout, she thought. A glance in the small shaving mirror attached to the bulkhead only confirmed Captain Spark's pithy observation about her skin, but revealed nothing about her clothes. Somehow they would have to do.

As she left the cabin, the sentry outside the door clicked his heels together smartly, presented arms, and then relaxed again. Eyes wide, she admired his red coat, which was stretched across his chest without a wrinkle, and then turned away in confusion when he winked at her.

"Oh, dear," she murmured under her breath, and looked up to see the surgeon leaning against a cannon, watching her obvious embarrassment.

They stood in the waist of the ship, with rows of guns made secure with a system of ropes and pulleys. The gunports were closed, but it was not dark, because the gun deck was open to the main deck above, like a skylight cut into a roof.

"This is a frigate," the surgeon explained, "with forty guns, eighteen to a side, and two carronades on the main deck and two bow chasers. We are not a ship of the line, but a commerce raider."

He led her down a companionway aft from the silent guns, and opened a door just beyond the last gun. She peered inside, taking in the gun there, too, the hammock slung above it, the gunport secured. She looked back at the surgeon for explanation.

"When we clear the decks for action, the gun crews knock down these bulkheads, and your cabin becomes another part of the gun deck. So does the captain's great cabin, and most of the other quarters." He patted the gun under the hammock.

"Miss Whittier, you are now residing on a killing machine. The *Dissuade* is a shark in international waters."

Hannah shuddered and eyed the hammock dubiously. "Suppose I should fall out of this thing?"

"Then you have the cannon underneath to break your fall," the surgeon replied, smiling at her wary expression. "Come, come, Miss Whittier! Have a little confidence in yourself!"

"Very well, sir," she said.

She looked around the tiny cabin and saw only a small sea chest. The surgeon opened it. "There are some more clothes in here, and whatever else that little beggar owned. This was not his cabin, of course. He slept on the floor in the galley. You have merely dispossessed two midshipmen."

"I am sorry for that," she said, noticing the ring bolts where the second hammock must have been secured and wondering how on earth there was room for two in a space for less than one. She looked in the sea chest, noting the extra shirt and canvas trousers, folding knife, and wooden flute. It was so little by which to remember a life. "How old was he?" she asked as the surgeon squeezed past the cannon and stood in the doorway again.

"He was ten," Lease said. His face was devoid of emotion, as though he steeled himself against a greater pain.

"So young," she murmured as she touched the flute and then closed the chest gently, wondering what was camouflaged by the surgeon's toneless voice.

He nodded. "That's the way of it. Captain Spark went to sea at ten. He has been more than twenty years in the navy, and all of them during the wartime."

"Thee cannot be serious," she said, startled. "What kind of life is that?"

The surgeon merely managed a small bow in the narrow opening of the door. "Who said it was a life? We live to serve the guns, and that is war, my dear." He looked beyond her to the great hulk of the gun. "Perhaps we would all fare worse on land. Good day, my dear. Go on deck, if you wish."

She nodded and he closed the door. Hannah sat down on the little chest and looked around her. She would only be able to stand upright because she was short. The gun was secured to the deck by a series of pulleys and tackle, necessitating that she watch her step to avoid stubbing her toes.

Hannah eyed the hammock for another minute, then rose. She stared at the gun, then climbed onto it and then into the hammock. Holding her breath, she lay back carefully and expected to be dumped out by the ship's movements.

Nothing of the sort happened. The hammock swayed gently from side to side and enfolded her in its generous cloth embrace. She relaxed and closed her eyes, perfectly at peace with herself as she listened to the shipboard sounds around her, the creak of the wood, the rhythmical scrape as the men holystoned the deck above. Every now and then, someone laughed, and voices murmured. Above this she heard the steady tread of someone on the quarterdeck, and then the humming of the wind in the riggings. It was a pleasant, low-pitched sound that seemed to harmonize with the slap of the water as the *Dissuade* cut through the sea.

When Hannah woke, she was still in the enveloping grasp of the hammock, swaying with the rhythm of the frigate cutting through the water. There was only the faint light of afternoon coming through the tiny porthole to indicate the passage of time. It was well that people kept watches aboard a ship, she thought as she lay there, *or we would lose all sense of time at sea.*

She lay there a moment longer as an enormous feeling of well-being washed over her. Her shoulders and knees still pained her, but she was alive and whole, and that was more than enough. *I really should thank the captain for his kindness to me,* she thought.

The idea took hold as she swung one bare foot idly outside the hammock. *I should just march boldly on deck and express* my appreciation, she thought, and then climbed carefully out of the hammock, onto the gun, and to the deck. Someone—it must have been the ship's surgeon—had placed another jar of ointment on top of the sea chest, and a hairbrush. She smiled at such a simple pleasure and untwined her braid. Humming to herself, she brushed her hair gingerly at first, and then more forcefully, when she discovered that her sunburned scalp was on a rapid mend. She replaited her hair, pleased with its chestnut color and thickness and imagining that her exposure to the relentless sun had given it those lighter hues that twinkled through it in the last light of the afternoon. She tucked in her shirt again, wished briefly for shoes, and left the cabin. The Marine clicked to attention outside her door, bringing his long musket to port arms, and then stamping it again by his side.

"Thee really doesn't need to do that," she said, embarrassed that a Quaker would elicit such military attention.

"Regulations require it, miss," he said, his eyes straight ahead.

"Well, if thee must ...." she said, and hurried up the gangway to the main deck above.

The sky was so incredibly blue that she could only stare in frank admiration as it contrasted with the white of the sails and the great tarred mast that seemed to go up and up, prepared to puncture the lazy clouds overhead. As she stared upward, shading her eyes with her hand, she saw the topmen balanced on the foot ropes that ran along each yardarm, reefing the mainsail and topsails above, and then on command through the speaking trumpet from the lieutenant on deck, unfurling them. They dropped with a bang and snap that made her jump.

They did it once, then twice, and then Captain Spark, who paced the quarterdeck, held his watch on them. When the last sail was reefed, they waited.

"By damn, that was slow as my fat Aunt Mabel," he roared, snapping his watch shut "Try it again, you sons of the guns, and put some back into it!"

The exercise was repeated four more times, Spark's eyes on his watch. Finally he clicked it shut and tucked it in his pocket. "Better," he hollered. "Your lives may depend on your speed, lads, mark you." He glanced at the lieutenant on the main deck with the speaking trumpet. "Tell them to stand down, Mr. Futtrell, lively now."

"Aye, sir." The lieutenant barked an order through the trumpet and topmen scurried down the ratlines to the deck one hundred and fifty feet below.

"My," Hannah whispered out loud as she watched them descend. She looked at the captain on the quarterdeck, expecting to see some show of appreciation. He stood, hands clasped behind his back, telescope tucked between his arm and his side, his expression sour. As she watched, he peered beyond her into the waist of the gun deck.

"Mr. Lansing, tomorrow we will run out the guns for target practice. I trust you will be more efficient than Mr. Futtrell and his nervous Nellies."

"Aye, sir!" came a voice from the gun deck.

Hannah sighed. My, but thee is difficult to please, she thought. Hosea would call thee a grouch. She turned away to look out across the water, but her view was obscured by the hammocks rolled into the netting that lined the railing. What an odd place to store one's bedding, she thought. It quite ruins the view.

She looked up the companionway to the quarterdeck, where the captain stood, telescope to his eye, gazing across the empty sea. I did promise to thank him, she remembered. And the view is better there. She crossed the deck to climb the ladder to the quarterdeck.

Her foot was on the first tread when she heard the helmsman at the wheel suck in his breath. She looked at him in surprise.

"Miss, I wouldn't ...." he began. "Not there."

She shook her head. Couldn't he see that was where the view was? And she did have a word of thanks to express to Captain

Sir Daniel Spark. She skipped up the narrow treads, looking over her shoulder in surprise as Lieutenant Futtrell bolted from his post by the mainmast and ran toward her, his hand raised.

"How odd these people are," she muttered under her breath as she stood on the quarterdeck. Mr. Futtrell had stopped now and was watching her, his mouth open.

The view was better. She strolled to the railing and stood beside the captain, who still had the telescope to his eye, his concentration intense on nothing that she could see. Hannah admired the play of the sinking sun slanting across the water, suddenly mindful that everyone on the main deck was watching her now. Even the seamen hung suspended in the ratlines.

"How peculiar," she said out loud, raising her face to the wind that ruffled her hair from the back. She cleared her throat, in case Captain Spark had not heard her remark.

The telescope came down slowly. How formidable he looks with that monstrous hat on, she thought as she watched him slam the telescope together with a cracking sound that could be heard all over the ship. I wonder why he stares that way.

"Captain, I wanted to thank you for—"

What she was going to say, she could not have remembered, not even one second later, not in the glare of Captain Spark's expression, which hardened into granite.

"What in God's name are you doing on the weather side of this quarterdeck?" he roared, his voice as loud as though he were addressing the topmen who still hung in the ratlines.

She stepped back in surprise, her hands to her ears in fright.

"You don't need to shout," she said. "I just wanted to thank—"

"You are a monstrous lot of trouble, Miss Whittier," he rasped, as though speaking over firing guns. His voice seemed to echo, as though the sails caught words as well as winds, and flung them back at her. Tears started into her eyes as she looked about for an avenue of escape. Everyone on the *Dissuade* was absolutely still, as though turned to stone in a fairy tale. She slowly backed toward the ladder. "I'm sorry," she began as her knees began to smote together.

He was at her side in two strides. She shrieked in terror as he picked her up and held her suspended in his arms over the railing onto the main deck.

"Mr. Futtrell! Do something with this!" he shouted and let her drop.

Mr. Futtrell caught her handily. She gasped with pain as his arms came in contact with her sunburned back, and burst into loud tears.

"I'm sorry, miss," he apologized as he quickly stood her upright on the deck. "You never stand between a captain and the wind. It just isn't done."

"I didn't know," she sobbed as she dabbed at her eyes with her sleeve and wished the sea would swallow her. Her face burned with shame as she looked around her, but the men had returned to their tasks. The topmen continued down the ratlines, and the helmsman, his feet wide apart on the slanting deck, steadied the wheel, his eyes on the sails.

"Are you all right, Miss Whittier?" the lieutenant asked, his eyes kind.

She nodded, too ashamed to give him more than a glance. "I just wanted to ... to thank him for pulling me from the water." She tried to take a deep breath, but she only hiccupped.

"Take it below, Miss Whittier," came the captain's voice from the quarterdeck above her. "I cannot conduct a poll here, but I suspect at least half of us go to sea to get away from women's tears!"

Without a word, or a glance in his direction, she hurried down the ladder, grateful for the darkness settling below deck. Her eyes filling with tears, she stumbled into her cabin and closed the door quietly behind her. She tucked herself into a little ball in the middle of the hammock and cried until her eyes hurt, her hands over her mouth so no one would hear. Exhausted finally, her eyes burning, she stared into the gathering gloom. Soon the smell of bilge that filled every cranny below deck was superseded by the odor of boiling coffee. It was time for dinner.

"I shall never eat again," she said and clasped her hands across her stomach.

Her eyes were closing again when she heard the sentry outside click to attention. "Miss Whittier," came that voice, softer this time, but still ripe with command, "eat with me tonight. We have to discuss your presence on this ship."

She waited a long moment. "I would rather swallow burning coals than take a bite with thee, Captain Spark," she said, her voice firm.

Her mouth grew dry at her own temerity, and she waited for him to slam open the door. The passageway was silent.

"Very well then," he said, and walked away.

She sighed in relief, overlooking the growling of her stomach.

A few moments later, the sentry clicked to attention again and she sucked in her breath and held it.

"Miss Whittier? It's Lieutenant Futtrell, ma'am. Would you ... could you ... take mutton with us in the wardroom?"

She let out her breath, sat up, and felt for the cannon with her foot. "I would be delighted, Lieutenant Futtrell," she said.

Chapter Five

Hannah dined in the junior officers' wardroom that night, washing down salty mutton with boiled coffee. She watched Captain Spark's lieutenants and the three midshipmen tap their sea biscuits on the table to drive out the weevils, and wondered why she ever complained about Mama's cooking. While the others looked on in amusement, she rapped her biscuit on the table, and gave a little shriek when two well-fed worms rolled out, and in the glare of publicity, huddled themselves into tight balls.

"Some prefer them in the biscuit," Lieutenant Futtrell observed. "They claim it gives the food more crunch."

Hannah shuddered at his words and gave a more vigorous tap to the biscuit. Another worm tumbled out. "When in Rome," she murmured, and took a bite, dreading the thought of any crunching.

"Bravo!" said the lieutenant named Lansing. The three midshipmen, none of them a day over twelve, looked at each other and giggled, then turned red.

"Don't mind them," Lieutenant Futtrell said generously.

"They've been at sea since they were ten, and don't know much about ladies."

Hannah sighed. "No one does. See here, sirs. I do not wish to continually be running afoul of Captain Spark. Tell me what I must do to prevent further disaster."

Futtrell pushed away his plate. "Stay off the quarterdeck unless invited. And that will never happen. But if it ever does, stand on the lee side with us, and not the weather side with him."

Lansing laughed. "I think coming between a captain and his wind must be like getting between a mother bear and her cubs."

She nodded. "And?"

Lieutenant Lansing stared thoughtfully into the mutton fat congealing on his plate. "Do not—I repeat—do not come above deck before eight bells. The captain likes a shower under the wash pump about then. God knows how he can tolerate it, but he washes in seawater, no matter the weather."

"Cleanliness is next to godliness," she reminded them, amused at the thought of the dignified captain capering about naked in cold weather. I wonder if he removes his hat, she thought.

"The captain inspects the ship on Sundays," offered one of the midshipmen, who blushed beet red and ducked his head when she looked in his direction.

Hannah smiled and crossed her heart. "I promise to keep my bed made and all my numerous possessions put away." She glanced at Lieutenant Futtrell, who was eyeing her, a smile on his own well-weathered face. "Surely he would not inspect my cabin?"

Futtrell shrugged. "He runs a taut ship, Miss Whittier." He nodded to the orderly hovering in the shadow of the bulkhead, who hurried forward to remove the plates. "He likes everyone on board to be useful, Miss Whittier. You might study in your mind how you can do this. We'll be another six weeks at sea."

"Six weeks!" she exclaimed in dismay. Six weeks to England, and at least another six weeks home. It would be months before her parents knew she was alive. "Six weeks," she repeated, her voice softer. "I could become most amazingly bored."

The lieutenants looked at each other and grinned. "Best make yourself useful," Lansing said. He took a last sip of his coffee before the orderly removed it and made a face. "And start by doing something about this coffee. I swear it is made of bilge water, or deck swash."

"Does the captain complain about his coffee?" she asked.

"It's probably the only thing he complains about, at least, until you came aboard," Lansing said, getting to his feet and ducking his head to avoid the deck above.

"Oh, dear," she said. "I wish one of thee could tell him that I didn't throw myself off the *Molly Claridge* with the expectation of being picked up by a frigate of the Royal Navy, Captain Spark commanding." She sighed. "But I owe him my rescue, at the very least."

Futtrell smiled and pulled out her chair as she made to rise. "One thing else, Miss Whittier. It might be better if you said 'you' instead of 'thee.' Makes me feel like a guilty sinner."

"Well, is thee?" she asked, her voice crisp. She reconsidered immediately. "I am sorry. I will try to remember. Can ... you ... think of anything else?"

"Only this," said Lansing as he ushered her toward the companionway. "When the captain gives an order, obey and don't ask why."

She put her hands on her hips. "That is fearsome undemocratic."

Futtrell bowed elaborately, to the amusement of the midshipmen. "Thee is in the Royal Navy now, Miss Whittier."

The air was much fresher on deck. As Hannah took several gulps of the brisk air, she vowed to spend as much time on deck as possible. She was not alone in this desire. Adam Winslow sat on a forward grating, deep in conversation with the other

Nantucket sailor. He raised his hand to her, but made no move to come closer.

Their voices low, other sailors had grouped themselves about the scuttlebutt for one last drink before going below to sleep. As she watched, they pulled their hammocks from the webs of rope lining the railings.

"Why do they keep their hammocks there? Isn't it dreadfully inconvenient to do that?" she asked Futtrell.

"You would think so, until those hammocks stored there deflect cannonballs during battle."

"Oh," she said, her eyes wide. "Does thee ... do you ... think we will run into trouble with the French between here and England?"

He nodded, not a trace of humor in his voice. "You can depend upon it, Miss Whittier. It is only a matter of time."

She took that bit of news below deck with her as she prepared for bed. She wondered what she would sleep in, as she said good night shyly to the sentry at the door and entered her tiny cabin. Draped across the cannon was one of the captain's nightshirts. It was not the one she had worn, greasy with salve, but a fresh one. She picked it up. "Captain Spark, thee is a strange man," she murmured out loud. She fingered the shirt and thought of her friend Charity Wilkins, recently married, declaiming on the simplicity of men. Thee does not know Captain Spark, if thee thinks men are simple, Hannah thought.

In a matter of moments, she was in the hammock, still dubious about dumping herself out, then reassured as it enveloped her again in its comfort. She squirmed into a comfortable position and folded her hands across her stomach. As she lay there, waiting for sleep, she thought of her list. It seemed so long ago that she had composed it. Now it was a meal for the fish, along with nearly everything else that had once comprised the *Molly Claridge*. But I won't think of that, she thought, for it makes me too sad.

She concentrated on the list. I asked for a handsome man with blond hair and blue eyes, she thought, and considered Captain Spark, with his rather fine curly hair and somewhat disturbing pale eyes. Perhaps I am too arbitrary, she considered. There is nothing wrong with dark, curly hair. "Not that I am for even the smallest minute considering thee as a possible husband," she said firmly. "But perhaps I should not be too picky about color of hair and eyes."

She turned gingerly onto her side, less from worry over her sunburn, than the lively fear of involuntary expulsion from the hammock. She tried to remember the other conditions on her list: patient, kind, devout, loves me. She stopped, her face even more red, thinking of her ejection from the quarterdeck. She was not a grudge holder; soon philosophy—and approaching sleep—took over. "Hannah Whittier, at least thee is now perfectly capable of telling the difference between love and pointed dislike, thanks to Captain Spark. As if thee had any doubts!"

She concluded that the way to finding a husband was fraught with true peril. I begin to wonder that anyone attempts it, she thought as her eyes closed at last and she slept.

She woke to the sound of the wash pump working on the deck and the clicking of heels outside her door as the Marine guard changed. She listened to the water pattering overhead as it fell onto the deck, and the sound of someone—it could only be Captain Spark—singing rather tunelessly. The air was cool and she shivered, wondering how he could stand to shower under that pump, and in seawater.

Her cabin was still dark, but it was a simple matter to climb from the hammock and dress. She tugged her hair back at the nape of her neck, tied it with a string salvaged from the sea chest, and opened the door. The guard, his face wooden, gave her a sidelong glance.

"Lieutenant, I wish you to escort me to the galley," she said firmly.

He grinned. "Ma'am, I am a corporal. This way."

She followed him silently, picking her way carefully through the gun deck, and overlooking those men still asleep in their hammocks. The clank of the wash pump ceased. She kept her eyes forward, hoping that the captain, in whatever state of dress, would not go below until she was out of sight in the galley.

Her hope was realized. She ducked through the door that the Marine held open for her, and sniffed appreciatively. A little man with a peg leg stood at the large galley range stirring vigorously.

"That you, Trist, you old bastard? Tell the captain to slow down and dry off them long limbs! I'll have his porridge in two shakes, and not before."

Hannah, her eyes merry, cleared her throat, and the cook spun about on his wooden leg. He stared at her in surprise, then hurriedly dumped the spoon back in the pot, muttering something about "losing ten years off me plaguey life."

Hannah ventured closer. "I didn't mean to startle you."

He continued stirring, as if too shy to look at her again. "Well, you did, miss, you did." He stopped then. "Is there something that you need?" he asked, as if eager to end her presence in his galley.

She nodded, wondered briefly if a small prevarication of good intentions was as bad as an outright lie, and plunged ahead. "I am under orders from the captain to prepare him a cup of coffee."

The cook gestured to the coffeepot on a back burner, its lid chattering away as the brew boiled and strengthened. "Already done, miss."

"No, you don't understand," she insisted. "I am to make it my way." She overlooked the mulish look on his face and dimpled her smile at him. "Oh, please, sir! I don't know what I'll do if you say no!"

She had no intention of crying, but there must have been a plaintive note in her voice that triggered the cook's immediate response. Without a word, he hurried to the ship's stores and pulled down a sack of green coffee beans. "Don't cry, miss, don't cry," he pleaded as he held it out to her.

It was a simple matter to roast the beans, grind them, and add them to a smaller pot of water simmering on the other back burner. She worked quickly; silently amused at how hard the cook watched her when he thought she was unaware. She added the ground beans to the strainer and returned it to the pot, wishing for a clock to time it precisely. She lifted the lid finally, and sniffed.

"Now you boil it?" the cook asked, his eyes hopeful.

"Oh, no," she said.

The cook turned back to the range, his back stiff with disapproval. "Then it can't be regulation navy, miss," he muttered, "and the captain is particular about the rules."

She opened her eyes wide. "I didn't know coffee had rules!" She waited until she thought he could not stand another moment of suspense, then poured a cup of the brew into a measuring tin.

"Wouldn't you agree that was better?" she asked.

He sniffed, his eyes suspicious. "Don't rush me, miss."

As she watched in amusement, he sipped at it, nodded, and turned back to the porridge. "Good enough for the king," he mumbled, "even if you are a Yankee."

He didn't say anything else, so she could only take it for a compliment. "Why, thank you, sir," she replied.

To her surprise, he turned about on his peg leg again and held out his hand. "Call me Cookie, ma'am."

"I will," she assured him. "And you may call me Hannah."

He drew back in shock as though she had grabbed him. "I could never!"

"Miss Whittier, then," she amended hastily. "And I promise only to invade your galley to make coffee for the captain."

His face rosy with shyness, the cook held out a large white

mug. "He says he likes it blacker than a coaldigger's arse, ma'am."

"He would," she murmured, mentally crossing the captain off her list yet again as she accepted the cup. Her eyes on the brimming mug, she left the galley, looking back only when the cook called to her.

"If you're ever bored, miss, there's always something to peel," he offered, and then ducked inside again, his face aflame.

She smiled to herself and kept her eyes carefully forward. Timing her stride to the roll of the ship, she looked up from the gun deck to see the captain, dressed and on his quarterdeck, hands clasped behind his back. He tapped his toe on the deck, and every line of his body seemed to scream out impatience.

Trist stood beside the gangway, eyeing her with vast disapproval. She held out the cup to him. "For the captain," she whispered, her eyes on the deck above.

Spark's orderly backed away, as though the cup contained hemlock. "Not unless Cookie brewed it," he declared, his voice as close to virtuous as possible, for a member of the Royal Navy.

"Oh, very well," she declared, took a deep breath, and mounted the steps.

Captain Spark had turned at the sound of her voice. He eyed her and the cup with suspicion, then pointedly turned his back again. She stifled the urge to throw the mug at him, and carefully crossed the deck to the ladder that gave onto the quarterdeck.

"Come to poison me on my own quarterdeck, Miss Whittier?" he asked, his back still to her.

"I doubt that even arsenic would have other than a sweetening effect to thy ... your nature," she said.

She climbed the first two steps of the ladder and the captain turned around, eyeing her with frosty distrust under frowning eyebrows.

"You seem to have a short memory, Miss Whittier," he began.

"And you are abominably rude," she replied. She leaned forward and set the cup down on the quarterdeck, then turned around and plopped herself onto the second step, coming no closer. With what she hoped was elaborate unconcern, she watched the seamen holystoning the deck, and waited.

After a long moment, he crossed to the gangway and picked up the cup. She heard him return to the weather side of the ship. He was silent. She couldn't tell if he was sipping the coffee, or if he had dumped it overboard. The minutes passed. She got up to go below again.

"Miss Whittier!" came the command from the quarterdeck. The mainsail boomed then, and the helmsman, who had obviously been watching his captain, grabbed for the wheel again as Captain Spark flung a curse and an order at him. The ship heeled quickly as the canvas flared and then filled again.

Goosebumps charged up and down her spine, and she stood still, her heart pounding so loud she looked down to see if she could watch it jump about in her chest. The captain's steps were firm on the deck above, coming closer. She shivered.

"Miss Whittier, have the goodness to look at me when I make such a racket," he said then, his voice mild and almost in normal speaking range.

She turned about in surprise. He squatted on his haunches until they were eye level, and held out the empty cup. "It may be that you have just justified the reason for your existence aboard this vessel," he said. "I'll have another, lively now."

She took the cup and hurried below, not daring to look at him again. She threw herself into the galley, startling Cookie into dropping the pot of porridge. He leaped back, surprisingly agile for a one-legged man, and swore as she poured another cup and darted out of the galley again.

The captain was waiting by the gangway. Without a word, she handed him the mug and sat on the ladder again. He drank the coffee slowly, his eyes on the sails, the expression on his face almost reverent. Finally he sighed and handed back the mug.

"I disremember when I have had a cup of coffee that excellent." he said. "If you will do that every morning, I expect that you and I will rub along quite well for the duration of this voyage."

"Aye, sir," she whispered.

He smiled then, and squatted by her again, his face close to hers, his blue eyes lively. "I think you are a scamp and a nuisance, Miss Whittier, but, by God, you can make coffee."

She thought he would rise then, but he remained where he was, balanced gracefully on his quarterdeck. "Now, if you can find Trist, my worthless orderly, tell him I am headed below for my basin of porridge. Join me, Miss Whittier?"

She shook her head, suddenly shy, and quite caught up by his blue eyes. "No—no, sir, I think not," she stammered. "I think I should make amends with Cookie." She slipped down the gangway until she was standing on the main deck again. "Do you suppose if I peel a lot of potatoes, he will overlook the fact that I startled him into spilling your porridge all over the deck?"

"By God, Miss Whittier, you are a trial," he murmured. "I wonder if your parents will want you back, given the choice. Tell Trist to poach me some eggs instead."

She hurried back to the galley, her heart pounding, where Cookie ignored her elaborately. On her tremulous request, Trist, with much wringing of hands and little moans, coaxed two eggs into a reluctant poach and charred the toast. Making herself as small as possible, she sat on the deck by a mound of potatoes and began to peel. Trist finally hurried forward with the captain's late breakfast, a large mug of coffee featured prominently. Cookie sat down and mopped his face. With a shaking hand, he pointed to the pile.

"Keep peeling!"

Hannah was still peeling potatoes an hour later when the

bosun's whistles twittered and the gun deck filled with seamen. Cookie, his rheumy eyes eager now, put down his knife and motioned her to the doorway. "There you are, missy," he gestured, his voice expansive. "Our reason for being."

As she watched, interested, the confusion of sailors resolved into separate crews standing beside each gun. The gunports were opened, and Mr. Lansing stood in the center of the deck, his watch in his hand. She looked up through the cut-out deck to see Captain Spark on the quarterdeck with Mr. Futtrell, his second officer.

"Mr. Lansing," he roared in that penetrating voice. "A complete exercise, right down to the sand. And if you're fast enough, by God, we'll blow up a few kegs."

The crews cheered and were silenced quickly by a sharp word from Mr. Lansing. While one crew member spread sand on the deck, another ran to fill a tub with water. A third stuck long wicks of slow-burning matches in the tub, while another readied the swab.

Hannah turned inquiring eyes on the cook, who stood beside her. "Sand?" she asked.

"For the blood on the deck," he replied, and laughed with some relish when she shuddered. "You'd be amazed how slippery it can get."

Small boys darted among the crews. She looked at the cook again.

"Powder monkeys, miss," he explained. "They get the powder forward from the magazine and hurry it back to the crews."

"They're so young!" she exclaimed in dismay.

The cook only shrugged. "Better than sweeping chimneys in Lunnon, I always say."

"I suppose," she whispered, her eyes on the crews. She saw Adam Winslow by one of the port guns. He looked at her and grinned. "I hope thee does not enjoy murder and death too much, Adam Winslow," she murmured under her breath.

The exercise began with a sharp command from the captain.

"Broadsides first, Mr. Lansing, then let them practice aiming and shooting as the guns bear."

In a fever of motion, the crews went through the exercises in silence, which ended with the gun elevated, the lanyard pulled and someone screaming, "Boom!" She knew it was only a drill, but as she watched from the companionway, Hannah felt a ripple of fear down her back, and recalled Mr. Lansing's quiet words of last night. It was only a matter of time before the guns spoke in earnest.

The crews drilled the better part of the morning, exercising the guns faster and faster until the men were drenched in sweat that dropped onto the deck, turning the sand dark. She wanted to go up on deck, where the air was fresh, but that would mean navigating across the gun deck, with the men working so feverishly. Hannah remained where she was.

She was joined by Andrew Lease, who nodded to her and leaned against the bulkhead beside her. He smelled pungently of oil of cloves. She sniffed the air, grateful for a smell besides sweating men, and the ever-present bilge. He waved his hands in front of her. "I broke a bottle in the pharmacy," he said. "I thought it was time to inventory my medicine." He sighed. "Not that much of it will do any good when the guns go off in earnest."

"You are so sure that will happen?" she asked, her voice low.

"It's only a matter of time." He looked at his hands again, the veins standing out in high definition, a surgeon's hands. "And then I go to work."

She looked at him, startled at the sadness in his voice. "Why do you do this, Mr. Lease?" she asked. It was rude question to ask a brief acquaintance, but she could not help herself.

He glanced at Hannah, but his eyes didn't seem to notice her. "It's the perfect career for a man who wishes he were dead, my dear." He touched her under the chin, leaving the smell of cloves as he went back down the companionway. "Maybe this cruise I will get lucky."

Chapter Six

Pushed along by the prevailing winds, the *Dissuade* sailed steadily on a course toward England. Hannah peeled great quantities of dead skin from her arms and legs and as far as she could reach on her back, and admired her golden tan, which was better than despairing over the loss of a ladylike complexion. She did not miss the confinement of her Quaker bonnet, with its long wings, like blinders on a carriage horse. The abandonment of corsets she suffered without a backward glance.

There were even moments, sitting on the deck crosslegged and barefooted, when she was perfectly at peace with the life that had been thrust on her. True, her first crunched weevil had sent her flying topside to lean over the railing, to the amusement of the junior officers' mess. She still held her breath until Captain Spark had taken his sip of his first morning cup of coffee, and pronounced it fit to drink. When she lay in her hammock at night, swinging idly over the great gun below her, she still agonized over what her parents must be going through. For a few moments, she would be wild to be home, and then the moment would pass, and she would remember the pleasure of the wind on her face, and the feel of the white deck under her bare toes.

She entered into the life of the commerce raider as far as she was able, secretly pleased that Captain Spark found her useful. After that first gunnery practice, when she had peeled enough potatoes to get back into Cookie's reluctant good graces, she had been summoned on deck by a peremptory command from the captain.

Hannah hurried up the gangway. The captain pointed to the afterhatch and she sat down, mystified. He nodded then, and the bosun's mate, grinning from ear to ear, deposited a large pile of old rope at her feet. Puzzled, she looked up to the quarterdeck.

"That, Miss Whittier, is oakum. It will be your task to separate the strands and place them in that sack."

Doubtfully, she took up a piece of rope and began to unwind it.

"Excellent!" Captain Spark said. "When you have finished, there is always more. You would be amazed at the amount of rope we go through."

"Captain, tell me ..." she began as she worked.

"What do we use it for?" he asked, finishing her thought. "When we spring a leak, we patch it with oakum. It has a thousand uses, I suppose, but that is the one we are fondest of."

She found herself observing Captain Spark from her usual perch on the aft hatch as she sat, day after day, picking oakum. He never sat down on deck, or even leaned against the railing, but ramrod straight, paced his quarterdeck, king of all he stared at. His eyes were often on the sails, and even more often on the brooding cannon below on the gun deck, which were exercised more and more often, the closer they came to England, and the dangers of a world at war for twenty years.

The hint of war came rushing to her the first morning they ran out the guns and practiced with live ammunition. Her heart in her mouth, she made herself small against the angle of the main deck and the quarterdeck and watched in terrified fascination as the guns boomed, the ship heeled to one side with the force of the discharge, then righted itself.

The men worked in silence for the most part, so they could hear the shouted orders of Lieutenant Lansing, who commanded the gun deck. There was only the screech of the gun trucks as the cannon were wheeled out to fire, and back to reload, and the sound of the explosion. The broadsides were painful almost, with the starboard guns and then the port guns roaring off together. Even worse, to Hannah's way of thinking, was when Lansing ordered his crews to fire as soon as they reloaded. The continuous roll of thunder as the guns belched fire set her whole body vibrating and her ears tingling in agony.

While the guns were roaring and the ship was heeling crazily from side to side, the lieutenant of Marines sent his detachment of men into the riggings with their muskets, where they clung to the lines, aimed, and fired at imaginary Frenchmen.

Accidents were an inevitable part of practice—powder boys tripping on the gun ring bolts as they ran with the cloth bags of powder; fingers crushed from a moment's carelessness in the hypnotic rhythm of swab, load, tamp, and fire. Andrew Lease was always there, a canvas bag of rudimentary medications and bandages slung over his shoulder, to help those in pain on the gun deck. He worked swiftly and surely, his face set, his eyes calm, then sent them back to their posts.

She had so many questions, but there was no one to ask. The surgeon spent most of the time on the lower deck in the pharmacy. In the evenings, he often stood on the coveted weather side of the quarterdeck with Captain Spark, conversing softly. When he did come onto the main deck during the day, Lease never failed to stop and talk with her, inquiring after her health, asking how she did, rather like they sat together over tea in a drawing room. She could only sigh after he left and continue picking at the endless rope, and wondering at the air of sadness he wore like a cloak.

Hannah kept her own counsel for the first time in her life. There was no one to giggle with, or share secrets, so she was silent for the most part, an observer. She began to anticipate the bells and the soft splash as the officer of the watch dropped the log in the water, then watched its speed to determine knots per hour before hauling it in. Even the twittering of the bosun's pipe resolved itself into distinct orders as plainly understood by her as by the crew that assembled to receive them, or carry them out.

She came to dread Fridays, when the bosun, at the command of the lieutenant of Marines, would pipe all hands on deck for floggings. To her way of thinking, the infractions were so minor: spitting on the deck; oversleeping when called on watch; exceeding the daily fresh water ration of one gallon per man. Eyes wide, scarcely breathing, she watched as the offender, shirt removed, was tied by the hands to the rigging.

The bosun took the cat-o'-nine tails out of a red bag and flourished them before getting down to the business. As crew and officers watched in silence, the lash came down quickly and thoroughly, turning the malefactor's back crimson. She watched in horror, forgetting to breathe almost, and then gulping air until she became light-headed.

It was on the tip of her tongue to protest. She glanced at the captain, standing tall in full uniform with his brother officers, his face impassive. He was watching her, too, as if expecting an outburst. She closed her mouth into a firm line and wished that the ship would stop spinning about. Dizzy and sick at heart, she watched as the sailor's comrades cut him down, sluiced him off with saltwater, and replaced him with another offender. He took his ten lashes with little gasping noises.

But she was the one making the noises. The ship seemed to whirl faster and faster until all she could hear was one continuous lashing after another. Hannah tried to get up from her customary perch on the aft hatch and make her way silently below deck, but her feet wouldn't move. In another moment, someone pushed her head between her knees and held it there.

"Now stay that way until you feel more the thing," said Captain Spark, his hand on her head. When she finally nodded, he released his grip.

Hannah sat up carefully; waiting for the verbal flogging Spark was so capable of administering. Instead, his eyes were kind as he looked at her.

"It's a sight that's felled strong men, Miss Whittier," he said. He motioned to Lieutenant Futtrell to help her below. "Perhaps we'll make a sailor of you yet."

She shook her head, and then groaned as it began to pound. Captain Spark turned his attention back to the misery on his deck, punishment which he had decreed. The lash whistled and popped and she went gratefully below.

But there were glorious days of sailing, when all the canvas was loaded on and the frigate ran toward home. The humming of the rigging became music to her ears. She watched the sailors climbing about like monkeys in the jungle, scampering up rigging that seemed to stretch upward and out of sight, like an Indian fakir's magic rope.

And then one morning, she set down the everlasting hemp in her hands and started toward the rigging herself. It wasn't a conscious thought that drew her there like a moth to flame, but more of an involuntary movement, the result of watching others climb up and down the rigging. She knotted her shirt firmly, so the wind would not whirl it above her head as she climbed, rolled her trouser legs to the knee, then began her ascent.

She kept her eyes ahead, looking steadily at the unoccupied lookout on the mainmast. There was usually a midshipman there, bare feet dangling over the edge, spyglass in hand, but they had all been summoned to the deck by the sailing master for a lesson in shooting the sun. The wind tugged at her hair the higher she climbed, until it was swirling about her face and in her eyes. "Drat and botheration," she said, wishing she had tied it tighter at the back of her neck.

She reached the lookout and was contemplating her next move when she heard a shout from far below, and made the mistake of glancing down. She gasped and clutched the rope tighter, astounded at the great distance between her and the deck. Lieutenant Futtrell stood far, far below, pointing up at her and waving his arms about. Then others were looking at her. She clung to the rope and stared at their upturned faces. As she watched in growing terror, the wind picked up and the mast began to sway. She closed her eyes and wished herself back on the aft hatch, safely picking oakum. Climbing the rigging had looked so easy from the deck.

As she watched Lieutenant Futtrell's antics, he picked up the speaking trumpet. "Come down right now, before you hurt yourself," he shouted to her.

It sounded like excellent advice. Hannah gulped and tried to move her feet. They would not budge, no matter how hard her mind willed it. She clung tighter to the rigging and prayed for rescue. As she clutched the rope, someone darted for the gangway and tumbled below.

In a few minutes, Captain Spark hurried on deck, stuffing his shirt into his pants, and then running his hands through his curly hair, anxious eyes on the mast. Hannah closed her eyes. "Oh, heavens, not him!" she whispered. He had been up for the early watch and had retired for a nap. She tried to move her feet again, but they were anchored like glue to the ropes. She dared herself to look down again, to see Captain Spark climbing steadily toward her. "Hannah Whittier, thee is an idiot," she said out loud.

Quicker than she would have credited, Spark climbed the rigging. He kept coming, as though to travel right over the top of her, and stopped only when he was standing on the same ropes, his body shielding hers from a fall. He was breathing heavily, and his breath ruffled the hair on her neck. She waited for the ax to fall.

He said nothing at first, only wrapped one arm through the rigging, gathered her hair back into a manageable handful and retied the string at her neck. "It helps to see what you're doing, Miss Whittier, if you have fancies of climbing the rigging."

"I am so sorry," she managed to gasp out through tightly clenched teeth. "I had no idea I would be so scared."

He didn't move, but rested his chest against her back until she relaxed a little. "You can't fall with me here," he said finally. "Just loop your arm through the rigging and listen to me. Do it now."

She forced herself to do as he said, afraid to look at him. She shivered and clenched her jaw tight to keep her teeth from chattering.

When he spoke, his tone was conversational, and she was grateful right down to her toes. "As I see it, we have three choices, Miss Whittier. I can have my men rig a block and tackle and we can lower you down, but that would be quite humiliating, don't you agree?"

She nodded, still shivering. He took her by the shoulder and gave her a little shake, then rested his hand beside her neck. His fingers were warm.

"I could also turn you around right now, and you could put your arms about my neck and your legs around my waist, and I could carry you down. But you will doubtless agree that such a maneuver lacks in dignity for both of us. You're a bit of a scamp, but I do have a position to maintain on the *Dissuade,* my dear Miss Whittier."

He was silent a moment more. Hannah cleared her throat, wondering if she could make her voice work any better than her legs. "The third way, sir?"

"I go back down to the deck by myself, and you follow me."

"But ... suppose I fall?" she whispered, looking at him at last.

His face was so close to hers that she could see interesting black specks in his pale eyes. "You won't fall, Miss Whittier. I believe you are made of much sterner stuff than that. Anyone who survives two days on a grating is not going to succumb so easily. By God, I did not realize it before, but your eyes are more yellow than brown. I had a cat like that once. Named her Lady Amber."

She giggled in spite of herself, and relaxed her death's hold on the rigging.

He took his hand off her neck. "Much better, Miss Whittier. Bear this in mind, my dear. When you get to the bottom on your own, I'm going to send you right back up and then down again, and I'll probably have my watch out timing you. Which is it to be?"

She raised her chin and looked him squarely in the eyes. "I … I will come down by myself, sir."

"An excellent choice, Lady Amber." He smiled at her then, the wrinkles deepening around his eyes. He sniffed the air around her ear. "What is that wonderful odor, Miss Whittier? I can't help noticing it at such close quarters."

She blushed. "My lavender water sank with the *Molly Claridge,* sir, but Cookie had some extract of vanilla that I am sure he is not missing."

He threw back his head and laughed. "Not only are you a rascal, but you are a sneaky one, at that. I like it, Miss Whittier. I can probably locate another bottle in my personal stores, if Cookie cuts up stiff. See you on deck, lively now."

Without another word, he was gone, scrambling down the riggings, a veteran of twenty years at sea. Her hands tightened as the ropes shook during his descent but she did not clutch them with the prospect of never letting go. She took a deep breath and looked across the yard to the foremast where three sailors stood, carelessly balanced on the foot ropes, ready to trim sail. There was no ridicule on their faces as they watched her, and she realized that at one time they had all been where she was now. As she watched, one of the men blew her a kiss then clasped both hands over his head in a triumphal gesture.

She nodded to him and started down the rigging, slowly at

first, groping for each new foothold, then more confidently, as each rope was right where it should have been. By the time she reached the deck, she was breathing regularly again.

The men in the sails cheered, and Hannah grinned. Captain Spark pulled out his watch and snapped it open. "Let's see how fast you can do it again, Miss Whittier."

Hannah took another deep breath and climbed back into the rigging. Her eyes on the pennant snapping out straight from the topgallant, she clambered up the rope, touched the lookout, and hurried down, reaching the deck again to cheers from all hands.

Captain Spark shut his watch. "Pretty good. It can be better, Miss Whittier, but we will let you rest on your laurels for now." He turned for the gangway. "And now, if you will excuse me, I will return to my cot. Miss Whittier, do stay out of trouble for at least another hour, if you can."

Only minutes ago, she would have taken offense at his tone. Now, she merely smiled. "Aye, sir. I promise."

"Sir, perhaps we could include her in the rum ration today?" Mr. Futtrell asked, his eyes lively with good humor.

The captain turned around, his eyes frosty again. "That is the last thing I would recommend for Miss Whittier! Mr. Futtrell, you know rum is for heroes. We will wait on that for this misguided bit of shark chum."

Futtrell chuckled and returned to his duty on the quarterdeck, and Hannah went back to the aft hatch and the pile of old rope that awaited her. Shark chum, indeed, she thought as she picked out the strands. You would not say that if I were tall and willowy, with a beautiful face. She sighed and flopped back on the hatch, surrendering to the sun. And why, Hannah Whittier, shouldst anything like that matter to thee?

It was foolish, she decided, as she sat up and applied herself more diligently to the oakum. Besides all this, he is so old.

"Beg pardon, miss?"

She looked up to see Trist standing before her, and hoped

she had not been talking out loud. "I am almost done with this batch," she said, indicating the oakum.

"Oh, no, no, it is not that, Miss Whittier." The little man cleared his throat. "Captain Sir Daniel Spark wishes your company at dinner tonight in the great cabin."

She remembered her last refusal of the captain and had the good grace to blush. She hesitated, and Trist continued.

"I was to tell you, if you looked indecisive, that he can arrange live coals, if you prefer, but all the same, he'd like you to eat with him."

Hannah laughed. "Very well, then! I will take mutton with the captain. When, sir?"

"Four bells, ma'am."

"Very well. Will anyone else be there?"

"Oh, yes ma'am, the surgeon."

She remained on deck all afternoon, picking oakum and watching the water. Captain Spark came on deck in midafternoon after his nap, nodded to her, and proceeded to his quarterdeck, where he remained, hands clasped behind his back. During the long afternoon, he stared out at sea, roared at the helmsman to pay attention, and then coached the midshipmen in the mysteries of navigation. She tried to listen, but the intricacies of the math involved eluded her, and she was grateful she did not have to suffer such a lesson herself.

As the sun began to slant across the deck and to set the water to dancing with new colors, Hannah went below. Dressing for dinner involved nothing more than changing to the other shirt, which, while still black-and-white checked, was not as faded as the one she had been wearing. She washed her face with her two-inch ration of fresh water and dabbed more vanilla extract behind her ears, then brushed her hair until it crackled about her face like a nimbus.

"Such a bother," she said into the tiny mirror, as she tamed it down and braided one heavy pigtail. Mama had told her once, when she had been in tears about her hair, that someday she would come to appreciate it. Well, that day had not dawned yet, she decided as she left her cabin, nodded to the Marine, and went to Captain Spark's door.

She knocked.

"Come."

She entered the room to see the captain and ship's surgeon seated by the table, drinking Madeira. They rose when she came closer, and the captain ushered her into a chair at the table. He sat down across from her, and Lease took the other place. Trist set the food before them, and it was the same as she had eaten for several weeks now, only served on rather fine Wedgwood. She smiled.

"Are you weary of ship's fare yet, Miss Whittier?" the captain asked, noticing her expression. "I hear from my junior officers that you do not care for surprises in your ship's biscuits."

"They told you truly," she said as he picked up his fork. "Sir, can we not say grace?"

The captain put down his fork, and Lease eyed her with a cross between amusement and respect. "Do you really think that an appeal to the Almighty will make it more palatable?" the surgeon asked.

"What? Have you no faith?" she teased.

"None whatsoever," the surgeon replied, his face quite serious. "And no hope, and precious little charity."

There was an awkward pause, and then Hannah plunged in. "All the more reason to ask the Lord to bless it. Bow your heads, gentlemen."

She asked a blessing on the food specifically, and the HMS *Dissuade* generally, said amen, and picked up her fork.

They ate in silence at first, then the captain looked up at Hannah, amusement on his face. "Forgive us, Miss Whittier, but we have been so long at sea that the art of dinner table conversation quite eludes us. What should we be speaking of? Affairs of state? The economy of the nation? Ladies' fashions? Price of corn whiskey? What interests Americans?"

Hannah smiled and tapped her biscuit on the table. "As to that, in Nantucket Mama tells us of her day, and Papa usually complains about the high price of everything."

Lease laughed. "I like that," he said, and then went back to eating.

"What did you talk about at table, Captain?" she asked when the surgeon seemed no more forthcoming.

The captain rested his elbow on the table. "I almost don't remember. I was ten when I went to sea, after all. I suppose my mother asked about my lessons, when she was there."

"And your father?" she prompted.

"He was seldom there, either," was the captain's short reply. He addressed his attention to the salt beef again.

How sad, she thought, remembering the lively conversations around the Whittier table. "We argued politics, made fun of our neighbors, and Papa generally wished James Madison to the devil. Papa is a Federalist."

The captain laughed and pushed away his plate. "Do you care about politics, my dear Lady Amber?"

"I think it is the duty of all Americans," she replied, taking another bite of the biscuit and wondering at his endearment.

"Even those females who don't vote?" he asked, twinkling his pale eyes in her direction.

She entered into his banter with no qualms. "Especially so, sir. Mama insists that someday I will be quite influential in helping some man cast *his* ballot!"

The captain nodded. "I don't doubt that for a minute, Miss Whittier. How is it that you have escaped parson's mousetrap thus far?"

"Sir, have a heart! I am just seventeen!"

The captain winced. "I had thought you older," he said, and poured another, deeper glass of Madeira. "What, then, was a tender Quaker lass of seventeen doing traveling unescorted to Charleston? Excuse me if I am nosy, but we don't get much good gossip on ship, and I don't care to discuss President

Madison myself, although my political leanings are Whiggish."

She smiled and held out her glass. He paused a moment, then poured the Madeira. "You're too young for very much of this," he warned.

She drank. "That's good."

"It should be. We picked that up from a Spanish coasting sloop out of Jamaica, didn't we Lease?"

The surgeon nodded. "Really, Daniel, this lady will think we are little better than pirates."

"You don't want to know what I think of you, sir!" she said, regretting her words the moment she said them, but forced into honesty by her nature.

"No, I suppose we do not," the captain murmured. "But for the sake of improving our dinner table manners, do tell us why you were bound for Charleston."

She told them of Hosea and his bride and the expected baby. "Which I am sure is born by now. I would like to have been there to help out."

Spark shuddered. "Children are a nuisance, Miss Whittier. I am grateful that to my knowledge, I have none. Always mewling and puking, I wonder that anyone tolerates them."

Hannah thought of her list and smiled to herself as she crossed him off it yet again. "Perhaps if you had your own, they would not seem so troublesome." She sighed. "And I suppose that was my other reason for Charleston. Papa and Hosea mean to find me a husband; someone steady with sufficient income."

Spoken like that, it sounded so bald. She stared into the Madeira. Perhaps it is good to lay one's cards on the table, she thought. It would be hard to do otherwise with present company.

"Is that what a woman wants?" Spark asked, leaning forward with both elbows on the table now, his eyes intense. "Sufficient income and a male—any male—as long as he breathes?"

She thought of her list again, weighed the probability of

ever seeing this man again once they reached Portsmouth, and sailed ahead fearlessly. "Do you know, Captain, I once assembled a list of the qualities I wanted in a husband?" She blushed when he chuckled. "Silly, wasn't I?"

"That would depend on what the list contained. You don't strike me as an empty-headed chit. Irritating, I own, but not slow of wit, Lady Amber."

As she looked into his disconcerting eyes, Hannah wished he would not call her that. "One thing was that he love me enough to place my welfare before his own."

The surgeon uttered a sudden exclamation, pushed his chair away from the table, and left the room without further comment. Hannah felt her cheeks burn, and absurd tears rushed to her eyes.

"Did I say something terrible?" she asked, her eyes wide with distress. "Oh. I meant no offense. I would not for the world hurt him."

The captain shook his head. "I think that what you wish is what everyone, man or woman, wants. Few have the temerity to list it. My congratulations."

"But ... why did he leave like that?" she asked, bewildered.

The captain sighed and filled her glass again, this time to the top. He pushed aside his own wineglass and pulled forward a tumbler, which soon was brimming with Madeira. "He'll have to tell you himself, Lady Amber. I don't uncloak others' intimacies. God knows, I can't understand my own."

It was a quixotic comment, and she knew better than to follow up on it. Hannah sipped her Madeira, the pleasure gone out of the drink. The captain downed his tumbler of Madeira and tipped the bottle toward his glass again. He looked at her, his eyes faint with amusement.

"You probably have something on your list about men who drink too much."

"Well, no, actually," she said, "but I could certainly add a rider."

He did not pour the wine, but set the bottle upright and pushed it away, clearing a space on the table in front of them. "I really had another reason for asking you here, beyond table talk and cornering you with my limp wit."

She watched him, her eyes wary.

"And don't look like that!" he protested, throwing up both hands. "I have no designs on your person! What I need is some help."

"Ask away then," she replied, trying and failing to keep the tremulous relief from her voice.

He noticed it anyway, and touched her hand. "Lady Amber, you needn't worry about preserving your virtue on this ship, not while I command. I know this is a difficult situation for you, but we will not make it worse. Please believe me."

"I do now," she replied softly.

"It is this, then. I am shorthanded since my last encounter with the French. I would like to use my midshipmen for other purposes, but I must maintain a watch in the lookout. Can you do that for us?"

She considered his request.

"I didn't think of it until this morning's little diversion in the rigging. If you could take one watch a day, perhaps even two, that would help me."

Hannah nodded. "I would be glad to." She hesitated then. "There is one condition, sir."

"Fire away."

"I will not call down to tell you I have spotted American vessels," she said. "But I can look for the French."

He took her hand again to shake it. "Very well, Lady Amber, very well. Your terms are not onerous, and I do respect your Federalist tendencies. Tomorrow then, the forenoon watch? I know you will miss the oakum, but after all, England is at war. You may use my glass."

"I shall do it, sir."

Chapter Seven

She slept well that night, full of plum duff and too much poached Madeira, eaten off Wedgwood and drunk from Waterford crystal. The hammock rocked her to sleep, and she succumbed to a pleasant dream that may have included a curly-headed man, but which, upon awakening, she could not quite recall.

Hannah put her hands behind her head and wriggled more comfortably in the captain's nightshirt. I should be practically bleeding with homesickness, and yet I am not. She considered the matter, staring at the deck overhead. My life has been so circumscribed, she thought. Everything I have done, has been at the instigation of others. But now ... I do not know what will happen.

The knowledge did not frighten her, and she wondered why, but only for a moment. It is that I trust Captain Sir Daniel Spark, she thought. He is a hard man in a hard service, but he is fair. He runs an orderly ship. She turned onto her side, and stared down at the cannon. I wonder if he can fight? She swallowed and felt the hair on her neck raise. More to the point, can I?

"Well, Hannah Whittier, thee can climb a rigging," she told herself as she carefully stepped onto the gun and then the deck below. "Such knowledge can only be expanded."

She dressed quickly and opened the door. The Marine clicked his heels and stood at attention, then held out a small parcel for her. "From Trist, ma'am," he said.

She took the package and went back into her cabin. She read the note: "For a change from the vanilla extract, Lady Amber. Yrs, Spark," and opened the package. Chortling with pleasure, she took out a bottle of extract of almond. She sniffed its sharp scent and dabbed a bit on her neck.

Cookie had the green coffee beans ready for her to roast, and she made short work of her morning ritual, humming to herself. Cookie sniffed the air suspiciously, then looked into his pantry, when he thought her attention was occupied elsewhere. Hannah smiled to herself as he located his own almond extract, and could make no complaint, or demand an extra peeling of potatoes.

The air was brisk with the feeling of a more northerly latitude as she came on deck with the captain's coffee. He stood as usual on the quarterdeck, his glass trained on the distant horizon. He wore the heavy woolen boat cloak that swept to his ankles, pulled back to reveal his impeccable whites. He turned around at her approach and nodded a greeting.

She set the mug on the deck by the gangway as usual, and as usual, he crossed to the rail and squatted gracefully beside her as she sat on the rung of the ladder. She watched as he took a sip and pronounced it successful.

"You could get yourself a cup, too," he offered. "This really is excellent brew, Lady Amber."

She made a face. "I do not care for it, sir. It makes me jittery and keeps me awake. And Mama claims I am not fit to live with when I am cross."

"I would not doubt your mother for a moment," he said after a good swallow. He sniffed the air around her appreciatively. "I think I like the almond even better."

She grinned up at him. "Except that I smell like dessert."

"Exactly so," he replied. "Do you know what I like to do first when I come off a long cruise?"

She shook her head, secretly pleased at his sudden talkativeness.

"I drink about a quart of water that comes fresh from a well, and then I have my housekeeper make me an almond cake with gooey icing, which I eat all by myself."

She clapped her hands in delight. "You do not share?"

"I might, with the right person," he said, then drained the rest of the coffee and handed the mug back to her. He nodded, and pointed to the aft hatch. "And there your oakum awaits. Lively now, Miss Whittier."

He turned back to stare at the ocean again, the interview over. A smile on her face, Hannah took the mug below deck and then returned to her task of picking oakum. She shivered in the early morning breeze and willed the sun to warm the deck soon. Sailors holystoned the deck around her, rubbing the already spotless planking with sandstone chunks the size of prayerbooks and then sluicing it down with seawater.

"Hannah, think what an oakum expert thee is becoming!"

She looked up in surprise at the sailor closest to her on the deck. "Adam!" she exclaimed. "Oh, sit and talk!"

He shook his head, his eyes on the bosun's mate. "I daren't. Are they treating thee well?" he asked as he continued by the hatch on his knees, scraping the deck.

"Oh, yes. And I will be sitting in the lookout soon, keeping watch for the French."

He chuckled. "Who'd have thought it? Not I, surely. Well, I do not believe thee was ever partial to sewing samplers, was thee?"

"Oh, thy sisters have tattled," she said and impulsively reached down to ruffle his hair.

"Belay that! Ship's discipline!" called Mr. Futtrell in ringing tones from his watch on the lee side of the quarterdeck.

To her embarrassment, Captain Spark looked down at them and frowned.

"He's my friend," she protested.

"And he is my crew," the captain reminded her, biting off his words. "Mind your manners, Miss Whittier! You may tousle his golden mane all you choose, once you're back in the United States."

The other sailors on their knees laughed and Adam blushed a rosy pink. "Oh, Hannah, thee is a rascal," he muttered, and continued along the deck.

Hannah cast a speaking look at the captain, which was entirely wasted, because he had already turned his attention back to the sea again. "Golden mane, indeed," she muttered to herself. "This is Adam Winslow, whom I grew up with." She nourished her feelings of vast ill-usage until the sun rose higher and warned the hatch she sat on. Then she abandoned herself to the pleasure of another day's sailing, wishing she could stretch like a cat and curl up for a nap.

At four bells, the midshipman in the lookout scampered back down to the deck and reported to Captain Spark on the quarterdeck. Hannah sat where she was, then tucked the rest of the oakum in the burlap bag at her feet as Spark took off his boat cloak at last and came down the gangway toward her.

"Well, Lady Amber, it is time for you to tempt the fates again. Mr. Futtrell? Will you fetch my straw hat from the great cabin, and my glass, and bring that copy of *Ships of Nations*?"

"Aye, sir," the lieutenant replied and hurried below.

He stood beside her on the main deck, and she patted the hatch.

"You could sit down, sir," she invited.

He looked at her in surprise, his eyebrows high arched. "Never, Miss Whittier. A captain does not sit on his deck, especially on a hatch."

"Don't you ever get tired?" she asked.

"I would never admit to it. Ah thank you, Mr. Futtrell. Sir, please take my place on the weather side until I regain the deck again."

He clapped the hat on his head and picked up the telescope, which he hooked onto his belt. He grasped the book in one hand and nodded to Hannah. "After you, Lady A."

She climbed the rigging, mindful that the captain was right behind and probably observing her at uncomfortably close quarters. The thought made her blush. She paused where the yardarm crossed the mast, feeling the old, sick fear of yesterday returning.

"Up you get, and lively now," came that brisk voice at her bare heels. "Please don't look down."

Without a word, she climbed higher until she was perched in the lookout on the topgallant. She took a deep breath and dangled her bare feet over the edge of the little platform, resting her arms on the modest railing. The mast swayed in the wind, and she gulped again.

"If you feel like heaving up an ocean, do it now, and not when I am on my way down," the captain admonished, his voice amused, as he held on to the rigging below her, a picture of grace. He edged higher until he knelt on the narrow platform with her, then took the straw hat from his head and put it on hers. "That should cut some of the sun," he commented and grinned at her. "I like it, Lady A. Makes you look even a more roguish scamp than usual."

She made a face at him and then clutched his leg when the mast swayed. Rather than utter some barbed remark, he laid his hand on her shoulder and kept it there until she loosened her grip, but did not release him.

"There now. It's something you can get used to," he said mildly. He unhooked his telescope and set it beside her in a small bucket intended for that purpose that was attached to the mast. He opened the book to a well-worn page and directed her attention to it.

"This is what you are looking for," he said, pointing out the pages of French men-of-war, all bristling with guns and painted black, with occasion gilt ornamentation. "The ensign is like this, and it may fly a pennant like this. Look for the tricolor."

She followed his finger, studying the pages. He smiled and leaned closer for a moment as the mast swayed. "I believe I do like the extract of almond the best."

She ignored his comment as his cheek just brushed hers. She knew she should scold him, but there was something so comforting in having him close by as she fought down her nausea and tried to make sense of the pictures that floated before her.

"Just take a good sweep of the entire horizon every so often, my dear, and that should suffice," he concluded, closing the book. "You'll probably wonder if you are really seeing things, after a while. And if you are not sure if it is a French ship, call down to the deck anyway."

"And if it is?" she asked, finally releasing her grip on his leg.

"Why, then, we fight," he said, almost surprised at her question.

"You'll let me come down from the mast first, won't you?" she asked, her eyes anxious.

He laughed out loud. "No, you silly chit! I'll keep you here and make you direct the laying of the guns! Of course you'll come down, and lively, too."

He started down the rigging and stopped when he was eye level with the platform. "Do you think you can occupy your time? It gets tedious."

She did not want him to go and leave her there, swaying in the wind. "What did you do to pass the time here when you were a midshipman?" she asked to detain his departure.

"I? It's been so long," he murmured, resting his hand on the platform. "I seem to recall singing ribald songs that I will never teach you, and memorizing the theorems of Pythagoras for navigational purposes." He started to pat her leg, then withdrew his hand. "Perhaps thee can use this time to recall improving scriptures," he teased. "Good day, Lady Amber. Remember, if you see a French ship, it's tally-ho."

She watched him descend, the wind tossing about his curly hair. Thee needs a haircut in the worst way, she thought, then pulled out the telescope and opened it. She discovered that by resting her elbows on the platform railing, she could hold the glass steady enough to scan the horizon. She looked all around, careful to balance herself, and then collapsed the telescope and used her eyes only. There was no other ship on the ocean. She sighed, feeling an emotion close to reverence. They were sailing quite alone on a wide sea, pushed ever closer to Europe by winds than had blown in that direction since the Lord Almighty had decreed it in Genesis. " 'The heavens declare the glory of God, and the firmament sheweth his handiwork,' " she murmured, and scanned the horizon again.

By the time the watch ended, Hannah was ready to come down. The sun had probably imprinted the black-and-white checks into the tanned skin of her sorely tried back, and she was thirsty. She resolved never to look in a mirror again, convinced that she would see that her freckles had multiplied like a many-headed Hydra. She had unbuttoned her shirt as far as she dared and rolled her trouser legs above her knees, but she felt like a duck basting under Mama's direction at First Day dinner.

"Miss Whittier!" It was Mr. Futtrell, calling to her with the speaking trumpet. "You may stand down now."

"Aye," she called down. She buttoned her shirt and knotted it securely before dropping the captain's glass down the front. I must procure a belt from somewhere, she thought as she carefully edged off the platform, onto the rigging, and then down to the main deck.

Captain Spark was waiting for her with his watch open. "Next time, come down faster," he ordered. "Your life may depend on it."

"Aye, sir," she said and reached into her shirt for the telescope, which she laid in his hand.

He took it with a smile. "It's been many places, Miss Whittier, but never there. I think Trist can locate you a belt," he said, then turned on his heel to return to the quarterdeck. "Thank you, ma'am. May I send you up again at four bells?" he asked over his shoulder.

"Of course." Stiff with sitting so long, she hurried to the scuttlebutt for a drink, wishing that she dared take more than one dipperful, but mindful of the Friday floggings. I am so thirsty, she thought as she went below to flop on her hammock.

Her tiny cabin was stifling with heat and thick with the polluted atmosphere that filled the lower decks, but she looked at the hammock gratefully. She glanced at the little sea chest, and smiled. There was the battered silver carafe and elegant stemmed Waterford crystal goblet from last night's dinner.

"Thank thee, Captain Spark," she said as she picked up the carafe and drank directly from it. In another moment she was asleep in the swaying hammock.

Hannah's late afternoon watch was relieved by one false alarm. She shouted, "Sail-ho!" to the main deck and Mr. Futtrell came charging up the rigging. He stood beside her on the tiny platform, and grabbed the glass. For a long moment he surveyed the place where she pointed, then lowered the glass with a grin.

"Well? Well?" she asked anxiously.

He put the glass to his eye again. "I think it is what you Yankees call a right whale, Miss Whittier," he said, unable to keep the laughter from his voice. "The Frenchies think they are so clever, but even they cannot spout."

She sighed with disappointment. "And now you will tease me," she muttered at last.

"I?" he asked, all innocence. "Oh, never, ma'am. My first ship sighting was an island, as I recall. My fellow midshipman named it the H.M.S. *Puerto Rico.*"

She smiled up at him charitably and took the glass back. "Very well, sir. I shall do better."

He started his descent. "You are already doing wonderfully well, Miss Whittier. Are all Yankee girls so useful?"

"As to that, I cannot tell. Mama always told me, 'Hannah, thee must make a difference.'" She frowned and then swallowed suddenly, thinking of her mother.

"Well, you have," he said, then paused and fumbled in his pocket. He took out two large pieces of ship's biscuit. "From Captain Spark."

She thanked him and munched the biscuits happily, swinging her feet over the edge of the platform, and wondering why she ever worried about the swaying of the mast, which was now only a pleasant diversion now.

When she descended to the deck again as the sun was setting, she shook her head at Captain Spark's dinner invitation. "I am too tired to be sparkling company." she apologized. "Besides that, it will take me an hour or two to unsnarl all these silly curls of mine."

The captain bowed, and picked up a handful of her hair that spilled in curls around her neck. "I could do that for you sometime, Lady Amber," he said softly. "I know you do not credit it, but I am a man of infinite patience."

She stepped away from him in sudden shyness, and he let go of her hair.

"Is patience on your list?" he added, smiling at her confusion.

She nodded and darted below deck, wondering what had ever possessed her to mention that dratted list. Ah, but I have long since removed thee from any consideration since you do not like children, swear to excess, drink too much, are generally blasphemous, and are not engaged in a profession designed to quiet the fears of a wife. And thee is vastly old, thirty at least. So there, sir. She was asleep almost before she climbed the gun.

Hannah watched for days, gradually extending her time aloft until she could manage for most of the day. Captain Spark,

while not saying anything about her service, made good use
of his midshipmen, sending one below with Mr. Lansing to
practice laying the guns onto a target, and sending the other
to follow Mr. Futtrell and study the setting of the sails. As she
watched from her perch, the second lieutenant drilled his
topmen over and over in the prompt reefing of sails to make
them battle-ready and less vulnerable to enemy fire.

Captain Spark remained on the quarterdeck with the third
midshipman, the two of them shooting the sun with his sextant,
and then spreading out the charts to determine landfall. She
watched all this with interest from her perch above the deck.

Adam Winslow climbed up once to sit with her. "I am off
duty, Hannah," he explained. "Mr. Lansing released us from
the gun deck, and I am glad of it." He nudged her shoulder.
"Hannah, is thee enjoying thyself?"

She smiled at her lifetime friend. "More than I would admit
to thee!"

He nodded. "And why not, I ask? The men talk about thee
and wonder if thee is ever out of sorts. I tell them no, that thee
was born with a sunny disposition." He took her hand then.
"But we have to get out of here, Hannah."

"I know," she agreed, her voice soft. "Thee has to return to
school, and I still would like to see Charleston. But how can
we do it?"

It was on the afternoon of the fourth day that she sighted
the French frigate. She was idly scanning the horizon, to the
north and east when she spotted the ship. She held her breath
to further still the movement of the telescope, and trained it on
the top mast of the distant ship where the pennant flew.

"Drat!" she whispered to herself. The day was calm and the
pennant drooped limply from the topgallant. "Blow, winds,"
she ordered, and to her extreme gratification the wind picked
up and the pennant streamed out straight as an arrow from the
mast. She took a deep breath. It was the tricolor of Napoleon's
France.

She kept the glass trained on the ship and watched in growing excitement as the frigate swung gracefully about. The *Dissuade* had been spotted at that moment, too. "Oh, God," she breathed, and slammed the telescope together, clipping it onto one of Captain Spark's extra belts that wrapped around her waist twice.

"Sail-ho," she screamed to the deck. "It is France!"

Futtrell, scarcely breathing heavy, was beside her in a moment's time, carrying his own glass. He looked where she pointed. "By God, Miss Whittier, it is the *Bergeron*, that gave us such trouble in the Windward Islands."

He leaned over the railing. "*Bergeron*, sir, damn them!" he called to Captain Spark, who stood in the quarterdeck riggings already, his midshipman's glass pointed to the northeast.

"All hands!" Spark roared to the bosun. "Beat to quarters."

"Come, Miss Whittier," ordered Futtrell, his face alive with excitement as the Marine drummer boy began to pound his urgent message.

"You first," she said. "I think you need to get to the deck first."

"I do," he said, already descending. "I'll be sending up my topmen on these lines. They'll run right over you, but don't be afraid. Hurry down, miss."

Her heart in her throat, she began her descent as the sailors were coming up the rigging. "Pardon, miss," each man said as he raced past her to a position on the footropes. When the last man had passed her she scrambled to the deck and made herself small against the aft hatch.

She looked below her to the gun deck, which was full of sailors. Everyone had a job and did it swiftly and silently. Mr. Lansing looked up at her and grinned once, then redirected his attention to the powder monkeys, who were already running to each gun with their first charges. She heard other men tearing down the bulkheads that divided the remaining cabins from the rest of the gun deck. Soon Captain Spark's furniture from the great cabin was carried on deck and lowered overboard into a dinghy tied to the stern, where it would ride out the battle.

She stayed where she was, fascinated by the urgency that swirled around her, and too afraid to leave her perch and get in anyone's way. Marines hurried past her and climbed the rigging with their muskets. Others, their faces steely, hauled up a swivel gun.

"Hannah!" She looked up to see Captain Spark striding toward her.

He was dressed in his best uniform, his fore-and-aft hat anchored firmly on his head, which set off something in her brain.

"Why don't you pin on all your medals, too?" she asked as he reached her side. "Then you would be an even better target, sir!"

"I always go into battle dressed in my best," he said. "It's such an insult, ma'am." He took her by the arm, and none too gently. "You are to go below to the cable tier and remain there until I come for you, and not one moment before."

"But it's dark there," she said, unable to keep the fear from her voice.

"Do it, Hannah," he ordered, lifting her off her feet with his hands clamped on her arms. He released his grip, but still held her there on the afterhatch. "You are going to hear the worst sounds you will ever hear down there," he said, his voice low, for her ears only. "When the guns run in and out, it sounds like the ship is tearing apart. You will also hear the screams of the wounded. I can't help what you will hear, but I can assure you that you will never again hear anything as bad, or be more afraid than you are right now."

She nodded, unable to tear her gaze away from his eyes. He touched her cheek with the back of his hand. "I was ten years old when I went into battle for the first time. Nothing scares me now. Go below, Hannah, and don't disobey me."

Still she hesitated. Without another word he grasped her

hands and swung her over into the gun deck, calling to Adam Winslow.

"You there, take her to the cable tier!"

Adam caught her and grabbed her hand, tugging her down two more decks until she was in the depths of the ship, and made her sit on the great cables that lay, wet with bilge, in the hold. "Do what the captain said, Hannah."

She nodded, afraid to trust her voice. In another moment he was gone, and she was alone. She shivered in the stinking darkness, listening to the rats that squeaked around her. Her mind was blank of all petitions to the Almighty. She locked herself into a tight ball and crouched on the cable, waiting for the battle to begin.

The first broadside sent her reeling off the cable and into the bilge when the ship heeled, righted itself, then swung quickly around for the port guns to bear. She screamed and leaped back onto the cable as the guns were pulled in, screeching on their tracks, reloaded, and then run out again, directly over her head. Through the heavy planking, she heard Mr. Lansing roaring at the crews to be lively now, but wait for the guns to bear again.

The next broadside was answered by the *Bergeron,* as the shot hurled into the gun deck above her. She clapped her hands over her ears and moaned aloud at the sound of the wounded and dying, and then the screech of the gun trucks again. Rats leaped about her, their fear as great as her own as they raced up and down the cable, seeking escape where there was none.

The third broadside from the *Bergeron* sent two balls crashing below the waterline. She held her breath in terror as the water began to rise toward the cable, and then let it out slowly when sailors with a lantern hurried below to patch the leaks with planking hastily retrieved from the carpenter's shop, and the everlasting oakum. She shivered on the cable and watched them. When they finished, they raced away. In another moment, she heard the clanging of the pumps.

And then the guns were firing at will as the ship swung
about, tacking to keep the weather gauge and continue a
relentless pounding of the *Bergeron*. The guns boomed, the
men screamed. Mr. Lansing was silent now, but still the guns
roared. They stopped momentarily with the cracking and
collapse of the mizzenmast over her head. She strained her
ears to hear Captain Spark roaring orders. The guns boomed
again.

The shrieking of the wounded grew louder, and she realized
with a start that they were being carried below. She thought
of the surgeon, and wondered how he could possibly manage
such carnage.

The roaring of the guns was a continual thunder that filled
her brain to bursting and threatened to send her screaming
along the cable with the rats. The water was still rising, but
much more slowly, now that the leaks were patched and the
pumps working. Soon the air space itself seemed filled with the
groans and screams of the wounded until it was too crowded
for her.

Hannah got to her feet and began to feel her way out of the
cable tier. I cannot sit here in the dark while people are dying
around me, she thought, and the thought gave her courage. I
must help. She thought briefly of her promise to Captain Spark
to remain where she was, and quickly discarded it. Thee was an
idiot to ask it of me, she thought.

She followed the sounds of the wounded to the orlop deck,
where there was light from battle lanterns. She looked down.
The deck was clotted with bloody sand and footprints. She
took a deep breath and came closer.

Fragments of men lay all around, some living, the lucky ones
dead. After her initial shock that sent her reeling back against
the bulkhead, she trained her mind onto Andrew Lease, who
stood over a table made of midshipmens' sea chests. A man lay
on the makeshift table, clutching what remained of his arm.
The surgeon looked up from his calm contemplation of the

ruin before him and nodded to her.

"Ah, my dear Miss Whittier. I can see I have lost my wager," he murmured, his voice scarcely audible over the moans of the wounded.

She hurried to his side, slipping once on the bloody deck, but hanging on to his calm words like she had once clung to the grating of the *Molly Claridge*.

"Wager, sir?" she asked, embarrassed that her voice quavered. She took hold of the writhing man on the table.

"Yes, hold him." Swiftly Lease bound a leather strap around the sailor's upper arm, then took her hand and clamped it over the screw apparatus attached to the strap. "Tighten when I tell you, and keep on until I tell you to stop."

She did as he said. The sailor screamed and tried to rise off the table. He entreated her to stop. "I am making him scream more, sir!" she pleaded.

"I will scream if you stop," Lease said, his voice still mild, his eyes on his patient. "Keep tightening. That's right. Yes. I lost the bet," he said companionably, as though they chatted between country dances. Amazed at his demeanor, she slowly screwed down the tourniquet.

"I bet Daniel you would remain in the cable tier until the all clear, and then join me here. He said you would disobey his orders and be in here before the battle was over. Obviously, I have lost a perfectly good bottle of Jamaica rum. There. Stop."

He reached across her to the tub of warm water that held his saws. He indicated the bottle of rum beside the sailor's head. "Pour some of that down the beggar's throat. As much as he'll take. That's a good girl. Now, look away, please."

Hannah stared at the surgeon's saw, and pressed her hands to the sailor's chest as the man clawed at her shirt, popping the buttons. The saw scraped on the bone.

"Tighten it again!" he ordered, his voice louder now, more urgent.

She did as he said, and he finished his swift work, dropped the shattered forearm in a brimming bucket and quickly tied off the artery.

The sailor was silent, his eyes closed. The surgeon looked up at her then, as if remembering some social indiscretion. He smiled apologetically, and extended his bloody hand to her across the table.

"Oh, do forgive my manners, Miss Whittier. Welcome to hell."

Chapter Eight

Hannah wasn't aware when the guns stopped, because there was no silence on the orlop deck where the wounded had been taken. She blotted all thoughts from her mind except the ordeal before her and did as Andrew Lease said. She only hesitated once, at the very beginning, when the surgeon took her hand and forced it against an artery that was cascading like a fountain to the deck above.

She had looked at him in terror as the droplets rained down, then did as he said.

"Excellent, Miss Whittier. Just jam it tight against the bone for another minute," the surgeon murmured as he continued his work. "Tell me, do you have brothers and sisters? I suspect you are the youngest."

She looked at him in amazement, then understood. "I have four older brothers, and yes, I am the youngest," she replied with scarcely a quaver in her voice. I will match you calm for calm, she thought, as she pressed against the artery. "Do you think I am the youngest because the captain contends I am a rascal, sir?"

Lease smiled as he sawed. "Yes, actually. You seem a bit used to your own way. Another moment, Miss Whittier."

"Perhaps I just resist bullying," she said as Lease took the artery in his hand and tied it off. "It is an American trait, I think." She gulped, too afraid to look down at what he was doing.

"He means well. Here, grab this fellow under the armpits. I think we can ease him to the deck."

Whatever his deficiencies in ordinary conversation, Lease knew his business. He worked his way through the wounded and the dying, moving so deliberately at times that she wanted to scream. "Haste never healed a wound," he commented mildly at one point. "Do quit gritting your teeth, my dear Miss Whittier. You might ruin an otherwise excellent facial structure."

The hours wore by, and then she realized that the last two men the Marines had brought below were French. She looked at the doctor. "Is it over?"

"You didn't hear the guns stop?" Lease asked as he surveyed the latest ruin on his operating table. "Why do they bring these wrecks below?" he asked no one in particular. "Am I God, to ordain a miracle? Just hold his hand, Miss Whittier. He will soon quit this life, lucky man. *Bon chance*," he told the sailor in French, bending over him and straightening his legs.

She took the French sailor's hand and held it tight until he died. Lease slumped against the bulkhead and sank to the deck, his face etched with exhaustion like acid on copper. He patted the deck beside him and she joined him, feeling oddly boneless as soon as she sat down.

"You are right, you know," he said at last when her eyes were closing.

"Right?"

"A husband should put his wife's welfare above his own."

If she had not already endured an afternoon and evening of strange commentary on fashion, customs, weather, and scientific discovery, delivered across an operating table,

Hannah would have been amazed. As it was, she regarded the surgeon's comment in the same calm in which it was delivered.

"My dratted list has already been a source of some embarrassment to me," she said. "I did not wish to cause you pain, sir."

Lease smiled, but there was no mirth. "I know you did not, and I was rude to walk out like that, particularly before Cookie's plum duff. Look far and wide, my dear, for a man who will not desert you when the sky falls in. Let me be your bad example." He closed his eyes and seemed to be reaching for a memory not usually touched. "My wife and baby would be alive today if I had possessed less pride in my skills to save them."

"Oh, sir," she said and tried to take his hand. He shifted away from her.

"I assured her that I could handle any situation, even as she pleaded with me to call in another surgeon," he continued, his voice dull, but with a wistfulness that went straight to her heart. "I was more concerned with my reputation than her welfare."

He said no more, but stared at the table with the dead man on it. In another moment, two sailors came onto the deck. "Captain Spark sent us, sir," said one, his face covered with black powder from the guns. "Can we help?"

Lease sighed and pulled himself to his feet. "Indeed you can. And I release you, Miss Whittier, from the underworld. These fellows and I will tidy up this little corner of Hades."

She left the orlop deck and climbed wearily to the gun deck, where the battle lanterns still glowed weirdly. She gasped the carnage there that had never even reached the surgery. She thought she saw Mr. Lansing, pale beyond belief, pulled into a corner, but she had not the heart to investigate. She continued her climb to the main deck, amazed at the effort it took to put one foot in front of the other.

There was no other ship on the ocean. Night had come and with it a certain tidiness as the darkness cloaked whatever still floated on the water from the *Bergeron*. She slumped onto the afterhatch, noting idly that the bag of oakum she had picked that morning was still there. She looked at the chaos about her, the bloody sand, the slanting deck, the ruined sails, the mizzenmast shattered at a height of ten feet from the deck, with the yards and sails drooping dangerously over the side. As she watched, sailors and Marines chopped through the mast and ropes and heaved it overboard. The ship righted itself, and the remaining sails filled as the sailors in the yardarms unreefed them. Order was replacing catastrophe as she watched, her eyes weary.

And there on the splintered quarterdeck, stood Captain Daniel Spark, calmly telling his crew what to do. He spoke quietly, and they moved to do his will. Soon the bosun's mate had turned the wash pump on the deck, sluicing it clean, except for the deeper stains. Hannah knew, as surely as she breathed, that the morning sun would bring out the survivors to holystone the deck back to its former whiteness. The mast would be replaced, the sails refined, and life would continue aboard the *Dissuade*. It was just another incident of war to these iron men who had contended against France for twenty years now.

A great wave of loneliness washed over her, bringing with it such pain that she could only get to her feet, climb to the quarterdeck, and huddle there against the comforting planking. If thee shouts me off this deck, I won't go, she thought as she gathered herself into a tight little ball. She listened to the captain's approaching footsteps, her heart aching, her mind blank.

Spark stood beside her. She waited for him to speak, dared him to, but he said nothing. He came closer until his leg touched her, and just stood there, continuing his orders to his crew as his boat cloak swirled around her, shutting out the dreadful view. She closed her eyes, relieved beyond words to be enveloped in darkness. He reached down once to pat her head when she began to shiver, then turned back to the task at hand as she leaned against his leg.

An hour passed, and still he stood on the deck, watching the evolution from upheaval to order. He spoke to her finally.

"Hannah, tell me if I won my wager."

"You did, sir," she said.

He knelt beside her. "You deliberately disobeyed me, didn't you?"

"Of course," she replied, looking him right in the eye. "You didn't really think I would stay there when all those men were screaming?"

He brushed her cheek with his own. "No, I did not." He stood up and moved away to the railing. "Cookie, find me some rum. Two glasses, or cups or whatever isn't broken."

She looked up. "Rum's only for heroes. You told me."

He nodded, but said nothing. In a few minutes he handed her a coffee mug full of rum. "Drink it all, Hannah. You're a hero."

Her eyes filled with tears as she took the mug.

"And for God's sake, don't cry!" he ordered, then knelt beside her again, his hands gentle on her shoulders. "How can I maintain order when my scurviest little crew member turns into a watering pot?"

She sobbed anyway, then took a great gulp of the rum. It furrowed a path down her throat and landed, glowing with a life all its own, in her empty stomach, where it warmed her all the way to her toes. She cried and sipped the rest of the rum until it was gone and she had no tears left. With a last shuddering sigh, she handed back the mug.

"Do you want some more?" he asked. Already, his voice sounded distant and thick, as though her brain were full of rum, too.

She shook her head. "I think it would make me drunk."

He poured another mugful and handed it to her. "Good. Have some more, by all means."

She set the cup on the deck. "I had not thought thee

unscrupulous, too," she protested, but her voice was light.

"I am that and worse, I suppose." He took another swallow and squatted beside her. "How is Andrew?" he asked.

She picked up the mug and drank it half down without pausing. She giggled and leaned forward until her forehead touched the captain's. "I think he is mad."

"I am certain of it, Hannah," was Spark's quiet reply. "But as he can still saw and tie with the best, I don't trouble him about it much." He looked around, and then sat beside her on the deck, leaning against the bulkhead. "Never thought I would sit on my own deck," he grumbled. "Let me know if you see Futtrell, and I'll get up. I have a certain standing to maintain in this community." He looked at her and chuckled. "That was a joke, Hannah. You're supposed to laugh when I make one."

She made a face at him and finished the rum. She held out the mug again, but he shook his head. "Oh, no! That's enough, even for a hero." He looked at her and flicked the hair back from her face. "Did he tell you she was my sister?"

"Oh, God," Hannah breathed, wide awake again. She took hold of Spark's arm. "Never that!"

He nodded. "She made that little sampler in my sleeping cabin."

"But ... why? Why would he want to serve with you?" she asked.

He shrugged. "Maybe that's part of his own mad punishment. After—well—after Melinda died, he disappeared. No one heard of him for a year, and I did check, whenever we came off blockade. Just gave up his practice and disappeared."

"Did he really cause her death?"

"Probably not, but who knows? He thinks he did." Spark stood up then and convened quietly with his lieutenant of Marines for a long moment while Hannah tried to gather her thoughts into one coherent shape. And then Mr. Futtrell, his arm in a sling, was on the deck, and the carpenter, too, wet from the waist down and smelling of bilge.

As she sat shivering on the deck, Captain Spark removed his boat cloak and slung it over her. "Go to sleep, Miss Whittier," he said. "You don't have a cabin right now, and this is the best place." He was gone then with the carpenter and the bosun, while Futtrell took his place on the quarterdeck.

She watched Mr. Futtrell pace back and forth, in imitation of his captain. Every few minutes he touched his bandaged arm as though proud to have a wound. How young thee is, she thought, and then was filled with the absurdity of her reflection. She was far younger than he, but she felt so old.

"Is Mr. Lansing dead?" she asked when he had stopped close to her.

He must not have seen her there in the shadows because he jumped back. "Lord, you scared me, Miss Whittier!" he exclaimed. "Place is full of ghosts. Thought you was another." He touched his arm again. "Yes, he's dead. Practically from the first."

She sighed and drew Spark's boat cloak tight around her. "And the *Bergeron* is sunk," she added as flimsy consolation.

"Aye, Miss Whittier, but do you know, weighing that against Mr. Lansing, I would rather fight her again and still have him roaring out orders from the gun deck." Futtrell moved away then, to smite the helmsman with a sharp order to trim the sails.

She watched him until her eyes grew heavy, then she lay down and arranged the cloak around her. She thought of Adam Winslow, and wondered if he still lived. And then Andrew Lease, with his desperate eyes and drawing room chatter, shouldered his way into her thoughts and stayed there, cutting and tying, as she closed her eyes upon troubled dreams.

When she woke, she was in her hammock again, but still covered by Daniel Spark's cloak. She snuggled deeper into the woolen warmth, loath to open her eyes on chaos by daylight. When she was unable to avoid the new day, she opened her eyes and sat up. The bulkheads knocked down so quickly before yesterday's encounter with the *Bergeron* were in place again, effectively shutting her off from the main gun deck. She sniffed the gun below her, which was still heavy with the odor of expended powder and shot.

She lay on her back, staring up at the deck, when she heard several heavy splashes. Her heart in her throat, she climbed from the hammock and wrenched open the tiny porthole. As she watched, another shrouded body slid into the water from the main deck. Hurriedly she dragged a brush through her tangled hair and ran onto the deck above.

She stood in silence as Captain Spark, dressed impeccably, and with all his medals this time, stood before another row of bodies sewn into their hammocks. " 'I am the resurrection and the life,' " he read from the little Bible in his hand, his eyes on the words without seeing them. "'He that believeth in me, though he were dead, yet shall he live.'" He removed his hat then and bowed his head. "Merciful Father, God of Battle, we commend these thy servants at the guns, to rest in the deep. God rest their souls and God bless the King and his Regent. Amen."

The next row of shrouded bodies was tipped off the deck and into the water. Hannah scanned the sailors standing alert on the main deck, her eyes anxious. She sighed. There was Adam, looking much older than his sixteen years, with a stained bandage on his neck. She looked around for the other Nantucket seaman who had been impressed, and sighed again. He was not in sight.

Another scripture, another entreaty to the Almighty, and a third row of bodies slid into the water. Her heart sore, Hannah looked at the captain and moved closer, alarmed at the agony on his face. *Why did I ever think him so hard,* she thought as she watched him, head bowed, feet wide apart on the deck, trying to retain what shreds of composure clung, tattered, about his tall form. She looked at the faces of the sailors and saw her own concern mirrored there. *How could I have seen* only rough men, she asked herself. They all have followed him to hell and back without a murmur. I have, too.

Then there was only Mr. Lansing left, sewn into a length of sailcloth, his hat resting at the head of the plank, his sword at the foot. She waited for Captain Spark, but all he could do was clear his throat over and over, unable to speak at the loss of his first lieutenant.

Hannah took a deep breath and stepped forward. She took the Bible from Spark's hands and turned to Job. Spark rested his hand on her shoulder and she looked back at him, wondering if she was completely out of bounds, and due for a scolding. She glanced at his face, a winter landscape, his eyes filled with tears, and turned back to the book. Her voice was calm. "'For I know that my redeemer liveth, and that he shall stand at the latter day upon the earth.'"

She paused, overwhelmed, and looked at Adam Winslow, who watched her, a half smile on his face. He nodded to her, and she gathered the courage to continue. "'And though after my skin worms destroy this body, yet in my flesh shall I see God.'"

The ship was silent. Even the riggings had stopped humming for once. There was only the slap of water against the ship, as though the sea were eager to receive another offering. Hannah bowed her head. "Heavenly Father, accept thy son to thy merciful bosom, where there are no guns, and no war. Let us live worthy to see Mr. Lansing again in the resurrection. God save the United States, the King, and his Regent. Amen."

Mr. Futtrell stepped forward and took the sword while Captain Spark tipped Mr. Lansing into the water. He stood beside the railing as the shrouded body, loaded with shot like the others, sank swiftly. Hannah hesitated. She longed to touch Spark, but she knew better. She stood next to Adam, who put his around her shoulder. They watched quietly, no one moving, as the captain stared at the water.

"Bosun, change the pump crew," he said at last, his eyes still on the water. "Send the starboard watch to Chips for orders."

"Aye, aye." The bosun's whistle piped and half the men hurried below to relieve the sailors at the pumps. The others gathered around the carpenter.

Spark turned around then; his composure restored, and settled his hat back on his head. He nodded to Hannah as she handed him his Bible. "Can you spend the day in the lookout?" he asked her. "I can't spare anyone to change off, and we must watch."

"Of course," she replied.

"My straw hat's in the cabin, and so is my glass. You can get them. Take this, too," he said, handing back the Bible. He turned on his heel for the quarterdeck, where a crew was preparing to jury-rig a new mast.

She hurried below deck to Spark's cabin. The black-and-white-checked canvas had been returned to the floor, the guns lashed down again, and the furniture arranged as before. She found the hat in the sleeping cabin and put it on her head. The telescope rested on the chart table in the great cabin. She looked at the chart on top, with the parallel rulers pointed to the Azores.

A half-finished letter lay on the chart. She picked it up, her mouth dry. "My dear Mrs. Lansing," she read, "please accept my consolation on the death of your son Edward."

She put down the letter, unable to continue. Imagine a lifetime of writing such letters, she thought. I could never. How does he? There was another such letter, and another, these finished and signed. As she turned away, a scrap of paper caught her eye. It was a narrow sheet, with pen wipings, blots, and doodles. She picked it up and read aloud. "Cheerful to a fault (Careful here: this could become tiresome). Courageous. Not afraid to argue. Lovely of face and body (at least to me). Places my welfare before her own." There were numbers scratched through and rearranged before each sentence, but she dropped the page as though it burned her fingers and hurried from the cabin.

I refuse to think about it, she told herself as she climbed the rigging. He cannot be serious, and I won't consider it. Numb with some emotion that was strange to her, she sat in the lookout and scanned the horizon, while the ship sailed more slowly toward Europe. She wished herself home in Nantucket and attempted a bargain. "Lord, if I am ever there again, I will not complain if my life is boring," she said out loud as she searched the ocean. "I promise to be very, very good and never write another list."

To her great relief, she saw no other sails that day. From her perch far above the deck, she watched as the crew juried a new mast to the stub remaining of the mizzenmast, working efficiently with block and tackle. The sounds of hammer and saw on the deck competed with the clanking of the pumps far below, as the men sweated to empty out an ocean that continued to seep back in through planks damaged by the *Bergeron's* direct hits. She trained the telescope on a quarterdeck conference between Spark, Futtrell, and the bosun, which ended with a sail being passed under the bow of the *Dissuade,* in another attempt to slow down the leaks. Still the pumps poured water over the side.

She remained in her perch until dark, then came down, stiff with sitting immobile for so long. Four more shrouded bodies waited on the deck for tomorrow's services. She stood by the still forms a moment, Spark's hat off, then hurried below to the orlop deck, which Andrew Lease had turned into a sick bay. The makeshift operating table of midshipmen's sea chests was gone, but there were ten men lying on the deck, some fairly quick, and others nearly dead.

Lease was bending over one crew member. He looked up and nodded to Hannah. She came closer, noting the exhaustion on his face. He smiled at her. "And how does our Hannah?" he asked in that drawing room manner of his that only increased her discomfort. He pulled her collar away from her neck. "Sunburned again? I recommend another regimen of salve, if Daniel insists on keeping you aloft."

"He has no choice," she said.

"Who of us does?" he asked in turn, then paused, his head cocked to listen to the sound of the pumps. "And now the ocean has turned on us." He took her arm. "Come sit, and tell me about your day."

It was all so weird that she backed away. "No, sir," she said, wishing that she did not sound so breathless. "I am too tired."

He chuckled. "Oh, you don't know tired, my dear! You and I get to watch Daniel and Futtrell turn into sleepwalkers."

"What do you mean?" she asked as she backed toward the gangway.

"With Mr. Lansing dead, and the sailing master, too, it's watch and watch about until we reach landfall. That's four hours on and four hours off, until they drop." He smiled. "We'll be lucky if the French don't find us again." His smile widened. "I am sure they will be kind to you because you are an American, but the rest of us?" He shrugged. "There are some who worry about things like that, but I am not numbered among them. Good night, Miss Whittier. Come visit again."

Hannah shuddered and hurried to the gun deck, and down the companionway to her room. The Marine sat outside her door this time, his bandaged leg resting on an overturned bucket. He held out a note to her.

She took it over to the ship's lantern and read, "Imperative you come to my cabin. We have a matter to discuss. Adam will be there, too. Spark."

Hannah folded the note and put it in her pocket. In another moment, she stood outside the captain's door. The Marine there clicked his heels to attention and opened the door for her.

Adam looked up from his contemplation of a handful of papers as she entered, his face grim. Spark stood beside Mr.

Futtrell in quiet conversation. Spark motioned her in.

"Come, Miss Whittier," he said. "Have a seat. There's something here you must read. Adam, give her that first page."

He was all business, standing there in his stockinged feet, far removed from the man who could not bring himself to bury his comrades that morning. She didn't understand his restless energy until she took the paper and began to read.

"Sit, Lady Amber," he said, pulling out a chair for her. She did as he said, her eyes on the paper, her attention caught.

"We found this document in a tarred shot pouch," he explained as she looked up, a question in her eyes. "I can only assume that the poor Frog was supposed to throw it overboard and sink it, but our lieutenant of Marines boarded too soon and spoiled his aim."

She turned back to the letter as the hair on her neck prickled. "This can't be what I think it is," she murmured when she finished.

He took the water-stained page from her. "It is a communiqué from William Darlington, the acting governor of Antigua, to Napoleon himself, damn his traitorous hide." Spark banged his hand on the table and she jumped. "I have sat at that man's table and eaten his food! And here he is, a traitor to the crown." He took the next pages from Adam, who was sitting quietly now and watching the captain. "There's more, Hannah, too much more."

She continued reading, distracted at first by Spark, who paced back and forth across the width of the stern, then absorbed and repelled at the same time by the document in her hands. It was pages of information about ship strengths of British commerce raiders and ships of the line that sailed in the Caribbean.

Spark stopped his pacing and stood behind her chair. He jabbed the page with his finger. "And look here! That damned Darlington names Lord Luckingham, another traitor within the government itself! I am astounded what men will do for money."

She put down the papers and Spark sat beside her. "We have to get this document to England," he said.

"But isn't that where we are headed?" She looked at the captain, wondering at his restless energy.

He took her hands. "Hannah, we're sinking. The pumps can't keep up, and we'll never raise Portsmouth. We're going to settle lower and lower in the water until we have to take to the small boats."

"Oh." She let that news soak in, then freed her hands from the captain's. "You had a chart on the table this morning. The Azores?"

He nodded. "That's our only hope, Hannah, and the trouble of it is, I don't know if they remain in Portuguese hands, or if the French have taken over. I think within a very short time, we will be prisoners of the French, even if we make that landfall."

He took her hand again. "I wanted you to know how bad was our situation, you and Adam. I'm sorry I ever got you two into this mess."

Hannah did not pull her hand away this time. "All I really wanted to do was get to Charleston," she reminded him gently.

He winced. "A hit below the waterline, Hannah!"

Adam stirred in his chair. "Thee has something in mind, doesn't thee?" he asked quietly. "And excuse me if I doubt it is an apology."

Spark gave Adam a measuring stare, and then a reluctant smile. "There are no flies on Yankees, are there?" he murmured.

"No, sir," Adam replied. "What do you want from me? I'd prefer thee did not involve Hannah, if it's to be dangerous. I at least have considerable regard for her welfare, even if thee does not."

His words, quietly spoken, hung in the air. Mr. Futtrell, who had been listening to this exchange, tugged at his chin and turned away.

"You think I have no regard for Miss Whittier's welfare?" Spark asked, his voice as quiet as Adam's.

"I don't trust thee," Adam said.

"Adam, what is thee saying!" Hannah cried.

Adam refused to look at her. She wriggled her fingers out of the captain's grasp and folded her hands in her lap. "Say on, Captain," she said.

"If we are soon prisoners of the French, you two Americans will likely be freed because you are not belligerents. I want you to get this dispatch to London."

Adam was silent for a long moment. "Let me think now. Thee raided the *Molly Claridge,* and took me off. Thee has probably been impressing others like me for years. We ought to be at war with England."

"Yes, you are quite right." Spark agreed.

"Thee has ruined my family's peace and frightened Hannah."

"She's equal to it," the captain said.

"By God, thee is a cheeky bastard, for someone seeking a favor," Adam burst out, his face red.

"I certainly am," Spark agreed, his equanimity unruffled by Adam's charge. "I am also in serious like with Hannah Whittier, and would never do her any harm." He bowed to Hannah, who sat dumbfounded. "I don't know you well enough to be in love yet, Lady Amber, but I fear I am dreadfully close. Is that cheeky enough, Adam?"

Chapter Nine

Adam regarded the captain in profound silence. Numb, Hannah stared at her hands in her lap, unable to look at anyone in the cabin. The captain stood behind her, resting his hands on the chair back. The very air seemed to crackle with tension.

Finally, Adam sighed. "Lord, what a muddle," he muttered. "Hannah, what should we do?"

She considered the matter. If, by some miracle, they managed to raise the Azores, the French would see to their release. At the least, they could request passage on a vessel to return them to the Caribbean. She could be in Charleston in a month or less. With any luck, this whole adventure would soon wear into a bad dream, and after all, what did they owe the British?

She looked at the dispatch resting in her lap, wishing it would go away. She thought of the men of the *Dissuade*, many dead, others wounded, and multiplied that number by the twenty British ships named in the dispatch. If Napoleon continued to be fed traitorous information about the Royal Navy in Caribbean waters, he would know how to harry the British there. Heating up the war in the Caribbean would mean Britain would be stretched even thinner in its blockade of the French and Spanish coasts. She could see only more death, more war. It is against everything I believe, she thought as she leaned back in the chair and felt Spark's fingers against her back.

Hannah scooted forward quickly and slapped the dispatch on the table. "Adam, we cannot be party to more death, and thee knows that would happen if this dispatch fell into French hands. I say we get the document to London."

Adam looked up at Captain Spark, who had not moved from his position behind Hannah's chair, and then back at her. "Hannah, we could be home in a month if we do not," he reminded her, his thoughts obviously traveling the same lane as hers. "And you think we should risk our lives getting this dispatch to London?"

"I do," she replied, her voice firm. She noted the skeptical look on his face. "And do not think for one minute it is because I am persuaded by this rascal standing behind my chair." She paused as Mr. Futtrell turned away again to hide a smile. "I do not feel anything for Captain Spark beyond admiration of his courage. Even you must acknowledge his courage. But I also do not love the idea of more death in the Caribbean. And I do not relish the idea of traitors. What American would?"

Adam was silent a moment more, then he looked at the captain. "Very well, sir, we will do as thee asks. I do not know how, but we can try."

Captain Spark reached around Hannah and shook Adam's hand. "We can work out the details as we run for the Azores," he said. He stuffed the dispatch back in its bag and handed it to Adam. "I think you and Miss Whittier should memorize this document. It may be destroyed, but one of you ought to get through with the message."

He took it. "Very well, sir. Hannah? Shall I have a go at it first?"

She nodded. Adam looked at Captain Spark. "With thy

permission, I will return to the gun deck."

"Granted, lad. And thank you."

He left the cabin. Mr. Futtrell cleared his throat. "As mine is the first watch, I believe I will go to the quarterdeck."

"Call me in four hours," the captain said. He sat down as soon as the door closed. "Well, Hannah?" He shook his head at her expression. "That mulish look on your face tells me that I may have run out my guns prematurely."

She wished he would sit on the other side of the table, and not practically knee to knee. She squirmed in her chair. Did he have to regard her with those unnerving eyes of his? Why were they so light and memorable? As she returned his unflinching pale stare, she knew that she could go to her grave and years from now and still remember the color of his eyes, and the graceful way he sat watching her. It was enough to try a statue. Thank goodness she did not love him.

"You can't possibly be in love with me," she said at last, when he seemed content merely to memorize her face and remain silent.

He wagged a finger at her. "I did not say I was in love, but only in serious like."

"You are absurd," she said, smiling in spite of her discomfort. "You just like the way I make coffee."

There, if she made a joke of his aspirations that should stop him. Instead, he leaned closer until she could have reached out and caressed his face, had she been of such inclination, which she was not. "I like the way your hips wiggle when you climb the rigging, and your cheerful way of doing things, even when your whole world is arse over teakettle."

"There you go!" she said triumphantly. "Your language is vile and you are a notable blasphemer."

"By God's wounds, I certainly am. Some things you'll just have to take. And I will have to get used to constant good cheer, which can be a trial at times. Are you even cheerful when you wake up? I can't wait to find out, Lady Amber."

"That is none of your business, and don't call me that!"

"Well, may I call you Hannah? Seems to me we have progressed to that stage."

"We have not!" she declared. Then she softened the blow by adding. "But since you have already been doing so, you might as well continue."

"And it is my desire to hear Daniel on your lips," he said.

"You want Mr. Futtrell to stand on the quarterdeck and yell 'Ship's discipline'?" she asked, unable to keep back the good humor that bubbled up in her. "I do not, sir."

He laughed. "Very well! Call me Captain Spark."

She stood up to leave and he rose, too, walking her to the door. "Really, these are paltry objections, my dear. I would have thought someone with your brains could do better."

"Of course I can," she said crisply, her hand on the knob. "You are an Englishman and much too old for me."

He leaned his hand against the door as she tried to turn the handle. "Those are weighty objections, Hannah," he agreed. "I'll always be an Englishman, but I assure you that no part of me is decrepit. Let me repeat a previous demonstration and add something more."

Before she could stop him, he took her face in his hands and kissed her. His lips were as warm as she remembered from their first meeting on the deck of the *Molly Claridge*. The ship yawed them and she grabbed him around the waist to stay on her feet. He pulled her closer until their bodies touched, murmuring something in her ear that made no sense. As she tried to regain her balance, he took her earlobe in his teeth, then ran his tongue inside her ear. The shivers that raced down her back made her moan a little, but only a very little. She wished he would stop, but when he did, she felt absurd tears tickling her eyelids. She wondered how her fingers could ever dig so into his back, and she hoped she had not scratched him.

He released her then, and turned away to the chart table. "Go to bed, Hannah," he said, his voice a bit dazed, "and don't try to improve on perfection."

She hurried from the cabin, her face flaming, grateful for the darkness of the companionway. The solitude of her cabin was a blessed relief, she decided as she closed the door behind her, and then sighed with exasperation. Captain Spark's boat cloak was still draped over the hammock. "I will not return it tonight!" she said out loud. "I would have to be crazy!"

She climbed the gun and crawled into her hammock, wrapping the cloak tightly about her, and gradually sinking into sleep. There is so much to worry about, she thought, her eyes heavy as she listened to the endless clanking of the pumps forward. We are sinking, the Azores are still so far away, the French are lurking somewhere, and I have to memorize a dratted document. She snuggled deeper into the cloak, which smelled of mildew, like everything else on board, and Captain Spark. Thank goodness I do not love him, or this voyage could become a real trial. And thank goodness Mama warned me about sailors.

She brought him coffee at first light, setting it as usual on the quarterdeck and assuming her customary position on the rung of the ladder. He crouched beside her as usual, his eyes weary, and sipped the coffee as he watched her face. "I was wishing you would come on deck sooner," he said when he finished and handed back the mug.

"I can bring your coffee sooner, if you wish," she replied.

He smiled. "I am not so sure I want coffee as much as I need conversation. It would keep me awake better, I think." He looked at the riggings, and then back at the jury-rigged mizzenmast. "Another night has passed, Lady Amber, and we are still afloat and somewhat closer to the Azores."

"Will we make it, do you think?" she asked.

He shrugged. "If you do not sight any French vessels, if the wind freshens, if the men can keep the pumps going. I don't hold out an optimistic report." He touched her shoulder then.

"But don't worry, I'll see you into one of the little boats."

"I wasn't worried," she said as she got up to leave. "I don't know why I should trust you, but I do."

The captain merely smiled and resumed his position on the quarterdeck, his eyes on the ocean. She went below deck again, retrieved Spark's boat cloak, and placed it on the quarterdeck before climbing the riggings for another day of watching. He nodded to her and wrapped himself in it. "Smells of almond extract now," he commented.

"Oh, I am sorry," she said. "Then thee should—you should—not give a girl a gift of scent."

"I will give you flowers in London," he replied, his eyes on the sails. "And diamonds, when you will let me. And children, drat them, and an estate with a view of the ocean."

"Sir, that will not happen," she replied, shy again and wishing he would not speak of such intimate matters.

"Oh, we shall see, Hannah," was all he would say.

The *Dissuade* moved sluggishly through the mid-Atlantic, weighed down by water in the hold, where the pumps clanked. Mr. Futtrell sent his crew aloft to raise as much sail as they dared, knowing that too much canvas crowded in the upper yards would sink them as surely as the ocean that lapped back and forth in the hold. When he was finally satisfied with the allotment of canvas, he sent the men below deck to the pumps again.

The shift in the hold changed every two hours, when the men, wet from the waist down, would come on deck and throw themselves down to sleep. Adam, his face drawn with exhaustion, climbed the rigging once to bring her some ship's biscuit and a flask of moldy water. They sat together in silence, for the most part, shoulders touching, staring out at the water.

"Hannah, tell me something," he asked finally. "Does thee love Captain Spark?"

She brushed off the crumbs from her shirt. "Thee is absurd! Of course not."

"He cares for thee." It was a simple sentence, delivered with Adam's usual lack of dramatics. "I see him watching thee."

Hannah put the telescope to her eye again and scanned the ocean. "He cares for thee." Adam's words so quietly spoken drilled into her brain. "Thee knows it is absurd, Adam," she said as she watched.

"So is our current situation, Hannah, and yet here we are. Who would have thought it?"

Without any more talk, Adam returned to the deck. As much as she liked her childhood friend, Hannah was not sorry to see him go. I must think this through, she thought to herself as she watched his blond head get smaller and smaller as he descended. She clasped her knees to her chest and leaned back against the mast, wondering what it was she had done to get the captain so convinced that he was in love.

Others at home had withstood her charms, she told herself wryly, thinking of the young men who came into the parlor there on Orange Street to sit and stammer and ask her how she did. Papa would talk of business, then leave her alone with one suitor or another, but nothing ever came of it. I must be speaking of the wrong things, she would think, or perhaps it is the way I look. There were no mirrors in the Whittier house so she went to the pond in the back field, and stared into its reflecting depths, wondering what there was about her features to prevent the return, beyond a few visits, of Nantucket's young men. She could see nothing in the reflection that would disgust a man intent upon marriage.

She finally asked her best friend Abigail Winslow. "It is that twinkle in thy eye," Abigail had confessed as they sat knitting once. "I suspect they think thee is a rogue at heart, Hannah. Is thee?"

She smiled at the memory, and her outraged reaction, and then her smile faded. Perhaps I am a rogue, she thought as she scanned the ocean again. I truly would rather be sitting barefoot in trousers in Captain Spark's lookout, my knees wide apart and my shirt unbuttoned.

It was more than that, and perhaps there was something to what Abigail Winslow had so artlessly declared. Last night when Captain Spark kissed her, she had not wanted him to stop. She lowered the telescope, wondering why her cheeks burned, even up here where no one could see her. I wonder, she thought, has this man taken my measure? Does he know somehow that I truly am a rogue, and more to the point, does this knowledge not frighten him off, as it did the young men of Nantucket? She rested her chin on the eyepiece of the telescope. "If thee knows these things about me, Daniel," she whispered softly, "then thee knows me better than I do."

She watched all day and into the night, when Mr. Futtrell finally called to her and she came down, weary with watching. Captain Spark had ordered the running lights doused before he went below to snatch a few hours sleep. If only there was some way to stop the noise of the pumps, she thought as she went below deck, shook her head at Cookie's attempt to feed her salt pork, and collapsed in her hammock. The thought of silent pumps made her sit bolt upright. "Oh, no," she said. "Let them make all the racket they choose." Silent pumps would mean that the voyage was over.

Each day passed into another one, similar and unrelenting, and broken only by the smallest of incidents that would have been soon forgotten, except that Hannah planned to remember the last, desperate cruise of the *Dissuade* for her whole life. She brought coffee every morning to the captain, hiding her alarm at his haggard expression and the exhaustion that seemed to seep out of his pores. One morning he handed her a boat cloak. "It's Mr. Lansing's. I see you shivering every morning until the sun climbs higher."

She took it, grateful for the warmth, remembering its owner. Another morning, there were two more bodies shrouded in their hammocks, which Captain Spark tipped over the side without a prayer. When she looked at him, a question in her eyes, he merely said. "I can't address the Almighty right now, Hannah. I wonder if he cares." Two days later, the forward pump broke, and all hands rushed to its repair. She watched from the lookout, wondering what was happening below, and then sighed with relief when the clanging began again.

Adam finished memorizing the dispatch, and it was her turn. She read over and over the letter in English from the governor of Antigua, with its traitorous catalog of ships and supplies of the Royal Navy in the Caribbean, destined for Napoleon. She knew it by heart at the end of a long day in the lookout, and returned it to Captain Spark when she saw him come on deck for the second night watch.

"Recite it for me, Hannah," he said, and she did, striking a pose with her hands behind her back, much as when she had attended dame school at home and had recited whole chapters from the Bible for Dame Oldroyd.

"Very good, my dear Lady Amber," he said when she finished, and applauded when she curtsied. "Now go get some sleep before you topple."

There was nothing of the lover in his voice anymore. That was gone after the first week of watch and watch about, replaced now by a dogged determination to see the thing through that shone in his pale eyes. He rarely spoke to anyone now, beyond the necessary commands, as though trying to preserve his flagging energy.

"You're the one who's going to topple," she protested. "I wish I could help."

He surprised her with a reply, instead of the usual noncommittal grunt that had become his latest mode of communication. "You can. Come on deck after Futtrell's watch. I have a hard time staying awake for that particular watch, and you can entertain me with stories of Nantucket."

"Very well, sir, except that nothing exciting ever happens at home," she said.

"Let me be the judge of that profound bit of infantile wisdom.

Until then, Lady Amber. Or perhaps I should brush up on my rusty French and say *à bientôt.*"

She came on deck in the early watch, when the stars seemed to be hanging just above the masts and there was no hint of welcome dawn on the horizon. The helmsman, his eyes bleary but his hands firm on the wheel, nodded to her as she tiptoed quietly to the quarterdeck and assumed her customary position.

"No, no. Come on deck, my dear."

Captain Spark stood in the shadow of the weather side, hanging on to the rigging, keeping himself upright by sheer force of will.

"You're wearing Lansing's cloak, I see. Good. Good. I am definitely feeling the chilly winds of Europe," he said as he motioned her closer.

She came to his side, and he put his arm around her, gathering her into his cloak and leaning on her a little until he regained his balance. He let go of the rigging and they stood, hip to hip, arms about each other's waists. It seemed too close to Hannah, but the captain shivered, and she moved in closer.

"I swear I'm cold right to the bone," he said, sticking his thumb into her waistband to anchor her more firmly to him. "Hannah, you're better than a hot water bottle."

Hannah chuckled. "Mama wraps a rock in a towel for me at home. She doesn't know, but sometimes I sneak in Hosea's old dog, especially in January when everything freezes."

"Tell me about your brothers, Hannah. Would I like them?"

"You would like Matthew," she said after considering the matter a moment. "He is a whaler." She laughed softly. "He and my sister-in-law have three children, each one born eight and a half months into his next voyage." She stopped when he laughed. 'Oh, but I should not talk about things like that, should I?"

"It will keep me awake," he replied with just a trace of good humor in his voice. "But why would I like Matthew?"

Hannah sighed and leaned against the captain, gratified that she fit just right under his arm. "He is devoted to the sea." She looked up at his face shyly. "I've watched you from the lookout, and sometimes you have such a dreamy expression as you watch the water."

"What makes you so sure I am thinking about the ocean?" he replied, teasing her.

"Of course you are," she insisted, even as his arm tightened about her waist. "Matthew is restless when he is on land too long. But I know it is hard for him to get to know his wife and children all over again, after every whaling voyage."

"I suppose," he said. "Perhaps children would not be so dreadful, if one got to know them."

"It will take a much better answer than that to get thee back on my list, Captain Spark," she said.

He threw back his head and laughed, and the sound was wonderful to her ears. "You and your bloody list!"

"Really, Captain!" she admonished. "I wish you would not swear."

"Wish in vain, my dear. And who is after Matthew?"

"Elijah, and he is a doctor near Boston. He is much too serious and treats me like a child."

"Well, you are, Hannah," the captain replied. "I can't imagine what I was thinking when I told you I loved you."

She stepped away from him instinctively, and he reeled her back in. "You ... you told me you were in like only," she reminded Spark.

"Oh, yes, how could I forget?" he murmured. "I'm sure that's all it is. A doctor, eh?"

"Yes." She thought of Andrew Lease, sitting patiently on the orlop deck every day, watching his sailors die. "How did you find Andrew Lease after he disappeared?"

"I never did finish telling you, did I? He found me, rather. We were in Deptford Hard for repairs and revictualing for the blockade. He just showed up one day and told me he was signing on as ship's surgeon." The captain shook his head and gathered her closer. "I think I am part of the punishment he has decreed for himself, but God knows I bear him no ill will. People die." He paused a moment, as though collecting himself. "Even lovely little sisters. Well Hannah, name me another brother," he continued, determined to change the subject. You dear man, she thought, looking up at him. You think nothing of staring into French guns and pounding away at close range until you sink a ship, but you cannot bring yourself to talk about your sister. How sad.

"William, who is a student at Harvard College." She leaned closer and whispered. "Mama thinks he is getting much too worldly."

The captain looked around at the deck, empty except for the helmsman. "I won't tell a soul, you silly nod."

Hannah blushed and straightened up. "It is a matter of some concern to my mother. Hosea comes before William, and he is a merchant like Papa. He has made it his business to find me a husband in Charleston among the other Friends there. I suppose that is why I saved him for last. He may prove the most vexatious."

The captain leaned over suddenly and kissed the top of her head. "Poor Hannah! Someone is always trying to tell you what to do. Do you get tired of it?"

"Isn't there always someone telling us what to do?" she countered.

He released her then and turned his back to her, staring out at the water again. "I suppose there is. Sometimes I think I have been working for Napoleon and France these past twenty years." He turned to her, his hands spread out. "I mean, they move, and I jump to the blockade, or sail the Caribbean, frightened right down to my toes."

She was silent a long moment. "At least thee is honest," she said at last.

"Only a fool would not be afraid, Hannah, or a madman like

Lease. He can't wait to get killed in the line of duty. I, on the other hand, would like to live a long time yet. At least, long enough to convince you that I am not too old for you."

She could think of nothing to say. "Thee knows it would never work, Captain Spark," she said softly.

"Why not?" he asked, his voice just as gentle. "I can bend and you can bend. I am sure ...."

What he was sure of, she never knew. With a cry, the helmsman let go of the wheel and dropped to the deck. Captain Spark rushed to the wheel, which was spinning wildly. His eyes on the sails, he corrected the course and called to Hannah. "See to that poor sod!"

She hurried to the sailor, who was lying on his back, arms outstretched. She gathered him into her arms, alarmed that he was dead, and then relieved to discover that he merely slept. When she pulled him in closer to her, he opened his eyes in surprise, startled to find himself in the embrace of a woman. He sat up, rubbing his eyes, to see his captain manning the helm. He staggered to his feet, only to drop to his knees again and then his hands. He swayed back and forth on the deck.

"God, Captain, I am so sorry!"

"Belay it!" Spark snapped. "You'll he more use to me if you sleep." He turned around, his eyes fierce. "And that is an order, Mitchell."

"Aye, aye, sir," said the helmsman, his voice scarcely audible. He crashed to the deck again and in less than a minute, he was snoring, as though he slept on a feather bed. Hannah stared at him, then covered him with Mr. Lansing's cloak.

"Should ... should I call someone?" she asked.

The captain shook his head. "No, my dear. Just sit on the deck close to me and tell me everything you know." He looked at the slumbering helmsman. "Sleep—what an innovation. I am resolved to try it sometime." He took a firmer stance behind the wheel. "Talk about the weather, your brothers, your church, every Bible verse you ever memorized, what you want in life. Keep talking. Keep me awake."

Chapter Ten

She kept him awake through that watch, and through the next night, telling him the same stories over and over until she wanted to cry at his exhaustion. The pumps clanged and sucked, and the seamen dragged themselves from pumps to sails, and then to the carpenter to continue their puny efforts below decks to keep out the rest of the Atlantic.

And then there was no more use in trying. Mr. Futtrell burst into her cabin one foggy morning and shook her awake. "Miss Whittier!" he hollered as though she stood half a ship's length away. "We must get into the boats! Captain's orders!"

She grabbed Lansing's cloak and ran topside. They still floated, but as she watched, the Marines carried the wounded onto the deck and lowered them over the side with ropes. Her hand to her mouth, Hannah ran to the ship's railing and looked down at the water, which was so much closer. Two little boats bobbed there, tied fast to the *Dissuade.* The surgeon balanced himself in one of them, receiving the wounded. "Come down the rope, Hannah," be called. "I want you in this other gig."

She looked at the quarterdeck, where Captain Spark watched her. "No," she said. "I won't, and thee cannot make me."

"Do it, Hannah," Spark said, nothing in his voice of compromise. "I want the wounded and you and Adam in the boats. We're lowering the launch and the dinghy, too, and you will all be tied to the ship. We will stay together as long as the ship floats, but it's safer this way."

Then Adam was at her side. "It's the wisest thing, Hannah. This way, when the ship sinks, we can just cut loose." He patted her shoulder. "Besides all that, Captain Spark thinks we will raise the Azores when this fog lifts."

'Thank God," she murmured, and grasped the rope that the bosun held for her. She was swung down into the other boat with the wounded and settled herself into the bottom, taking one of the men in her arms. He looked at her through eyes cloudy with pain, then closed them again and relaxed against her. Adam was soon beside her in the launch.

"When this fog lifts, I think the wind will freshen," he told her, his eyes on the deck above them. "And then I think Captain Spark will finally crowd on all sail." He grinned at Hannah. "We could be in for a Nantucket sleigh ride. Is thee ready?"

She nodded, thinking of her brother Matthew and his tales of racing in small boats alongside a harpooned whale. She pulled the wounded sailor closer to her and tucked the blanket around his still form. "Adam, I thought to live a quiet life on Nantucket."

Adam laughed. "I never thought thee would, Hannah. Not once. There is something about thee ...." He paused as Captain Spark's head appeared over the railing, a pouch in his hand.

"Andrew, take this," he called to the surgeon busy in the other boat. "Put it in your medicine satchel." He tossed the captured dispatch in its bag to the surgeon. "If you can keep it, fine, but if it is in danger of discovery, you must destroy it."

'I'll not fail you this time. Daniel," the surgeon said quietly as he put away the dispatch.

"You've never failed me, Andrew," said the captain. "I wish to God you would not speak so." He leaned on the railing as though he wanted to say more, but suddenly he raised his head, sniffing the air. "By God, the fog is lifting, and damned if I don't feel a breeze." He blew a kiss to Hannah. "Tally-ho, Lady Amber. I'll see you in Terceira, or be damned."

Hannah looked at Adam, a question in her eyes.

"It's the largest island in the Azores," he explained, his eyes on the sails for a sign of the wind Spark prophesied. "Captain Spark's been moving through this fog by dead reckoning. Hannah, he's quite a navigator."

"Then what?" she asked. "I know you have been planning something."

He scooted closer to her. "We'll surrender with the wounded, and ask to be taken to the commandant in charge, French or Portuguese."

She looked behind her at the other two launches, which were still empty and tied to the stem of the *Dissuade.* "Who goes in those?"

"As many sailors and Marines as they can carry, and they won't be heading for the harbor, but somewhere else on the island." He looked at the quarterdeck, and the captain who was no longer in sight. "Captain Spark means to give them a merry chase."

Hannah sighed. "I wish I were not afraid."

They sat another half hour, bobbing on a calm sea, and then the fog lifted as though raised all at once by a giant hand. Hannah gasped at the sight before them. It was Terceira, rising out of the Atlantic like the welcome beacon it was.

Adam couldn't hide his admiration. "He may be an Englishman and a damned rascal, but I defy any Yankee skipper to call that landfall any better!" He touched Hannah's shoulder. "But is Terceira friend of foe?"

At a sharp command from Mr. Futtrell, the sailors raced into the rigging as the wind picked up, stationing themselves along the footropes for his command. At a signal from Captain Spark, who manned the helm, the sails in the upper yards dropped with a boom, and the *Dissuade* perked up for one last attempt. The little boats tied alongside jerked forward and Hannah grabbed for the gunwhale and took a firm grip. Adam stuck his hand in the back of her trousers and braced his feet against the floorboards.

It was a gallant effort by the *Dissuade*. The sinking ship crowned on all sail and beat its way to the harbor's entrance, picking up speed until they were skimming over the water. Adam looked up at the sleek commerce raider, wounded but gallant to the end, struggling through the sea. "Thank God the tide runs in our favor," he said, shouting over the slap of the water. "What a ship, Hannah!"

They reached the harbor entrance, and Hannah stared at the stone fort, trying to determine what flag flew from the pole. She could not tell; they were too far away.

"Ahoy all boats!"

Mr. Futtrell hung in the riggings of the *Dissuade,* the speaking trumpet to his lips. "Cut all cables! Good luck and good hunting!"

Adam reached over and cut through the cable that tethered their small boat to the *Dissuade*. Picking his way among the wounded, he hurried forward to the small sail and raised it, calling to Hannah over his shoulder. "Take the tiller!"

She scrambled to do as he said, grateful down to her bare feet that Papa had insisted that his only daughter, the child of an island, knew how to handle a small boat. And thee taught me to swim, she thought, as the wind caught the sail and she leaned against the tiller. They rocketed past the final pit of land that spared Terceira's harbor from the brunt of the Atlantic swells. Hannah looked behind her to see the two launches in the stem of the *Dissuade* cut across to the Atlantic side.

The *Dissuade* was sinking now. Hannah looked back in alarm as the frigate turned bow down into the water and began a slow death spiral. "Jump!" she whispered fiercely, her hands clenched into fists. She watched, her heart in her throat, as the remaining men who could not fit into the small boats leaped off the rising stem.

"Can you see the captain?" she asked Adam anxiously. "Or Mr. Futtrell?"

Adam squinted into the sun. "No, Hannah. But he will come about. Surely thee doesn't think that is the first time something like that has happened to him?"

Hannah shuddered and hung on to the tiller. "I think all I want to do now is get home to Nantucket!"

Adam just grinned at her as they sailed into the harbor at Terceira. As they warped toward the dock, Andrew Lease's boat right behind them, two launches pulled out from shore.

"Tally-ho, indeed," Adam said under his breath. He handed the sheet to a wounded man who could sit up and scrambled back to take the tiller. Hannah handed it off gratefully and grasped the wounded man again. She looked back at the *Dissuade* in time to see it sink in a maelstrom of whirling bubbles. Heads bobbed in the water as another launch, this one with a swivel gun mounted on the bow, moved toward them.

The launches sailing toward them bow abreast warped and then backed their sails beside each boatload of wounded. Hannah looked at the soldiers hopefully. "What uniforms are those?" she whispered to Adam, who was eyeing the deck gun swiveling about to face them. But then the man with the most gold braid spoke to them in French, and she knew it didn't matter. Captain Spark had lost his gamble.

He leaned toward the boat, taking in the bloody bandages of the wounded, and goggling at her as she sat in the stem next to Adam, head high. He removed his hat, bowed—no easy feat in a bucking launch—and placed his hat over his heart. "Messieurs, mademoiselle, I must with regret place you under rest. Please follow me to the dock."

His English was quaint at best, but his meaning was unmistakable, as he pointed to the deck gun, then toward the stone fortress that crowded the hill. Hannah smiled her sunniest greeting and nodded.

Adam looked on, amused. "Why doesn't thee blow him a kiss, too?" he asked.

"I would if I thought it would help," she whispered back. Hannah turned around for one last look at the launch loading on the survivors from the *Dissuade,* then devoted her attention to the lieutenant in the French boat, who was still grinning at her.

Crowded by the French launches, Adam ran his gig up onto the beach. Hannah hurried from the boat and helped one of the wounded men into the shallow water that lapped on the beach. He sank onto the sand and lay there, covering his eyes with his hand for protection from the sun. In a few minutes when all the wounded were lying on the beach, she looked up at the soldiers who surrounded them, more curious than belligerent. "See here," she began, her hands on her hips, "these men need to be taken to hospital. Can one of you authorize that?"

The soldiers and fishermen who were gathering looked at each other and shrugged. She turned to the officer with the gold braid who had hailed them from the harbor, but he only shrugged his shoulders, too. Obviously, his challenge at the bay's entrance had exhausted both his English and his authority to respond.

Hannah repeated her entreaty as Andrew Lease approached, dragging his own wounded onto the beach. Adam turned to help. "Sir, can you not get these men out of the sun at least?" she asked the Frenchman one more time.

The French lieutenant shook his head. "The colonel is coming," he said. "We can wait with patience."

"Save your breath," murmured the surgeon. "The fun begins when Daniel hits the beach." He took her by the arm. "Whatever they do to him, you are not to object. He told me to tell you that, and he did not make a bet this time."

Hannah sighed and sat down on the sand, creating shade with her body for the wounded man who had no arms to protect his eyes. The sun was hot on her face, and she wished the captain's straw hat hadn't gone down with the *Dissuade.*

The launch with the *Dissuade* survivors was soon docked. As she watched, the captain, hands tied behind his back, was hauled off the boat, followed by the sailors who had jumped from the stem of the sinking ship. She looked for Mr. Futtrell, but he was nowhere to be seen.

"Stay here, Hannah," Adam cautioned as she got to her feet, her eyes on the captain. " Oh, and look who's coming."

She gulped and looked away from Captain Spark, who was on his knees now in the sand, a pistol pointed directly at his head. It could only be the colonel, who was covered with gold braid and wearing a vastly ill-fitting wig stylish in the last century. Sweat streamed down his face, and he appeared to be in a foul humor, stalking on short legs toward the crowd of soldiers and fishermen.

"Did we interrupt his luncheon?" Adam whispered. "Well, here goes."

Adam hurried forward, shouldering aside the French soldiers who tried to drag Captain Spark to the colonel first. He stopped in front of the colonel. "Sir," he began, shouting to be heard over the tumult of voices behind him. "My friend Hannah and I are American citizens and we demand the protection of France from this monster who wears a British uniform."

Hannah gasped and started forward, but Lease grabbed her hand. "Leave him alone," he hissed. "He knows what he's doing! Do you want to get out of this place with a whole skin, or not?"

She stood where she was, watching Adam speaking so earnestly to the colonel, who listened intently, then motioned her forward. She hurried past the captain, hesitating only when the soldier guarding Spark kicked him in the stomach and he flopped onto his side, gasping for breath.

Adam grabbed her and held her close to him. "Sir, we demand your protection!"

The colonel looked at her from her disheveled hair to her bare toes, interest replacing irritation. "It is true what he says? He was impressed by this scoundrel and your ship was blown from the water?"

Adam had apparently left off the finer point that it was a French ship which sank the *Molly Claridge*. She thought to correct the error, but as she was trying to figure out how to express this diplomatically, Captain Spark raised up on his knees again. "Yes, and I sank your damned frigate *Bergeron*," he shouted. "I'd do it again in a minute!" He disappeared then in a crowd of soldiers.

Hannah cried out and tried to pull away from Adam, but he refused to let her go. The colonel, undone by her tears, patted her on the back.

"There, there, *ma chère,* I am certain we can do for you what you wish," he consoled as his troops beat Captain Spark and the other sailors rescued from the *Dissuade.* "We shall return you promptly to the United States, if that is your desire."

"It certainly is mine," Adam said fervently.

Hannah looked back at the captain, but he had sunk out of sight, obscured by the French troops surrounding him. She wiped her eyes on her sleeve and clutched at the colonel, who was perspiring even more freely. "Oh, sir, we should go to London, I think! We have such a claim to lay before the Lords of the Admiralty."

The colonel leaned forward, smelling of sweat and salt pork, and took her chin in his fat fingers. "*Ma chère,* did that beast lay a hand on you?"

You're the only beast, she wanted to say, as he pulled her closer. She could hear the soldiers screaming behind her. They will kill him if I carry this charade further, she thought. She shook her head, and threw herself into the colonel's arms. "No, no, but this has been a dreadful experience! I am so grateful to be safe in your protection!"

Her heart breaking as the soldiers continued to beat Captain Spark, she forced herself to look up into the colonel's sweating face and give him a teary smile. He clutched her to his ample chest, then drew her back and kissed her soundly on both cheeks. "*Ma petite chère,* consider yourself and your brother under the protection of Napoleon himself!"

She sighed with gratitude and kept herself by force of will within the damp circle of his arms. "Thank you, sir. Now, sir, if you please, even if they come from a hated race, these wounded men do need to be tended."

"As you wish, my dear. Anything else?" The colonel dabbed at his face with a grimy handkerchief.

"I think your soldiers should lay off the captain now," she said, trying to keep the desperation from her voice. "I mean, wouldn't Napoleon be chagrined with you if he missed the privilege of guillotining such a beast?"

The colonel looked up from his contemplation of her face and motioned to his soldiers. "Ah, yes, of course." He barked his orders in rapid-fire French and the soldiers stopped. He said something else, and they dragged the captain, unconscious now and bleeding from his mouth and nose, onto a cart where he was thrown with his sailors and trundled toward the fortress.

The colonel released her finally from his sweaty embrace, and offered her his arm. "Come, *ma chère,* and you, sir," he added, bowing to Adam. "Let us offer you the comforts of the French nation. This is a godforsaken Portuguese hole, but we do our best. They make an excellent blood pudding here, and the Madeira is superior."

She nodded, her face pale as she strolled arm in arm with the colonel to the fortress, following the bloody trail left by Captain Sir Daniel Spark and the men of the *Dissuade.* The sun seemed so hot, and she began to perspire as the ground rose and fell as though she were still on the *Dissuade*. Her knees buckled and she fainted for the first time in her life.

When she woke, there was a cool breeze playing over her body. Hannah looked into the eyes of a black child swinging a fan on a pole as tall as she was. When the child saw that her eyes were open, she dropped the fan with a clatter and ran from the room.

Hannah raised herself up on one elbow and looked around. The high-ceilinged room was large and airy, with delicate lace curtains attempting to soften the medieval stone of the fortress at Terceira. She sat up and stretched, looking down at the simple chemise she wore. "It appears thee has come up in the world, Hannah Whittier," she said out loud as she went to the window.It opened onto a balcony, and Terceira spread below her. The protected harbor was busy with ships of all sizes, and the air hung heavy with sea birds competing for chum from the fishing boats. The water was the deepest blue imaginable and there were palm trees lining the shore. She sniffed the air. Honeysuckle. It had to be.

"Mademoiselle, you are better?'

She turned around to see a woman in the doorway. "Why, yes, much better," she said. "Thank you for your kindness."

The lady came forward, extending her hand. "I am Madame Aillet, wife of Colonel Aillet, who rescued you from those beastly English."

"Then I am doubly grateful to make your acquaintance," Hannah murmured as her brain screamed at her to ask about the beastly English. "I do trust, however, that the wounded among the English have been cared for."

"Mais oui!" Madame Aillet exclaimed. *"We* are not the barbarians here." She returned to the hall, and then motioned in a servant, who carried a bath, and was followed by a line of slaves with buckets. "You will like to bathe now? I have laid out a dress for you. It belonged to my daughter when she was much younger, so forgive us if it is out of mode."

"My other clothes?"

Madame Aillet made a face. "We will burn them, if you say so."

"Oh, no!" Hannah declared, and then added hastily, as she noted the woman's startled expression. "I mean, shouldn't one keep a souvenir?"

"I suppose, if you choose …." said Madame, and then left the room, shaking her head, and muttering. "Americans are strange."

When the bath was full, Hannah shooed the servants away, assuring them that she was perfectly capable of washing herself. She scrubbed herself with Madame's lavender soap, relishing the chance to bathe in something besides seawater. Her skin was a source of some dismay, brown as it was, and with freckles popping out on her bare shoulders.

It felt good to get into a dress again, to stand in front of a full-length mirror for the first time in her life, and admire the way the simple muslin of palest blue fit so well across her breasts and hung in graceful folds to the floor. The face that smiled back at her truly did have eyes with a twinkle in them, as Abigail Winslow had assured her so many months ago. "I suppose I am a rascal," she said to her image. "I know I should not get such pleasure from what the mirror tells me. Mama would call it vanity of the grossest sort."

She turned away then to open the door upon Madame Aillet's personal maid, who spoke no English, but who entered with a handful of brushes and combs and a seriously determined expression on her African face. Hannah submitted with pleasure to having her hair arranged in curls high on her head.

Madame Aillet returned to survey her maid's handiwork and pronounce it fit. She clapped her hands in delight. "My dear mademoiselle, you must find a husband to give you diamonds for your hair! Surely there are such men in America!"

Hannah thought of her earnest Quaker gentlemen acquaintances and chuckled. I wonder if Hosea's sailmaker suitor for me would deck me in diamonds, she thought, and immediately discarded the idea as moonshine. Daniel Spark would, however, she thought, and tumbled out that impish idea, too.

She turned to Madame Aillet. "Could I possibly be allowed to see the surgeon and the wounded?"

"I cannot imagine that you would wish to," Madame protested, her hands fluttering in agitation.

"Oh, but I helped tend them," Hannah said, "and I am concerned." Her chin went up. "It is an American thing to do."

Madame thought a moment and then shrugged. "I cannot imagine what harm this would be. Come with me."

The wounded lay on pallets in a narrow, high-ceilinged room deep within the fortress. Andrew looked up as she entered.

"You are a welcome sight, Miss Whittier," he said and nodded to Madame Aillet, who refused to enter. "I will send her out soon, Madame, but I do appreciate your allowing her here."

Hannah's eyes scanned the two rows of wounded, stopping on one shrouded figure. "Don't tell me that is Daniel Spark," she whispered, her hand digging into the surgeon's arm.

"No, no. He is over there. I do not wonder that you could not recognize him." He took her hand and led her to the end of one row.

She knelt by Spark's pallet on the floor, appalled at the damage the soldiers had done. The surgeon knelt beside her. "I think that once the swelling goes down, he will appear much more presentable, but there isn't much I can do about his nose. He will have to resort to appearing interesting from now on, rather than handsome."

She leaned closer, touching Spark's face. "Is he unconscious?"

Lease shook his head. "I think he is just sleeping now. It's been too long since he has done that. You could wake him up."

"Oh, no, I wouldn't dream of it," she whispered, her hand on his chest. The captain stirred and moved his legs, and Lease removed her hand.

"Gently, my dear. His ribs are broken in several places." He pulled back the blanket to show her the bandages wound tight around his chest.

To her surprise, the surgeon took her hand and placed it on the bandage just above his waist. "Feel that."

A question in her eyes, she cautiously prodded Captain Spark. "It feels like paper under there." She looked at Lease then, as the color drained from her face. "The dispatch? But why didn't you just destroy it?"

He leaned closer to whisper in her ear. "You need that dispatch to convince the Admiralty that Antigua's governor and Lord Luckingham at the Horse Guard are traitors. Otherwise, it is just the word of two Americans who have no love lost on the Royal Navy." He smiled at her. "At least, I think this is Adam's case. About you, I am not so sure."

Hannah regarded him seriously. "I am not sure either, sir."

"Well, so it sits. I have received a message from Futtrell. He had commandeered a fishing boat and plans a rescue tonight."

She gasped. "Do you think he can do it? Someone has to get the captain out of here!"

Lease regarded her with a smile. "Precisely my thought. Colonel Aillet is quite prepared to forward our captain to France and the guillotine, as soon as he is able to stand the rigors of the voyage."

"But Mr. Futtrell!" she protested, and then lowered her voice when Spark stirred in his sleep. "He is so young!"

"You will be amazed what people can do, if they have to, my dear Miss Whittier," he replied, his tone mild, his eyes touched with that weariness again that went beyond mere physical exhaustion. "All I ask is that you stay close to Adam tonight and be ready to do what he tells you."

She nodded, her eyes on the captain. Lease watched her a moment, then turned away to a sailor who called for a drink of water. "Remember, my dear Miss Whittier. Stay close to Adam."

Hannah knelt another moment beside Spark's pallet, and then covered his bandaged ribs with the blanket again. She surveyed the wreckage before her, one eye swollen shut, a nose beaky now at the bridge where it had once been so straight. "Well, thee will certainly look more fearsome on the quarterdeck," she whispered, resting the back of her band against his neck.

To her surprise, Spark opened his one good eye and looked back at her. "Bosoms," he mumbled and then closed his eye again, as though the effort was too great. "I was getting awfully tired of that black-and-white check, Lady Amber. Bosoms. Much better ...." He was silent then.

I should be offended by thee, she thought as she watched him another moment, then carefully removed her hand from his neck. I wonder why I am not?

"Thee is a pitiful specimen," she whispered and kissed his hair. "Perhaps we should chum thee for sharks."

He opened his eye again. "I intend to mend rapidly, Hannah."

She patted his neck again and rose without comment, pausing in the doorway, wondering if she would see him alive again. My dear captain, she thought, once you told me that the worst fear was the sound of the guns firing and running in and out. It is worse, far worse, to fear for the life of another.

Chapter Eleven

Hannah would have given the world for a glimpse of Adam Winslow, but he was nowhere to be found. As it was, she endured a tour of Terceira's fortress of São Miguel by Madame Aillet, who had a tendency toward the morbid, and dwelt at length on prisoners who had suffered torture in the dungeons. It was not an itinerary designed to soothe her concern over Daniel Spark's probable fate. She had asked, at the end of the tour, if she could return briefly to the makeshift hospital where the Americans lay, but Madame Aillet's raised eyebrows ended that attempt. She allowed herself to be escorted to her room, where Madame admonished her to lie on her bed for relief from the enervating heat that rolled across Terceira in late afternoon.

She told herself she was not tired. Hannah paced the room as the little slave skipped after her, fanning, wishing there was something she could do for Daniel Spark besides worry about him. She stopped finally, when she noticed the child was out of breath, sighed, and lay down on the bed, certain that she would never sleep when someone so dear to her suffered. She was asleep almost before she finished castigating herself.

When she woke, the sky was cloudy and thunder rumbled across the choppy water of the bay. She sat by the window in her chemise, staring out at the palm bent by sudden gusts of wind. When the rain finally began, it was almost a physical relief for her. She continued to stare at the water, wondering what Lieutenant Futtrell had planned, and wishing it were Mr. Lansing, older and more seasoned, still alive and in charge of a rescue attempt. She knew Adam Winslow well, and could only hope that the events of the past month had given him the maturity he would need for whatever part he played in the events about to unfold.

And what about thee, Hannah Whittier, she asked herself. Is thee capable of instant action? What length will thee travel to see to the safety of Captain Spark? She did not know the answer, beyond a fervent desire to see him alive and stalking many another quarterdeck, the wind at his cheek, and his eyes on the sails. It is not because I love him, she assured herself. He meets none of my requirements for a husband, beyond the fact that he is patient with me, and kind, and listens to what I say. I wish I could say that I was indifferent to his kiss, and the warmth I feel when he is very near, but that appears to be the nature of rascals.

Her unprofitable thoughts were given a new direction by the summons to dinner. She followed the servant down the polished stone hallway to a charming banquet room with a balconied view of the harbor. Adam Winslow, wearing a handsome coat of French cut that almost fit him, beamed at her as he stood conversing with the Aillets, and a tonsured Dominican soon introduced as Madame's confessor. Other officers, some in French uniform, some in Portuguese, made up the dinner guests. She found herself seated between two Frenchmen, whose English was rudimentary at best, and whose sole occupation appeared to be gazing down her bosom without drawing attention to the fact.

Dinner was delicious, especially the fish garnished with

lemons from Terceira's orchards, and concluded with a robust Madeira already so highly praised by the colonel. Hannah ate what was set before her and wondered why it tasted no better to her than sea biscuits, salt beef, and Cookie's heavenly plum duff.

When the last plate was removed, the colonel nodded to his wife, who rose and gestured to Hannah.

"My dear, let us leave these men to their politics and cigars," she said, holding out her hand.

No, Hannah thought in sudden panic. She looked at Adam, who rose and held out a closely written paper.

"Colonel, please indulge us." he said, after bowing to Madame Aillet. He pointed to the paper. "I have taken the liberty of enumerating all the wrongs done to us on the *Dissuade*." He looked at Hannah. "I would like to read it, and then request that Captain Spark be brought here to sign it."

"But, my dear boy, he can hardly walk!" the colonel protested. "I must save him from all exertions for the guillotine."

Adam's chin went up, and Hannah suppressed a smile. Ah, Colonel Aillet, she thought, you do not know how stubborn this young man can be. She sat down again, content that Adam would prevail.

"I think you owe it to us," Adam said. "I want that beast to hear this, and then I want him to sign it. And I hope he hurts. It would only be a slight recompense for all the wrong he has done us. If you are of a mind to return us to the Caribbean, I want to slap this in the hand of England's ambassador to the United States, once we are home again. The doctor can bring Spark here."

Hannah watched her young friend, secretly impressed by the set of his jaw. She leaped to her feet. "I can only second what my friend has said. We have grievances which must be addressed, if not in London, then in Washington, D.C."

The colonel considered the request, then motioned them closer. "Come, you two! I will do as you say."

Hannah hurried to Adam's side. He took her hand and held it close to his chest. "Let us hope he does not come with a squad of soldiers," he whispered to her as the colonel conversed with his fellow officers, then sent them from the room.

"He will be with us soon," said the colonel. "Some more Madeira?"

While the colonel returned to the table to pour another glass, Adam leaned closer to Hannah. "All I know is that Dr. Lease told me he had arranged some kind of diversion."

She looked at him, a question in her eyes, as the thunder, louder now, rolled across the bay. "Thee must be ready for anything," he told her, then accepted the Madeira with a smile from Colonel Aillet.

They seemed to wait forever, and Hannah writhed inside, wondering if Captain Spark was too badly injured to mount the stairs. Madame Aillet finally retired to the chapel with her confessor, and the colonel went to the window to smoke his cigar and watch the progress of the storm.

"I wish thee knew what Dr. Lease has in mind," she whispered to Adam.

"So do I," he replied, his eyes on the doorway. Suddenly his grip tightened on her hand. "Well, at least we will know soon. As the captain says, 'Tally-ho, Lady Amber.' "

She turned to the door to see the captain, leaning heavily on the surgeon, enter the room. The swelling had lessened, but he still could open only one eye. His usually impeccable white trousers were bloodstained and dirty, and Lease had thrown a shirt about his shoulders. She sighed. There was no guard. This was no surprise; in his present condition, Captain Sir Daniel Spark was no threat to anyone. She peered closer, that look of dogged determination in his one open eye was familiar to her. She crossed her fingers, hoping that Colonel Aillet would not realize what a fire burned within the battered man before him.

"Ah, my dear Captain Spark." the colonel said. "So good of you to join us."

Spark grunted and sank with a groan into a chair. Lease set his medicine satchel on the table and glowered at the colonel. "I do not know why you have summoned us here, but I must protest such treatment of the wounded," he said, and then pointed a finger at Adam. "Don't you think the guillotine punishment enough?"

Hannah gasped as Adam slapped the surgeon across the mouth with the rolled up document. "I cannot stomach your English arrogance," he shouted back. "We have suffered grievously at this monster's hands, and I will be satisfied!"

It was a convincing performance. The colonel, bristling with indignation, stepped between Adam and the doctor. "Monsieur, remember that you are a guest in my dining hall!" he protested to Adam.

Lease turned a cold stare upon Adam, who glared back. "It is what I expect from American rabble!" the surgeon said, his voice heavy with disdain.

They glowered at each other while Captain Spark rested his forehead on the table. The colonel chuckled. "Captain, you have reminded us of the reason for this visit. I am sure that my dear American guests will look forward to that moment when your head is situated just so under the blade before it drops."

"Bastards," the captain muttered, not raising his head.

"Why you ...." Adam reached for Spark, but Lease grabbed the back of his coat.

"Now, now, gentlemen!" the colonel admonished again. "Monsieur Winslow, I suggest that you read your document, so the captain can sign it." He giggled. "At least, if he has enough unbroken fingers to sign it."

Adam snapped open the paper, stood in front of the captain and ship' s surgeon, and read his catalog of injuries, some real, most imagined, dealt them on the last voyage of the *Dissuade*. He paused to scowl at the captain, who leaned back in his chair now, silent in the face of such accusation.

When Adam finished, his last words still ringing in the hall, he slapped down the paper in front of Captain Spark. Colonel Aillet procured quill and ink from the buffet and set it on the table before the captain, after clearing a space among the dishes. "I wonder that England allows such men as you to go to sea," he said as he dipped the quill in the ink and handed it to Spark.

The captain looked up from his own contemplation of the document spread before him. "And you have waged a humane war?" he asked quietly as he took the pen awkwardly in his hand. Hannah winced to see his swollen knuckles and the way he sucked in his breath as he applied pressure with his arm.

The scratch of the pen seemed loud in her ears. She turned away, unable to bear the sight of Spark in such pain. She met Lease's glance, wondering at the lights that flickered in his own eyes. She had seen nothing but defeat and melancholy mirrored in them before, but now they glowed with a brilliance that made her shiver. Is thee truly mad, she wondered as Colonel Aillet presented the document to Adam with a flourish.

"Yes, yes, soon his head will roll," Aillet assured them. He nodded in Lease's direction, too. "And yours, doctor."

Lease whirled around, his mouth open. "And what have I done to deserve such a fate?" he asked, his voice rising unpleasantly.

Colonel Aillet spread out his hands, palms up. "Surely you do not think Napoleon will be inclined to spare you? I am certain that Dr. Guillotine will be happy to extend professional courtesies to you, too."

Lease grabbed Aillet by the front of his uniform. "I think not, Colonel," he hissed, "especially when I show you what is in this bag. I believe I have a dispatch from the *Bergeron* that you will be grateful to see in Napoleon's hands. Only consider how he will thank you."

Spark looked up from the table then, and tried to rise. "Good God, Andrew," he said, the devastation in his voice unfeigned. "You were supposed to destroy that!"

Hannah looked from one man to the other, and then at Adam, a question in her eyes. Adam shook his head and edged closer to her. "Sits the wind in that quarter?" he murmured. "I think our surgeon is playing a deep game with France."

Hannah shook her head. "Thee doesn't understand, Adam!" She stared at the surgeon, wondering why he had told no one else about the infamous dispatch, which he had bandaged to the captain without his knowledge.

His eyes burning into the surgeon, Captain Spark tried to rise from the table, only to sink back in pain. "Damn you, Andrew," he shouted. "I think you are mad that you would betray your king and country!"

Lease only smiled and turned his full attention to the colonel, retrieving his medicine satchel from the table and leading the colonel to the buffet. "I merely wish to maintain my head's connection with my neck," he said with a backward glance and a smirk at the captain.

"Hand it to me," the colonel said, snapping his fingers in his urgency.

"Patience, *mon* colonel," the surgeon said. "I had thought the French liked ceremony. What say you to offering me one of those cigars you have been smoking, and then I show it to you? Over here, too, where the light is better."

The colonel smiled and selected a cigar, and a match, which Lease took from his hand. Smiling broadly, he led the colonel to the balcony and struck the match against the stone tracery.

Captain Spark stirred uneasily. "He doesn't smoke," he murmured. "I wish you would stop him, Adam."

"And he doesn't have the dispatch," Hannah said, her voice low.

"Tally-ho," the surgeon said distinctly as he opened the medicine satchel and dropped the match inside.

Everything happened at once. Hannah looked at the captain, and then with a strength Hannah wouldn't have credited, he grabbed her and pulled her to the floor. He tugged her under the massive dining room table and fell on top of her at the same time Adam dropped beside them and the medicine satchel exploded.

The concussion from the blast seemed to ricochet from wall to wall and then inside her head, even though Captain Spark clapped his hands over her ears. Chunks of stone crashed onto the dining room table, and all the glasses and china on the sideboard tinkled into shards as the three of them huddled close together. When the room was finally silent, the captain took his hands from her in time to hear a similar explosion in the harbor, and another.

Adam was the first to stand. He dragged Hannah from under the table, his hand trembling, his voice high pitched. "Hannah, was this his diversion? Oh, God, how could he?"

The two of them helped the captain to his feet. "How could he not?" said the captain, looking at the gaping hole where two men had been standing only seconds before. He took Hannah's arm. "I do not wish to appear callous, but let us not look a gift horse in the mouth. Lead on, Adam. Andrew showed us the way out, and I think he, Mr. Futtrell, and the Marines have created enough diversion for us to get to the harbor."

They descended the stairs slowly, a step at a time, clutching the captain between them as soldiers raced past them, hurrying toward the sound of the explosion in the banquet hall. Hannah held her breath, wondering why the French soldiers did not stop them, but they appeared intent upon reaching the dining room to report to the colonel. Hannah shuddered to think how fast they would come down those stairs again when they found the colonel in as many pieces as the chinaware and crystal. Somewhere deep within the walls of São Miguel, she heard a woman screaming. "Poor Madame Aillet," she said out loud.

They were met at the outer archway by a phalanx of red-coated Marines and sailors waving cutlasses. "Thank God," Captain Spark said, and pitched forward, unconscious. The Marine with the broadest shoulders picked him up and threw him over his shoulder like a bag of feathers and set out at a dogtrot for the harbor, which was ablaze now with burning shops and fired boats.

"Begging your pardon, ma'am," said a sailor Hannah recognized from her days aloft in the lookout. He picked her up and raced after the Marine, while Adam ran alongside, grinning from ear to ear.

Soon they were in the harbor and surrounded by more Marines and sailors returning from other parts of town. They carried with them squawking chickens and piglets trussed within an inch of their lives and other souvenirs of a sleepy town which, until the *Dissuade* sank in its harbor, must have thought itself far removed from the troubles in Napoleon's Europe.

Her rescuer ran on board the ship just behind the captain and Adam jumped from the dock as a sailor cut the cable and they swung out to sea. The seaman set her down, apologizing for his rude behavior, but Hannah could only wring his hand in gratitude while he towered over her and blushed like a schoolboy.

"Someone take the captain below," snapped a commanding voice from the deck. "Lively now. We don't know how bad he's hurt. Miss Whittier, where is the doctor?"

Hannah looked up at Mr. Futtrell, who stood, eyes stern, feet planted widely apart, on the darkened deck. "He was the diversion," she said simply.

Futtrell nodded, but said nothing. Adam helped her below deck, where a sailor had already wrapped the captain in a blanket. Without a word, she sat down and leaned back against the gunwales as the sailor deposited the unconscious captain in her lap then raced back on deck again. The harbor shook with another explosion while Futtrell steered a course out into the Atlantic, taking them out of harm's way and far from the wrath of a French garrison destroyed by a handful of shipwrecked members of the Royal Navy.

Hannah took a deep breath and then another. What ship was this, she asked herself as she pulled the captain closer and looked about her. Everywhere were barrels of fish, and nets. Captain Spark stirred in her arms and opened his one eye. She touched his face. "I think Mr. Futtrell has commandeered a Portuguese fishing vessel;" she said.

Spark nodded and then closed his eye again. "Lady Amber, it is nine good sailing days to Lisbon," he said. "Only think of all the ways you will discover that you can cook tunny." His voice was scarcely audible, but it carried a conviction that put the heart back in her. "I told you I was a rapid mender." He chuckled, and then winced. "But I think I will sleep now, my dear. Don't wake me until we get to Lisbon. I could sleep a week."

Captain Spark slept for two days as the *Maria la Rainha,* a fishing smack from Terceira, plowed a course for Lisbon, some nine hundred miles distant. Hannah found an old mattress from one of the forward cabins and with Adam's help, rolled him onto it. He made no comment beyond a stifled groan and another lapse into unconsciousness. When he was conscious, he seemed intent on what was happening inside his body. She held his hand, fearing this inward preoccupation and praying that it did not require a doctor. And then one morning he sat up and demanded something to eat.

"We have lots of tunny, and it's not getting a moment younger," she said.

"Why then, I'll have some, Miss Whittier," he said. He made a face. "You would think Mr. Futtrell could have commandeered something with a keg of salt beef and sea biscuit on board."

"Oh, you are a difficult patient!" she teased. "You are complaining, and here we are under all sail and proceeding to Lisbon, where I trust we will see no more ugly customers."

He nodded and rubbed at the stubble on his chin. "Only

a court martial board, Lady A, and they can be decidedly unpleasant."

She stared at him. "Surely thee will ... you will not be castigated for losing the *Dissuade.*"

"It is standard procedure. You still remember the dispatch you memorized?"

She nodded.

"Good! That will help. I only wish I had the original."

"But you do," she said and tugged at the blanket around his waist.

He grinned. "Hannah! Mind your manners! Ship's discipline!"

"Oh, hush," she said, blushing. She pushed on the bandage and was rewarded with the crackle of paper. "Dr. Lease bound it around your waist."

"By God, so he did," Spark replied, fingering the dispatch layered between the muslin strips. He leaned his head against the gunwale, looking suddenly old. "And all he had in that medicine satchel was gunpowder, I suppose."

"I suppose," she echoed, her voice soft. "Why did he do it, Daniel?"

The captain touched her face. "You have never called me that before."

"I was forward. Forgive me."

"You are charming, and I won't forgive you." He let his hand drop to his lap, serious again. "I don't know why he did it. Maybe some people have to beat themselves over the head with their sins, real or imagined. I am not numbered among that sensitive lot." He gazed into her eyes. "Put that on your list, Hannah. A rascal is always a better bedfellow than a man with a guilty conscience."

She was silent, looking at her hands. "I wish I had never mentioned that list," she said finally, and got up from the deck where she sat. She quietly left the lower deck, even as he called to her to return.

The ate tunny for a solid week—boiled, stewed, soupy, fricasseed, roasted, poached, and sautéed, while Mr. Futtrell and Adam, their eyes almost gluey from lack of sleep, stood watch and watch about and Captain Spark grew stronger. He could open both eyes now, and wiggle his fingers without flinching, and when he laughed at something she said he did not have to hold his side. She would have shaved him, but no one on board had a razor.

The *Maria la Rainha* had been captured at the end of its voyage, and the water barrels were all but empty. The sailors and crew went on quarter rations immediately and began an elaborate deception to make sure Captain Spark had plenty to drink. Hannah was touched by their solicitude, and by the way that at some point during the day or night, everyone on board managed to wander by the lower deck to see that he was getting better. I wonder how I could have thought them rough, barbaric men, she asked herself when she came on deck one night, relieved by a sailor who insisted that Captain Spark was well enough for her to leave his side.

Mr. Futtrell was standing the watch. He motioned to her to give him a progress report and then invited her to join him. "Soon we'll be in Lisbon and this adventure will be over," he said. "Do you think you'll try to go to Charleston then?"

Hannah smiled to herself. "Charleston seems like another world, Mr. Futtrell."

"It isn't. You can pick up your life where you left off."

She couldn't answer him. She knew she could never return to what she was before. Perched on the railing, her arm looped through the rigging, she examined her character and realized with a shock how much she had changed. I know that I can face the worst kind of trouble, she thought. I also know better than to let Hosea or Papa bully me into marriage, no matter how good their intentions or how good the man, if he is not right for me. I also know that I cannot put people in lists or categories. We are all governed by so many different circumstances. I hope this will make me more tolerant of others and leave me flexible enough to see good, no matter how well disguised it may appear.

It was not something to tell Mr. Futtrell, of course. "What about you, sir?" she asked. "What will you do?"

"Oh, I hope to ship out again on another raider with Captain Spark, if he'll have me." His face clouded over for a minute. "Of course, it won't be the same without Mr. Lansing on the gun deck, but that is war."

She considered him. The night was dark, so he could never see blushes. "Mr. Futtrell, do you think Captain Spark might be induced to leave the sea?"

He stared at her. "I think he would sooner sprout wings and fly to Madagascar, Miss Whittier." He groped in his inarticulate fashion to explain. "On land, he's just the younger brother to a baronet who's pretty well managed to ruin the family."

"Dear me," she said.

Mr. Futtrell was just warming to his subject. "I've seen him in drawing rooms and even at Almack's, ma'am, and it's not a pretty sight! All he does is pace about and wish himself elsewhere." He peered at her in the darkness. "The sea becomes a bit addictive, Miss Whittier. Perhaps you've noticed?"

She thought of those glorious days under full sail, perched in the lookout, barefoot, wearing canvas trousers and a loose shirt. She sat now in the dress Madame Aillet had given her, covered with a long shirt one of the Marines had removed from his own back when he noticed her shivering that first night as they fled Terceira. Soon I will be dressed properly again, she thought, but I can never forget how nice it was to be barefoot on a sunny deck, the wind in my face, listening to the rigging hum.

"Yes, I suppose it is addictive," she replied.

"Captain Spark will die before he will give up the sea."

She found a pair of shears in a forward cabin and cut the captain's hair one morning while Adam snored on the mattress and Mr. Futtrell trod the deck above with firm footsteps. She had no comb, so she fingered his curls out as straight as she could, and made a good attempt. "You know, you could go on deck and relieve Mr. Futtrell, I believe," she whispered, her lips close to his ear so as not to awaken Adam.

"I could," he agreed, "but it is good for Futtrell to feel the full strain of command. It is an important part of his nautical education that I will not deprive him of."

"He has done well, Daniel," she reminded him as she gathered the shorn curls into a corner.

He took her hand. "So have you, my dearest Hannah," he said, and tugged her closer. "I think I will never forget this voyage."

"Nor I," she replied, suddenly shy. She closed her eyes and leaned forward for his kiss, even as she told herself not to.

It never came. From the mainmast came the cry, "Land-ho! Mr. Futtrell, we have raised Lisbon!"

"Damn!" said Spark as she drew away. He tugged her close again and his lips just grazed hers. "Damn," he said again, and it was more of a caress than a curse.

She pulled back then. "I don't understand you, sir. You practically kill yourself to get to Lisbon and now listen to you! I do not pretend to understand men."

He smiled, but there was a bleakness in his eyes now. "My dearest Hannah Whittier, my sort of proper Quaker miss, I have discovered to my great chagrin that I really do love you, want you beyond all bounds of propriety, and yearn for you like a mooncalf. Damn! And now we have raised Europe and my life is not my own anymore. Neither is yours."

"What do you mean, sir?" she asked.

"You are probably about to find yourself at the center of an international incident, Miss Whittier," he said as he struggled to his feet, draping the blanket about his shoulders. He leaned on her and then grasped the deck above. "Soon there will be ambassadors, and ministers of state, and accusations hurled about and ...."

"Not from me, Daniel," she said quietly.

"Nor I," he said. "Just tell me that you love me. It's not enough, but it will do until I can get a more firm commitment. And I will, Hannah."

She opened her mouth to speak when the lieutenant of Marines hurtled down the gangway. "Sir, Mr. Futtrell requests your presence on deck, and I am to help you."

He was gone then, with a backward glance that seemed to through her like a hot poker. I do not know if I love you, she thought as she returned his gaze. You are still too old, and you will not give up the sea for me, and there is this matter of our nationality. If I consider all these objections and still love you, I am a bigger fool than any of us thought.

Chapter Twelve

I believe that I will soak and soak until my skin is wrinkled, and still smell of tunny, Hannah thought as she sat in the hip bath in Lisbon's American Consulate. The consul's wife had brought in lavender bath salts, and then verbena and lily of the valley, and they had even changed the water once, but Hannah still smelled fishy.

"Miss Whittier, you must put the best face upon this," said the woman as Hannah wrapped herself into a towel.

"Yes, by all means! At least I did not drop into a tanner's vat or irritate a skunk," Hannah teased. "And my hands and feet are very soft from all that fish oil."

"I am sure that the essence will fade," assured the woman, with no indication that she appreciated Hannah's joke.

"*L'eau de poisson*," Hannah said. "I do not think it will overtake rosewater or patchouli as the scent *du jour*, except among cat lovers."

The woman managed a grimace that Hannah charitably called a smile, and went to the door. "I am sure my maid has left something on the bed that will fit you," she said. "When you are dressed, please come downstairs to the bookroom. My husband says that he has more questions."

Hannah suppressed a sigh and turned to the bed, sorting through the clothing until she found a chemise that appeared to be her size. She tugged on the smallest petticoat, and was chagrined to see that it was too large. If I ever had a womanly figure, I have lost it on my diet of tunny and ship's biscuit, she thought as she gazed into the mirror. And horrors, I have never had so many freckles! She sat cross-legged on the bed, refusing to go any farther. If I find some clothes, I will only be subjected to more questions in the bookroom, she thought, her mind high on rebellion.

"I have told thee everything I know," she said out loud, and flopped back on the bed to stare up at the ceiling. "Thee cannot squeeze any more blood out of this Quaker turnip."

She folded her arms across her chest, scrutinized the ceiling, and blamed Adam Winslow for her current difficulties. As soon as Captain Spark had been taken off the fishing vessel on a stretcher, Adam leaped from the ship and demanded to see the American consul. Before she could protest, she found Adam and herself occupying a litter on its way to the consulate.

She would like to have shunned Adam for this betrayal, but it was difficult to overlook someone sitting knee to knee with her. She made herself as tall as she could and fixed him with a stare that would have wrung a cry of ill usage from a sculpture. "Adam, what fly was buzzing in thy brain when thee thought to bring in the American consulate?" she demanded finally.

He returned her stare for stare. "Don't be a dunce, Hannah! I was thinking I would like to get home," he declared in round tones. He stopped, skewered by her outraged expression, and slumped forward, exhausted. "Captain Spark has the dispatch, and we ...."

His jaw dropped as he fell asleep in midsentence, leaning forward until his head touched his knees. With a sigh, Hannah pushed him back against the side of the liner. "Thee is the dunce, Adam." she said, even though he was past hearing. "I have the dispatch now!" She wished for the hundredth time that she could have convinced Adam to let them stay with Mr. Futtrell. But that would have been futile, too, she realized as the liner swayed up to a mansion overlooking Lisbon's magnificent harbor. Blasted with exhaustion himself, Mr. Futtrell had merely waved Adam on and stepped aside for the consul when he came on board the *Maria la Rainha* to retrieve these errant children from Yankeeland.

"But how *is* thee, Captain Spark?" she asked the ceiling in the consulate. The question energized her and she sat up and pawed through the simple muslin dresses on the bed. The sooner she finished with the questions, the sooner she could petition a visit to the hospital where Spark had been taken. She had to return the dispatch from the *Bergeron*.

Don't let thee get a swelled head, Captain Spark, she thought as she pulled on a primrose-colored muslin cut a bit lower than she liked, but otherwise acceptable. I merely mean to see that thee is taken care of, and that the dispatch is safe. Then it would suit me fine to be on a ship bound for home.

She burst into tears, wondering why it did not suit her fine, and decided that her nerves were as tangled as her hair and needed a good comb out. She only cried harder, remembering the time Captain Spark had so gently combed her hair when she was stricken with sunburn and could not move. And now he is lying somewhere in this dirty city full of shifty characters of Mediterranean extraction, and I am not with him!

She slapped cool water on her face and lay down until the moment passed, then brushed her unruly hair until her shoulders ached. She was tying back the gleaming mass of hair when the consul's wife returned.

"Miss Whittier, the consul would really like to speak to you."

"Very well," Hannah sighed.

Adam was still deep in exhausted slumber and could not be wakened, but that was no reason for the consul not to question her again about the entire escapade, beginning with the hailing of the *Molly Claridge* and the impressment. She gave the same answers to the same questions, only this time a clerk took down every word. His pen scratched and grated on her nerves until she wanted to swing from the chandeliers, babbling gibberish.

When she finished again, two more men came into the room and were introduced as the incoming and outgoing ambassadors to Holland. They requested her story, and she told it again, fighting back tears this time. Each word she spoke seemed such a condemnation of Captain Sir Daniel Spark and the *Dissuade*, however unintentional. How could she tell them of his many kindnesses, the days of glorious sail aloft in the lookout? They would never understand how safe she felt when she sat on the quarterdeck after the battle, covered by his boat cloak, or how the gallant Mr. Futtrell had steered them safely to Lisbon. She knew she would never mention the dispatch. It was not the business of the United States.

"There, sirs," she said finally. "I have told this story over and over and it does not change."

"No, it does not, Miss Whittier," replied the consul at last, after observing her over his laced fingertips as he sat at his desk. "Why do I think that this is not all the story?"

"I cannot imagine," she said, sitting up more straight in her chair, hoping that she had tucked the dispatch into a safe place in her room.

"Perhaps Mr. Adam Winslow, when he finally wakes up, will have an augmented edition?" the consul asked.

She nodded, hoping they would not notice the sweat that suddenly beaded on her upper lip. "It's entirely possible. He saw the whole adventure from the gun deck, and I did not."

"Adventure? Was it an adventure, Miss Whittier, to be terrified out of your mind?" said the incoming ambassador to Holland, his voice heavy with disbelief. "I think you are too kind. We will lay this 'adventure' on the desk of David Erskine, Britain's ambassador to the United States, and see what comes of it."

"I wish thee would not." she murmured. "It was—" she paused and smiled, thinking of Captain Spark—"it was truly an adventure." It was something to remember when I am married safely to some dullard and living the life I was born for, she thought, but you stodgy ambassadors would not understand.

The men looked at each other. "Well, it is over now, my dear," the consul said. "I am sending you and Mr. Winslow to Holland with the ambassador, where you will be transferred to a ship for Boston. You'll sail in two days."

She flinched as though someone had slapped her. "So soon?" she managed.

The consul stared at her. "My dear Miss Whittier, did you notice the fortifications that the Viscount of Wellington is ringing around this city?'

She shook her bead.

"He expects this city to be attacked by Napoleon's marshals this fall. Even now British troops are falling back into Lisbon and bringing hordes of wounded. God knows where they are putting them all. I am sending my own wife and family to safety with the ambassador. Of course you will go. This is not a matter for argument."

Hannah rose and the men stood up. "Then I would like to say goodbye to Captain Spark before we sail," she said. She stared down their amazed expressions. "I owe him that for his kindness to me."

"Out of the question!" the consul exclaimed slamming his fist on the desk for emphasis. "We should be at war with those rascals and you want to pay a hospital visit? Miss Whittier, you are out of order. Go back to your room, please."

She turned on her heel and hurried from the bookroom, her face blank of all expression. She stood in the empty hallway, shaking with rage and helplessness until she felt more calm, then moved slowly toward the stairs. She put her hand on the railing and stopped. "No," she said distinctly and looked back at the closed door to the bookroom. "I will not, and thee cannot make me."

The hall was still empty. She walked swiftly toward the front door, holding her breath as she passed the parlor where the consul's wife sat at the piano with her daughter. She opened the front door carefully and slipped out into the Lisbon afternoon.

It was downhill all the way to the harbor, past large residences shielded behind walls with iron gates, and then smaller houses, and finally shops. She moved purposefully, trying to walk along with the crowds of shoppers, her mind in turmoil over how to find one wounded man in a foreign city swollen with the injured. She had no money to tempt anyone to help her, and nothing beyond a fierce desire to see that he was alive and well.

The docks frightened her, filled as they were with milling soldiers and sailors wearing uniforms of many countries. The men eyed her as she hurried past, calling out remarks that made her ears burn. She hurried on, wondering where to look, who to speak to, praying that no one would touch her or drag her into one of the numerous dark alleys that bisected the waterfront like veins.

"Miss Whittier! I say, Miss Whittier!"

She whirled around to see Mr. Futtrell, clad in a new uniform, shouldering his way through the crowds toward her. She gave a sob of relief and threw herself into his arms, hugging him and crying at the same time. "Mr. Futtrell, you have to help me find the captain!"

He held her off from him and peered down into her tear-stained face. "I thought I left you safe in the hands of the American consul," he said, pulling out his handkerchief. "My God, madam, we can't have you wandering about the Lisbon docks."

She nodded and thanked him for his handkerchief. She blew her nose and let him lead her to a bench in front of a chandler's shop. "You did leave me with the consul, but he was beastly and kept asking me the same questions over and over again, and when I said I wanted to see how Daniel did, he said it was out of the question and I ran away," she finished in a rush of words.

"Miss Whittier, I do believe you have changed a great deal since you came on board the *Dissuade*," he said, a grin on his face.

"What has that to do with anything?" she demanded, and clutched his arm. "I have to know how Daniel is. They are going to put me on a ship for Holland and then home, and I have to know. I still have the dispatch, and he needs it."

He stood up then and offered her his arm. "Miss Whittier— Hannah—let us find the captain."

She burst into tears again and had to blow her nose more heartily before the lieutenant would allow her to accompany him. "After all, I have appearances to keep up," he told her, his voice stem, but his eyes merry. "You certainly are a tenacious bit of shark chum." He paused a moment "I suppose if the American consul finds us, I will be clapped in irons and charged with attempted kidnap."

"I suppose it's possible," she said, twinkling her eyes back at him. "I suggest we hurry."

His grip tight on her arm, Lieutenant Futtrell led her through the crowd of sailors and soldiers and onto a quieter side street leading up from the harbor. "Lord Wellington is in the city," he explained as they hurried along. "He is supervising the construction of breastworks around Lisbon to keep Boney from pushing us into the sea. We will see some hot work here soon."

Hannah hurried to keep up with his long stride, and he shortened his steps obligingly. "What will happen to you?" she asked.

"I'm to be shipped out on the next tide back to Portsmouth," he said, and stopped before a church. "He is here, Hannah, at All Saints." He tipped his tall hat to her. "I would come in, but he and I have already spoken, and I have to catch the tide. I'll probably see you in London quite soon."

"Not if I am bound for Holland," she said, retaining her clutch on his arm.

He leaned down and kissed her cheek, gently tugging off her fingers. "What little I know of you tells me that you will find a way to get to London, Hannah. Do you know you still smell of tunny?"

She laughed and dabbed at her eyes, hugged him one last time, and slipped into the cool gloom of the church. When her eyes became accustomed, she looked around in shock and horror. The nave was filled with wounded men from the entrance to the chancel, lying practically shoulder to shoulder on pallets and tended by nuns, who glided up and down the rows. "War, I hate thee," she said softly, clasping her hands tightly together.

There were doctors here and there, kneeling beside the patients. She thought of Andrew Lease, swallowed a huge lump in her throat, and went from surgeon to surgeon until she found an English physician. His eyes red from lack of sleep, the surgeon pointed to a side door and turned back to his patient.

There were more pallets in the lady chapel off the main sanctuary. She gasped with relief when she saw a redcoated Marine sitting on the floor by a pallet closest to the altar. He looked up at her approach and grinned, and she recognized him from the *Dissuade*.

"Well, as I barely live and faintly breathe, it's Lady Amber," came a voice from the pallet. "Corporal, go find someone else to watch for a while, will you?"

With another grin and a tip of the hat, the Marine left the chapel as she ran forward and flung herself across the man who lay on the pallet.

"Ow! Gently, my dear," Captain Spark said. "My ribs are still sore and look out for my arm. But before you get discouraged, let me add that my lips are fine, however."

She sat up, put her hands gently on each side of his face and kissed him. His good arm went around her and he pulled her back down to the pallet, kissing her with a fervor that belied his convalescing condition. One kiss was not enough; two scarcely served to slake her own thirst for him. Thee is an idiot, Hannah Whittier, she told herself as she ran her tongue inside his eager mouth and wished the world somewhere else.

Spark finally stopped for breath. She sat up then as he sighed and grasped her hand. "My dear Hannah, I hope the next words out of your mouth are 'I love you,' or I will think you an unconscionable tease."

"I love you," she said. "And I've never kissed anyone like that."

"I am profoundly grateful," he said. "I would have to call him out."

"Come to think of it, Captain Sir Daniel, I've never kissed anyone but you," she said.

"Better and better," he said, pulling her closer again. "Let's keep this Yankee abandon our little secret, all right?"

She nodded and rested her head carefully on his chest. "The American consulate wouldn't let me come to see you, but I did anyway. Mr. Futtrell showed me the way."

"That boy continues to rise in my estimation," he murmured, his hand in her hair. "I see a brilliant future for him in the Royal Navy. And a future for you in my Dorsetshire manor."

The moment the words were out of his mouth, she wished he had not said them. It was as though they were a cold dousing of seawater from the wash pump, a brutal reminder of her situation. As she lay in his arms in the chapel in Lisbon, she thought of her home, and a wave of agony washed over her. "Oh, Daniel, I don't know," she whispered.

"Trust me. I do know," he replied. When she said nothing, he sat up. "You have the dispatch?"

"Not with me," she replied, sitting up more decorously

and moving away slightly, wondering at the power of words to make her feel so dispirited suddenly. "This expedition was decidedly spur of the moment. I can get it to you tomorrow, now that I know where you are."

"Good. I probably will be here a few more days, at the very least."

She sat closer again and told him of the consul's determination to ship her and Adam to Holland tomorrow. "I do not see how we can avoid it."

"Avoid it any way you can," Spark replied firmly. "Didn't I once promise you almond cake and fresh water in my home?"

So thee did, she thought as she left the hospital in the careful company of the Marine. We have talked about a great many things, and I have kissed thee too much for my own peace of mind. I do not know what I was thinking, but does anyone think enough, under those sweet circumstances? She doubted it.

"I think we'll have to walk, ma'am," the Marine said, intruding on her thoughts. "Seems like every spare conveyance is already taking someone to or from the earthworks."

She nodded and followed his lead through the streets crowded with a weird collection of local citizens haggling in the marketplaces for their supper, soldiers heading for the fortifications, wounded coming from distant battlefields, and sailors prowling the waterfront All around was noise and confusion; she longed for the quiet coolness of the church where she had said goodbye to Daniel after another kiss that went on far too long and left her feeling restless.

"A bit disorderly," the Marine commented, looking about him with some distaste. He kept his hand at her elbow and hurried her along through a crowd of drunken Light Bobs. "Give me the open sea any day, where the decks are well scrubbed and the canvas tight."

Hannah nodded. She looked up at her protector. "Thank you

for your help. I can put that dispatch in your hands as soon as we get to the consulate."

"And I will take it right back to the captain," he replied. He hesitated a moment, whether to confide something, and then continued. "He called for you last night. I think he had a touch of fever."

And I wasn't there, she thought. Nor will I be there if he should call again. "I will trust you to see that he gets the care he needs," she told the Marine, her eyes on the long driveway up to the consulate. "I do not think he and I will meet again. I am bound for Holland."

The Marine frowned down at her. "I call that a bl ... blinking shame, ma'am, if you'll pardon me. He really is a good man. I wouldn't have served with him through three cruises, if I didn't know that."

They climbed the hill in silence as the sun set over the harbor, turning the water into a silver sheet. So many ships rode at anchor, so many troops streamed ashore to continue the fight against Napoleon. She thought of her own peaceful home on Nantucket, where each day was pretty much like the one before it. Her life could take its own quiet course there, with no more of the rude shocks she had experienced during this summer's adventure.

The consul's house was brightly lit and the door wide open, discounting any hopes Hannah may have harbored about sneaking back inside. As she walked wearily up the front steps, her Marine in tow, the consul stormed out the open door.

"Where have you been?" he thundered after a look at the Marine behind her.

"You would not let me go to the hospital, but I went anyway," she said, raising her chin up to look him squarely in the eyes.

Before she could protest, the consul grabbed her and pulled her inside, slamming the door after him. The Marine knocked on the door and then pounded upon it, but the consul ignored his efforts. "Go away!" he roared at last, not relinquishing his hold on Hannah.

He let her go when the knocking stopped and shook his finger in her face. "You will go right to your room and remain there, Miss Whittier! Don't you know there is a war on out there?"

"I know better than you do!" she stormed back. "The British have their backs to the sea here and no one to depend on but themselves."

He pulled her further into the house toward the stairs and gave her another shake for good measure. "One would think you sympathized with those who destroy our shipping and impress American citizens. I do not want to see your face again until the ambassador sails for Holland, Miss Whittier."

With a sob, she ran up the stairs and into her room, slamming the door behind her. She sat on the bed a moment to collect her thoughts, then hurried to the window drapery, where she had hidden the *Bergeron* dispatch in the wide hem. It was still there. She flung open the window, but the Marine was long gone. "Drat!" she exclaimed and threw herself down on the bed. Somehow she would have to leave the consulate again in the morning, this time with the dispatch, and take it to the captain.

She sat up. Perhaps Adam could do it. She went to the door, and turned the handle, but it was locked. She pounded on the door. No answer. "I was better treated by the British!" she shouted through the heavy oak paneling.

The house was silent. She went to the window again, looked down two floors to the paving stones below, and sighed. She lay down on her bed and curled herself into a little ball.

The morning brought breakfast on a tray, delivered by a tight-lipped servant and followed by Adam Winslow. The maid set the tray on the table by the bed and Adam lifted the cloth that coveted it. He whistled and rolled his eyes at her.

"At least it is not bread and water, which I am sure is all the consul thinks thee deserves," he observed as she rubbed the sleep from her eyes. "Hannah, what is the matter with thee? I disremember thee ever behaving like this on Nantucket."

She ignored him, eating her way steadily through the food on the tray, and looking around for more. When she could find none, she went to the drapery and pulled out the *Bergeron* dispatch and slapped it in Adam's hand.

"We have to get this to Captain Spark." she said.

"I can assure that the consul has no intention of letting thee wander the streets of Lisbon again," Adam told her. "And don't get those tears in thy eyes and look so stubborn! Hannah, this is still not our fight"

"How can thee say that?" she replied. "There is a traitor in the British government."

"What is that to us?" he asked baldly, taking her by both hands. "Hannah, thee is behaving like a school miss."

She shook off his grip. "Thee will not help me, Adam Winslow?" she asked.

"I will not help thee," he replied. "We sail tomorrow morning for Holland, and then home." He left the room then. In another moment, the key turned in the lock.

Her first impulse was to bang on the door, and rage and scream until her voice was raw, but she quickly discarded both ideas as unproductive in the extreme. All that remained was the window. She went to it again and opened it wide, hoping that during the night the house had shrunk two floors and the ground underneath her window was flowerbeds of soft dirt instead of paving stones. Nothing had changed. If anything, the ground looked farther away. This is not fair, she thought, resting her chin on her hands and staring out the window.

She noticed the narrow ledge that ran from her window to the next room, which had a balcony, and climbing ivy. It was a matter of some twenty feet along the ledge, which was tenanted now with doves, cooing and puffing themselves up and strutting back and forth as though they strolled on a broad highway.

It wasn't a moment that demanded deep thought, she decided as she stuck the dispatch down the front of her dress and climbed onto the window ledge. A moment's thoughtful consideration would only lead to rejection of the plan as dangerous as it was foolhardy. I must seize the moment, she thought as she inched along the ledge, her eyes on the balcony, and not the ground. I must pretend I am in the rigging and not look down. At least the building does not sway. Oh, the things I have done for thee, Daniel Spark, she thought as she edged along. She reached for the balcony finally and pulled herself onto it.

Adam Winslow stared back at her from the other side of the glass. With a shake of his head, he opened the door onto the balcony. "Thee is certifiable, of course, and I suppose I am, too," was all he said as he straddled the balcony railing and started down the climbing ivy. "I will test it first and then thee should follow. If we are both hanged for aiding and abetting the enemy, I will make sure thee swings first so I can have the satisfaction of watching thy neck stretch!"

He wouldn't speak to her all the way to the hospital, but kept his eyes straight ahead. Not until they entered the sanctuary of All Saints did he make a sound, and then it was a sigh that went all the way to his toes as he stared at the rows and rows of wounded men from Wellington's last encounter with Marshals Soult and Ney. He took her hand then. "Hannah," was all he could say as he tugged her closer.

She leaned against his shoulder. "Adam, doesn't thee see? If we can help unmask a traitor in the British government, perhaps it will even the odds here in Portugal and Spain."

He nodded. "And there would not be so many wounded, eh, Hannah? Well, let's get this dispatch to our captain and be done with it."

She hurried toward the lady chapel, squinting into the gloom as she saw the pallets of wounded there, each space filled. She frowned. The Marine corporal was nowhere in sight. Her mind filled with disquiet, she tiptoed to the pallet last occupied by her captain. Someone else lay there now.

Captain Spark was gone.

Chapter Thirteen

Her first fear was that he had died in the night, but she quickly discarded that notion. Anyone who could kiss like Captain Spark was firmly planted on the road to recovery. Her second thought was anger. So you could not wait to leave, she considered as she stared down at the pallet and its sleeping new occupant. This was replaced quickly by despair. They have shipped you out for London and a court martial, but I am not there.

With eyes that scarcely saw, she went back into the main chapel. Adam followed her. He touched her arm. "Is it Holland now?" he asked quietly.

She gave him a searching look that made him turn red and stare at his shoes. "Adam, where is thy backbone? We have to get to England! That's all there is to it."

A brief conversation with the hospital steward confirmed her fear. "Oh, my, yes, he was shipped out on last night's tide, miss," the clerk assured her, looking down through bloodshot eyes at his endless list of dead, wounded, and misplaced. "Something about a court martial at the Admiralty in two weeks." He chuckled, remembering. "Damned ... er, excuse me ... bless me if he wasn't a bit exercised over being so rudely hauled up from his bed of pain. I do believe that was how he put it."

"Then you have considerably cleaned up his conversation for my benefit." she replied, her voice crisp. "Has he sailed?"

"Yes, miss. You're too late."

She left the building in a rage, too angry to cry over this latest misfortune. She was at the bottom of the stair, fuming, before Adam caught up with her. He grabbed her and sat her down on the bottom step.

"Hannah, thee is not fit for society!" he said, his demeanor more commanding than usual. "We'll never get anywhere with thee in a total rage."

He was right of course. She leaped to her feet and walked to the broad stone banister leading down from the church. She wanted to pound on something, but the only thing there was a chestnut horse, its reins looped over the carved marble flowerpot. She turned her face into its shoulder instead and cried, standing there until she felt calm enough to look at Adam again. The animal was obliging in the extreme, wickering softly at her as she stood there.

"He *is* a good horse, madam," said a voice behind her.

She whirled around to stare at an elegantly tall officer with more gold on his shoulders and sleeves than probably was deposited in the whole U.S. Treasury. His tanned face was in no way marred by his beaked nose. He looked like a man who could lead armies, and here she was sobbing into his horse.

"I am sorry, sir," she managed, and scrubbed her hand across her eyes and backed away from his horse as though she had been attempting its theft.

He shook his head and smiled down at her, taking off his lofty hat. "Don't worry, my dear. I have cried into Copenhagen a few times myself, and not so long ago."

His words were spoken quietly, so none of the equally gold-braided men who followed him down the steps could hear. "May I introduce Copenhagen, Miss ... Miss ...."

"Hannah Whittier of Nantucket," she said, and held out her hand shyly.

He took it in both his gloved hands. "You are a long way from home," he said.

Her eyes teared again at his words and without saying anything else, he whipped out a handsome monogrammed handkerchief. "Perhaps I should not have mentioned that, Miss Whittier," he said while she blew her nose. "Obviously I don't need to remind you of the miles between this dirty city and what I am sure is a more pleasant existence. Here, sit down."

He indicated the bottom step again and she sat, her eyes on his face. He dusted off the step and joined her, waving on the officers around him. "Gentlemen, find something to occupy yourselves, if you will. Miss Whittier, my name is Wellesley, Arthur Wellesley."

She heard Adam's soft whistle behind her. "Mr. Wellesley?" she asked.

"Not precisely. I command this ragtag army, my dear. I am the Viscount of Wellington."

"Oh, my," Hannah said, her eyes wide. "I didn't mean to cry all over thy horse!"

He threw back his head and laughed, and it was the most extraordinary laugh Hannah had ever heard, high-pitched and somewhat horselike itself. Copenhagen tossed his mane at the sound as though horse and master shared a conspiracy.

"My dear, I am sure he will dry," said Wellington. "Now tell me what is troubling you."

Adam tugged at her arm. "Hannah, thee cannot bother this gentleman!"

She shrugged off his hand. "Sir, I am perplexed at how difficult it is to do a good deed for the British."

Wellington took off his gloves. "I did not know it was so hard, my dear."

"It's no wonder thee lost the War for Independence," she continued steadily, ignoring Adam, who had thrown up his hands and stalked up the steps to sit behind them, his head in his hands. "All I have been trying to do is help Captain Sir Daniel Spark—do you know him, sir?—get a dispatch from a French ship to London, and I am scotched at every turn."

Wellington absorbed this bit of information without a blink. "I know the Spark family. Does he not command a commerce raider?"

"He did, but it sank in the harbor on Terceira. And now he has been sent to London for a court martial, and I still have the dispatch. He needs me, sir."

He looked at her. "I don't doubt that for a moment, Miss ... Whittier, did you say? And are you a Quaker, miss?"

"I think I am," she replied, some doubt in her voice, "although I have not been acting precisely as a Quaker should lately. I mean, I'd like to murder the Lords of the Admiralty for being so pigheaded about this court martial. I mean, couldn't it wait?"

Wellington laughed again. "I am sure you are not alone in your wish to see the First Lords to Hades, my dear. Show me the dispatch."

She took it from the front of her dress, but did not hold it out to him. "See here, sir, can I trust thee?" she asked.

One of the British officers standing close by laughed. 'That's enough, Beresford." the viscount murmured. "Obviously this little lady has been through a few trials for this dispatch."

"Oh, we have, sir," she agreed. "More than thee knows." She hesitated another moment, then held it out to him.

"You can safely assume that I have the good of England in mind, Miss Whittier," Wellington said as his hand closed over the dispatch. "We are waging a lonely battle against the Corsican tyrant, and we have few friends in the world. Unfortunately, your nation is not among them. Perhaps I should be suspicious of you?"

She turned shocked eyes on him, and then smiled to see that he was grinning at her. "Thee is a dreadful tease, sir," she said, to the silent enjoyment of the officers around the viscount. "Go ahead and read it."

He did, leaning back on the step and propping himself up with his elbow. She could see how tired he was and could only wonder at the terrible responsibility he shouldered. *And now he is digging trenches around this city, and I am bothering him with one more little detail.*

He looked up halfway through the dispatch and motioned to one of his officers to sit beside and read, too. "My God, sir," said the officer, his voice low, as he scanned the closely written page. They continued reading in silence, then Wellington folded the dispatch and handed it back.

"Yes, you do have to get to London. Miss Whittier," he said after another moment's reflection. "And promptly, too. Beresford, what do you know of the Navy? Are not court martials at the Admiralty conducted the last week of each month?"

"I believe so, my lord," the officer said. "That would give her two weeks, wouldn't it?"

Wellington nodded. "My dear, do you have any objections to a prompt removal from Lisbon?"

"The more prompt, the better," she replied. "We had to climb out of a second-story window at the American consulate this morning to get here, and I do not think the consul will want to see us again in this life."

The viscount winced. "To the contrary, I strongly suspect he will be looking for you."

"I should think he would be glad to be rid of her, sir." Adam spoke up then, coming closer to the steps. "I am Adam Winslow. Hannah and I have known each other forever, and I was impressed from my ship by Captain Spark."

"Worse and worse," murmured Wellington. "And still you wish to help him?"

"No, I don't." Adam said bluntly. "But Hannah won't let it alone until she does, and believe me, thee doesn't wish to be nibbled to death by this particular duck."

"Adam!" she exclaimed as the viscount laughed again. "He will think I am a pest."

"Thee is."

They glowered at each other. Wellington shook his head. "Temper, temper," he said, and got to his feet. He pulled up Hannah after him. "My dear, I know I can get you on board a fast packet to Portsmouth, if you don't object to a bit of subterfuge."

"Sir, I am well acquainted with subterfuge by now. Haven't I been in close company with the Royal Navy these six weeks and more?"

He clapped his hands together, his mind made up. "Very well, then, since the American consulate had probably alerted the waterfront, Miss Whittier, we will have to be a bit smarter. I would like to avoid an international incident, if I can, so would you mind terribly dressing as a cabin boy?"

Hannah and Adam looked at each other, their eyes merry. "Sir, that was what she did on the *Dissuade,* and do you know, Captain Spark even sent her into the lookout to spy for French cruisers?"

Wellington shook his head and lifted the reins from off the flowerpot. He mounted Copenhagen. "I am continually amazed at the resourcefulness of the Royal Navy, Miss Whittier. I recommend that you remain here until Adam can find you some suitable kit. Then I expect to see the two of you—and that infamous dispatch——at the H.M.S. *Dauntless* in an hour or less. The navy is dashed particular about wind and tides."

He wheeled Copenhagen around and held his hand out for Adam to mount behind him. The other officers found their horses and mounted while she stood on the steps of All Saints. "I must make a flying nip to London and a conference with the small brains at Whitehall. You can be my cabin boy, Miss Whittier, since you are so good at it. See you soon. And don't murder anyone until Adam returns."

She watched them leave, then returned to the chapel, where she sat in a shadowy corner until Adam returned an hour later with clothes draped over his arm. He held them out to her.

"Wellington is a great gun, Hannah, for all that he is British," he whispered. "Hurry now. We have to catch the tide."

She took the clothes and ducked into the narrow stairway leading up to the bell tower. It was only a moment's work to pull off her dress and petticoat and get into sailor's canvas pants and shirt, wool this time. She balled up the dress and petticoat and wedged them under the lowest step, wondering what the priests of All Saints would think when a housecleaning eventually uncovered them.

Adam knocked on the door to hurry her along. "I'm coming!" she hissed, and rebraided her hair down her back. Someday I will wear my own clothes again, she thought as she hurried from the chapel with Adam and ran with him, hand in hand, down the steps.

Wellington stood on the dock waiting. She ran toward him, out of breath, and he thrust his valise into her hands, commanding her to follow closely by his side. "The American consul has been stalking up and down the docks for the past hour and more, Miss Whittier," he whispered under his breath as they strode along to the jolly boat. "And I have been perjuring my soul and assuring him that the British would never be party to any deception regarding an American female of tender years."

He lifted her into the boat, luggage and all, and hurried to sit beside her, obscuring her from any view from the waterfront. Adam scrambled in behind them as the helmsman cast off the rope and raised the sail for the *Dauntless*.

"Of course, we could have simply given thee the dispatch to take to the Admiralty," Adam said as the boat skimmed over the water, outlined by the setting sun.

Wellington nodded. "You could have tried, my young friend," he said, "but why do I have the feeling that would not have been good enough for Miss Whittier here?"

"Because she is a totty-headed female," he replied. "I have known her for years as a sensible Nantucket girl, and now see what happens when she gets one ocean voyage!"

Yes, indeed, Hannah thought as the jolly boat swung around to meet the *Dauntless*. I do not know that I would recognize myself if I saw me on the street. I used to be biddable, like Mama, never saying boo to a goose, and here I sit beside the Viscount of Wellington, one of the great men of Europe. She rested her chin in her hand. And somewhere Daniel Spark needs me.

Hannah spent the voyage from Lisbon to London in the great cabin that the captain had vacated for Wellington, listening to rain scour the deck of the cruiser, and working her way through a great pile of darning. "Thee does not have a pair of socks without holes," she grumbled to the viscount as he sat day after day in the cabin, bringing his journal up to date and writing reports.

"My dear, that is yet another unglamorous consequence of war," he murmured as he wrote. "Does 'attrition' have one 't' or two?"

"It has three," she replied, and he threw down his pen. "Well, it does."

He shook his head, smiled at her, and picked up the pen again. "Captain Spark must be a man of considerable patience to tolerate you," he said, his eyes on the report spread before him.

"Oh, he has no patience at all," she said, cutting the thread with her teeth and picking up another sock, quite unruffled by his jest. "He calls me dreadful things like 'shark chum,' and blasphemes and uses expressions that would make my mother go into spasms."

"And he has no qualms about impressing Americans," Adam added from his corner by the stem galley.

"Has the man any good qualities?" Wellington asked, putting

down his pen at last and rubbing his eyes.

Hannah was silent as she bent over her darning. He loves me, she thought, and that shows right good sense. He kisses most excellently, and that is nothing to tell the Viscount of Wellington. "He is fearless in a fight," she said at last. "And ... and when I am afraid of something, like climbing the rigging, he makes me face down my fear until it does not scare me any longer."

"Excellent man," Wellington said. He rested his head in his hand. "I could use him when I visit Whitehall next week and try to explain to the armchair generals why I lost so many men at Vimeiro and why we struggle now to hang on to Lisbon." He was silent then, his sharp features shadowed and then revealed by the swaying lamp.Hannah put down her darning. "Captain Spark would say that once thee has faced the guns, nothing can frighten thee," she said, her voice soft.

Wellington looked at her and nodded. "You are right, of course." He reached across the table and touched her cheek. "And I think I understand why Captain Spark tolerates you."

She blushed and picked up the sock again. "Sir, I think if thee would cut thy toenails more regularly, thee would have better socks."

"Hannah!" Adam groaned. "Won't thee ever be still?"

She grew quieter as they reached the coast of England and sailed into Portsmouth Harbor, wondering why she had not just given the dispatch to Wellington, as Adam had suggested. We could be on our way home, and I would eventually forget Daniel Spark, she thought as she stared out the stem gallery windows to the gray ocean, rising and falling on oily swells. As the anchor chain ran out of the hawser hole and the sailors furled the sails in Portsmouth Harbor, she told herself that once she knew for certain that he was well, she would have no trouble leaving. Not a bit.

The further benefit of being pressed into the service of Arthur Wellesley, Viscount of Wellington, showed itself as soon as they drew up to the wharf, where a post chaise waited. Wellington flipped a coin to the helmsman while Adam lifted Hannah onto the dock. He bundled them inside the post chaise and nodded to the coachman. "These are good horses?" he asked the coachman.

The man grinned and bowed. "Oh, yes, my lord."

"Then spring 'em, my good man," Wellington commanded. "We have a date at the Admiralty."

They drove all night, Hannah asleep against the viscount's shoulder as they raced through the silent countryside. When she woke in the morning, her neck stiff and her back aching, she wondered if he had slept at all. He was staring out the window, his eyes half closed, his expression unreadable, as though his body was here in the coach but his heart remained in Lisbon with his troops.

She sat up, and he glanced at her, then resumed his stare out the window. "Have you ever considered, my lord, how often in life we find ourselves wishing we were where we are not?" she murmured. "It seems that is all I have done lately, and I think thee has the same difficulty."

He nodded. "I should be in Lisbon. Oh, Beresford knows his business, and mine, too, but I am commanding." He clapped his hands together in a frustrated gesture. "It is so hard to convince people that I truly know what I am doing. I know how to fight Napoleon, and it is not by explaining my every move to the First Minister!"

He paused then, as if surprised at his vehemence. "Well, we all have our troubles. Hannah, what will you do once you have given Captain Spark the dispatch?"

"I expect I will return to America," she replied, wishing the idea had more appeal.

"I wonder," he said, then stared out the window again.

Her first view of London was hazy smoke rising from countless chimneys, to drift, dirt-colored, around low clouds that promised rain again. She looked for St. Paul's Cathedral, which she had seen in books, but it was obscured by the fog that settled everywhere. She shivered. "When did summer end?" she asked of no one in particular.

"I think when you were below deck darning socks," the viscount said. "I trust you have better weather in America. I know we do in Spain." His voice sounded wistful, as though he wished himself back to the hot summers on high plateaus.

It was well past noon when the post chaise slowed to a stop in front of the three heavy pillars distinguishing the Admiralty House from other, less dramatic government buildings. The viscount helped Hannah from the carriage and stood there a moment, his hands in his pockets. "Perhaps I should come in with you," he said at last. "My own business can wait, and I worry about what kind of reception you Americans might get from the porter."

They hurried up the steps, just ahead of the rain that had been threatening all morning, and into the antechamber with its black-and-white marble floor. Wellington set his hat on straighter and strode to the porter's desk, looking down at the man who sat scratching away with his pen. "Are there any court martials in session right now?" he asked.

"Yes, sir," said the porter, "but they have begun after noon recess, so you cannot enter."

"We have come from Portugal with an important dispatch," the viscount replied, rapping his knuckles on the desk. "We demand entrance to Captain Sir Daniel Spark's court martial."

"Well, you cannot have it," the porter replied, turning back to his paperwork. "The rules apply to the army as well as the navy."

Wellington stepped back, surprised. Hannah tugged at his cloak. "I told you how difficult it was to do a favor for the English people," she said.

The viscount nodded and withdrew to the chairs by the large windows. He thoughtfully regarded the porter, who was deep in his forms again. "I am forced to agree with you, Miss

Whittier. This calls for a classic army response. Adam, can I trust you to make an appropriate diversion in this antechamber while I whisk Hannah into the trial?"

Adam grinned and held out his hand. "Does thee have a match, my lord?"

The viscount smiled back and handed Adam a box from his pocket. "Make it a good one, Adam. I'll go your bail if the navy hauls you away."

"What can they do? Impress me?" Adam asked as he struck a match and held it under the nearest drapery.

"Resourceful chap," Wellington said as he watched the smoke rise in a choking cloud from the ancient cloth. "Come, my dear. We have an appointment with the First Lords, whether they know it or not."

By now the porter was staring at the window, where smoke billowed. Screaming, "Fire! Fire!" he scrambled from his chair, knocking over the inkwell, which spread ink all over his precious paperwork. Adam went to the next window, set another fire and darted out the door as the viscount grabbed Hannah by the elbow and steered her down the hall.

The first chamber yielded nothing more than a clutch of clerks, busily working over another stack of documents. "We should send Adam in here," Wellington said as he closed the door. "Think what a bonfire that would make. Do you suppose anyone actually reads that stuff? We could be doing the navy a favor."

Hannah laughed and let him tug her along the hall to a massive doorway at the end. It was guarded by two sailors, but the viscount didn't even pause. He slammed the door open and looked around him in satisfaction. "Ah, yes," he said and patted Hannah's shoulder. "Well, here you go, my dear." He bowed over her hand. "I am certain my wife would thank you for darning all those socks. And I will try to trim my toenails more frequently."

She let him kiss her hand, her eyes merry. "Good luck with

Napoleon, sir. I think thee will win."

He winked and left the room, his cloak billowing out behind him. Hannah turned her attention to the chamber before her, sighing with relief to see Captain Spark, handsome in full uniform and with his arm in a sling, standing by his chair, a grin on his face. Others rose, among them Mr. Futtrell and several Marines from the *Dissuade*. She started down the aisle, but was stopped by the sailors from the doorway.

"Let me go!" she shouted. "I am so out of patience with the Royal Navy!"

And then Spark was beside her. "I recommend you release her at once," he said, scarcely raising his voice to the men who held her arms. "Lively now," he added and the sailors let go.

"What *is* the meaning of this!" shouted a loud quarterdeck voice from the long table at the front of the chamber. The First Lords were standing now, too, craning about for a better view. "Is that a woman?"

"Yes, my lord, quite a woman," Spark replied, tucking her arm in his good one and pulling her toward the front. "Hannah Whittier from Nantucket, Massachusetts. She has a little present from the *Bergeron* for you, my lord." He turned to Hannah and whispered, "Where is Adam?"

"Setting fire to the curtains in the antechamber," she replied.

He stopped and put his hand on her shoulder. "And whose idea was that?"

"Why, Arthur Wellesley, the Viscount of Wellington. He thought a diversion would get us past the porter."

Spark stared at her. "Hells' bells, you have been keeping excellent company."

"He is a fine man, Daniel, and I wish thee would not swear," she said as she took the dispatch out of the front of her shirt. "Who do I give this to?"

"Give it to that red-faced walrus with the pop eyes," he whispered. "That is Lord Tichenor." He hurried her toward the long table, where the lords all stood, surrounded by lesser ranks of officers. "My Lord Tichenor, we request permission to approach the table."

"This is highly unusual, Sir Daniel," bellowed the admiral, his voice still equal to any battle or hurricane. "God bless me, it *is* a woman!"

"Well, more of a young lady, actually, but she will grow," Spark amended. "Give him the dispatch like a good girl, Hannah."

She handed it over. "This is from the *Bergeron,* which Captain Spark sank. It makes excellent reading, sir, so we saved it for thee."

Spark looked around the room until he located Lord Luckingham. He leaned across the table. "My Lord, you may wish to set a stronger guard at the door before you begin reading."

"As you were!" the first lord shouted. "Find that ... that young lady a chair. My God, madam, have you no shoes?"

"Why, no," she replied, unable to keep the laughter from her voice. "We could not find any that small in ship's store, and it was warm in Portugal when we left."

The officers in the room laughed. The admiral banged on the table with the flat of his hand, and then stopped suddenly, sniffing the air. "Do I smell smoke?" he demanded in the same rasping voice.

"Yes, sir," she replied. "My friend Adam had to set fire to the curtains to distract the porter long enough for me to get in here."

The admiral stared at her. Captain Spark shrugged his shoulders. "Americans, sir. What can one say?"

The admiral clutched the dispatch to him and sat down slowly. His eyes narrowed. "Madam, you come from a distempered race."

"Exactly what I have been telling her, my lord," Spark said cheerfully. "Come, Hannah, you can have my chair."

She sat down next to Mr. Futtrell, who flashed her a grin and then turned his attention to Lord Tichenor as he read the dispatch. Captain Spark found another chair and pulled it next to her. "You made it," he said simply, and took her hand.

Halfway through the dispatch, Lord Tichenor looked up and cleared his throat. He gestured to the *Dissuade's* Marines. "Stand by the door, men," he ordered, then returned his attention to the paper. The two other lords stood behind his chair, reading over his shoulder.

"We were almost through," Spark whispered, leaning close to her. "Naturally, I could not say anything about the dispatch, because I did not have it." He looked into her eyes. "You are a wonder, Hannah."

"I am nothing of the sort," she protested, but her voice was soft. "How could anyone stand in the chapel at All Saints and see all those wounded men, and not want to do something to end this bloodshed faster?"

He nodded, then turned his attention to the front, where Lord Tichenor was on his feet now. He clasped her hand more firmly, twining his fingers through hers as though he did not wish to let her go again. "About those kisses in the chapel," he whispered, his eyes still on Lord Tichenor. "I meant every one of them, Hannah."

Lord Tichenor rapped on the table for silence. He held out the dispatch toward Lord Luckingham, who sat in the front row, supremely unconcerned. "Lord Luckingham, perhaps you might find this document interesting," he said, and gestured for him to come to the table.

Luckingham strolled to the front, a question in his eyes.

"He doesn't have a clue," Hannah whispered.

Lord Tichenor's voice was all affability now. "Start reading here, my lord. It's a letter from the governor of Antigua. Take your time; savor it, you bastard."

The chamber was silent now, as a hundred officers, men, clerks, and barristers stared at Lord Luckingham. Luckingham snatched up the document from the table. The paper began to rattle in his fingers and the color drained from his face, leaving behind the wide-eyed stare of an animal in a trap. "You can't possibly believe a document delivered by an American, my lord," he said at last, turning the word into an epithet.

Hannah was on her feet in a second. "We have dragged that document through hell, my Lord Tichenor!" she shouted. "I have seen men die for it! I don't care if thee are all pettifogging, arrogant Englishmen! No nation deserves to suffer a traitor!"

Her words rang out in the chamber. Lord Luckingham threw down the document and leaned against the table, as if his legs would no longer support him. He covered his face with his hands as the *Dissuade's* Marines led him away. Hannah sighed and sat down again.

Lord Tichenor watched the traitor until the door slammed. He sat down again, a frown on his face, and looked again at the other papers before him. "Now where were we?" he murmured to himself. "Ah, yes, Captain Spark, I believe we have to deliberate now and conclude your court martial."

Hannah leaped to her feet again. "My lord, I hope thee is not going to cut up stiff because the *Dissuade* sank. Thee was not there to see all that water pouring into the hold and hear those pumps clank."

The first lord's lips twitched, but he managed a stern face. "Miss Whittier, sit down!" he ordered. "One doesn't get to be first lord without hearing pumps. Captain Spark has already been ably defended and does not need American counsel from some barefoot chit."

"Very well," Hannah muttered and let Spark pull her back into her chair.

The first lords rose and left the chamber. "They could be gone all afternoon deliberating," Spark said.

"Then they are perfect idiots," she replied.

"Hannah, be quiet," he said, but he was smiling. "Thank you for all you have done."

The clerk announced the return of the first lords, who filed right back into the chamber almost immediately. Captain

Spark rose to his feet on their command. Lord Tichenor took Spark's sword, which lay on the table before him, and turned the hilt toward the captain. "You are exonerated of all charges, Captain Spark. The lords admiral are of the opinion that your defeat of the *Bergeron* and subsequent removal to the Azores showed the sort of verve and pluck that England expects of its navy. You are honorably acquitted, sir. You need only wait for further orders."

Spark smiled and stepped forward for his sword. He saluted, then put the sword back in his scabbard. He bowed. "Thank you, my lords admiral."

Lord Tichenor bowed in return, then gestured to Hannah. "Thank you, Miss Whittier, for your service to our nation," he said, his voice softer now and his eyes more kindly. "Perhaps somewhere in London, Captain Spark can find you some shoes."

Chapter Fourteen

Triumphant in victory, Daniel Spark rescued Adam Winslow from the clutches of the navy. "Sirs, he had to create a diversion to get beyond the porter," he told the first lords, when he stood with them in the antechamber, looking at the charred draperies. "Miss Whittier told you how hard it was to do a favor for the British, my lords," he added. "And after all, they are Americans, used to dealing with problems on a more primitive level."

Lord Tichenor leveled his most ferocious quarterdeck stare at Adam, who grinned back. "You appear to be most unrepentant, young man," he began, the words rumbling out of him.

"I think this little bonfire is just recompense for being impressed and forced to sail to England entirely against my own wishes," Adam said, returning stare for stare. "And I think Captain Spark should pay to replace the draperies."

Lord Tichenor rumbled again, but it sounded more like a laugh desperate to escape from his insides. "You are as cheeky as this young lady."

"Almost," Adam replied, grinning at Hannah. "I think it is in the blood, my lord. And we want passage home from thee as soon as it can be arranged, don't we, Hannah?"

She took a deep breath and nodded, not looking at Captain Sir Daniel Spark. "Yes, we do," she whispered.

Lord Tichenor threw up his hands. "Very well! I will arrange for vouchers to be sent to ... My dear Miss Whittier, where are you staying? I would certainly prefer that the American ambassador, God bless his fractious soul, not get wind that you are in London."

"They will stay with my mother and me on Half Moon Street," Spark said. He looked at the draperies again and sighed. "And I will replace the draperies in the antechamber."

"Excellent!" Lord Tichenor declared. "Then we can call this matter closed."

"You two are expensive, indeed," Spark grumbled as he helped Hannah into the hack after Adam. "And you, Lady Amber, I suppose you will expect me to find some clothes for your back."

"And shoes, please," Hannah said, laughing at the expression on his face. "Above all, shoes."

Thee has found me shoes and too much more, Hannah decided as she sat crosslegged on her bed in the Spark mansion on Half Moon Street. A week has passed and I have more dresses and hats than all my Nantucket friends put together. She looked around her at the unopened packages on the bed, delivered only moments before and borne triumphantly past the butler and upstairs by the maid that Daniel Spark's mother had loaned her. Only a day or two ago, she would have pounced on the packages and opened them, to exclaim over the beauty within. Now she could only shake her head at such extravagance as a vague feeling of unease gnawed at her Quaker scruples.

She sighed as the maid closed the door behind her. Soon Lady Spark would come up the stairs to exclaim over her son's latest purchases for Hannah Whittier. "He is usually such a clutch-fist," she had earlier told Hannah with a pout. "He keeps my household expenses on a tight rein, and I find it such a restraint! But look, he has bought you morning dresses and walking dresses, and hats that are much handsomer than my own!"

On Captain Spark's command, a French modiste, complete with sneer and superior manners, had arrived the very next morning, when Hannah still lay in bed, wearing one of Lady Spark's nightgowns and contemplating the handsome plaster swirls in the ceiling. It was a view far removed from the plaster and beams of her own little bedroom under the eaves on Orange Street. But Madame LeTournier could not be ignored, especially when she threw back the covers and demanded that Hannah rise and do her duty. Protest that all she needed was one or two serviceable dresses was useless argument, Hannah soon discovered. Madame LeTournier walked around her, taking measurements and announcing her plans for Mademoiselle's complete wardrobe.

"But I do not need so much!" Hannah exclaimed. "One or two dresses, some shoes, and perhaps a cloak …."

"I have my orders from *le capitaine*," Madame LeTournier insisted. " 'Rig her out like a ship of the line,' he said, and so I shall. Hold still, Miss Whittier. How can I measure your foot?"

She resumed her protests two days later when the first of the lovely confections began arriving, sure indication the seamstresses at LeTournier's salon were burning their candles right down to the holder to fulfill their commission from Captain Sir Daniel Spark, 'hero of the Caribbean, savior of England from the hands of traitors,' as Madame had put it.

"Oh, I cannot accept these," she demurred as Lady Spark buttoned her into an especially attractive blue morning dress of the lightest wool. It hung in neat folds to her ankles, with slippers of the softest Moroccan leather, dyed to match.

"Don't be missish," Lady Spark insisted. "Now, turn around. Perfection!"

She went into the hall and called her son, who arrived in shirtsleeves, with a physician trailing after him, who was trying to resplint his arm. Holding his arm, the captain walked around her, spending more time in the back than she liked, and then faced her. "Shipshape from all points of the compass, Hannah," he pronounced. "By God, you are enough to stop a man's breath! Just keep eating that stuff Mama's cook thinks we need, and you'll soon have sufficient meat on your bones. The cut of your jib is truly a marvel."

"I wish thee would be serious," she said.

"I am, you silly nod!" he replied, his eyes merry. "Ask Mama how tight I am with her accounts. I expect a good return on my investments, and you have amply fulfilled that promise."

"It's too much!" she insisted. "How can I wear these clothes among my own people in Nantucket?"

Daniel sighed and rested his broken arm on her shoulder so she would not move. "Mama, take Dr. Sanford to the blue saloon for some port. I must reason with a stubborn Quaker." When the door closed behind them, he kissed her so thoroughly that she could be only grateful he was hampered by a broken arm.

"Humor me, my dear," he murmured into her hair as she rested her head against his chest. "I go for years with nothing to look at but gray biscuits and green drinking water and seamen in canvas trousers. You can't imagine what a bright spot you are in my life. Now stop cutting up so stiff over this wardrobe, or I will have to take more drastic steps and kiss you until your knees buckle." He kissed her again, his good hand gentle against her breast. "Perhaps I will do that anyway."

Later, when the clothes were put away lovingly in the dressing room by the maid, and Spark had returned to the ministrations of the surgeon, Hannah went in search of Adam. He sat in the library wearing some of Spark's civilian clothes and looking over the guidebook the captain had loaned him.

"Adam, what am I to do?" she asked, sitting down beside him.

He looked up from the guidebook, his expression somewhat distant. "I have tried to give thee advice before, and it is never what thee wishes to hear," he told her, biting off his words. "So I think I shall not waste my breath. Thee knows what to do."

Of course she knew what to do, she thought two days later as she lay in bed and stared at the ceiling again. It was becoming an old friend to her, considering how often she woke up at night now to stare at it. Only last night she had been so proud to have Captain Spark, resplendent in his uniform and even more dashing with his arm in a sling, usher her around the great room at the Admiralty House at a reception for some minor European royalty lately escaped from the clutches of Napoleon Bonaparte. She knew she looked fine in her low-cut dress of primrose-watered silk, her hair piled high on her head and twinkling here and there with diamonds from the Spark vault.

Burdened as he was with a sling, Daniel had required her help to dress for the affair. "Lady Amber, if you could just tie this for me, I could have ample leisure to stare down into your rather fine cleavage," he said with a grin as he stood in the hallway outside her open door, neckcloth in hand.

"I wish thee would not talk so," she said with a grimace as she stood on tiptoe to arrange the stock about his neck. "And I should not have allowed the maid to toss my hair with your diamonds."

"Why not?" he asked as she stepped back finally to survey her efforts. "Better on you than unnoticed in some dark vault." He came closer and touched her shoulder. His voice was gentle, caressing even. "Have you heard that my friends are saying that Captain Spark, commerce raider and scourge of the French Caribbean, has finally struck his colors for the American Quaker?"

Eyes wide, she shook her head. "Thee does not encourage such rumors, does thee?" she demanded.

He winked at her. "I just smile mysteriously and change the subject. It drives people crazy."

He was standing so close to her that she could smell his shaving soap. If she had felt so inclined, it would have been so easy to put her hand on his neck and pull him down to kiss her. She knew he would succumb without a struggle, and the knowledge made her uneasy, because it was more power than she knew what to do with.

"Thee knows I am not ready for such rumors," she murmured and stepped back into her room.

"I think you are," he said, and leaned against the door frame. "I seem to remember some fervent kisses in front of the altar in All Saints, and don't try to tell me I was delirious and imagining things."

She blushed again and put her hands to her cheeks. "I wish thee would not speak so."

Before she could stop him, he encircled her with his good arm and kissed her. It took more strength than she possessed to resist him as she eagerly raised her face for another kiss, and then another. I wish we did not fit so well together, she thought in exquisite misery as his lips traced her jaw line and came to rest against her ear.

'Talk's cheap, Hannah Whittier," he murmured into her ear. "Maybe you had better decide just what it is you want from me. You can't protest and then kiss me like that."

He let her go, then suddenly reached forward and took her around the waist again. "I am thinking of an American expression, Hannah," he said, his voice breathless. "Either fish or cut line."

He left her then, and went back to his room, whistling. She watched him go, torn between vexation at her own body's perfidy, and amusement to see that he still walked as though he expected the deck to rise up to meet him. He was in perfect harmony with the ocean, even on land, and it gave his walk a certain swagger that she remembered when her own brother returned from a whaling voyage. I could watch thee all day, she thought, as she closed the door softly, and leaned against it, wishing that she didn't want to follow him down the hall and into his room. That he would never object multiplied her own discomfort.

She stared down at her chest, red now where she had been pressed so tight against his uniform buttons and medals. What does thee want, Hannah Whittier? She forced herself to think about it in the baldest terms possible, hoping to disgust herself. With this man's wonderful body come all sorts of entanglements, she thought, her lips pressed tightly together. He would make love to thee until thee no longer felt so restless, but it would be in an English bed, in an English house, with an English view out the window. And then when thee knew his and his mind better than thy own, he would leave thee for the sea, and thee would be alone among the enemy.

"Why am I doing this to myself?" she asked her reflection in the mirror. The unhappy face that stared back at her had no answers. She felt the acutest longing for her mother, wanting more than anything to see that face that looked so much like her own. She was desperate to crawl into her mother's lap like a child, sob out her misery, and ask for advice. She understood now why her mother had paced the house, waiting for her father to return from month-long trips to Boston and New York to buy for the store. It was not so much concern for his safety, as it was a longing for the comfort her husband brought her.

Thee wants that same comfort, she told herself, but does thee want it from this man? He has not one quality that thee felt was so important in a husband that thee would add it to a list, beyond a curious patience with thee so out of reckoning with his usual style. And he is kind, so kind, and brave beyond what is reasonable. And when I am with him, I am these things, too.

So she had gone to the reception, and glittered and simpered and smiled at Captain Spark's officer-brothers, and listened to Mr. Futtrell, his face flushed with too much champagne, tell of her exploits in the lookout and below deck during the fight with the *Bergeron*. She tried to remember to say "you" instead of "thee," because she did not wish to be thought quaint, but it was as though she stood outside her body and watched someone else sparkle and shine. All she truly wanted to do was make love to Daniel Spark, but she could only laugh and bloom, and hope her longings for him did not show.

He proposed on the ride home, sitting carefully across from her in the carriage, not touching her, but looking steadily into her eyes. "I do not suppose there is ever a good time to do this, Hannah," he began. "I've never proposed before, so I cannot claim any skill."

She reached out and placed her fingers on his lips. "Don't do it, Daniel," she whispered.

He shook his head and took hold of her hand. "I am compelled to it by your face, your body, the way you think, the feelings you have, your courage, your silliness, your impish tongue. This is not something I can resist." He smiled at her confusion. "I suppose I should go down on one knee, but with my arm in a sling, I fear I would overbalance myself. Hannah, marry me, please. I know all your good qualities and all your faults and I am content to live with both of them forever."

"Or until you go to sea?" she asked, her voice breathless.

He did not blink. "Yes, until I go to sea. We're at war, Hannah—I need scarcely remind you—and I am not deserting my country, not even for you."

He moved over to sit next to her. "But I love you powerfully, and I will always return every year or so from the blockade, or the Caribbean. I wish I could promise more now, but I cannot."

She was silent, appreciating his plain speaking, even as it twisted her insides like a knife. "I need to think about this, Daniel, because right now my answer is no."

He considered her words. "And you do not wish it to be no?"

She shook her head, unable to think of words to express herself. There is so much we Quakers leave unsaid, she thought as she looked at Daniel, and thee would never understand such silence.

"I truly would like to know how you feel about me, Hannah," he asked at last. "You kiss me as though you want me, but you have never said so. Tell me in words, my dear."

"I could lie to you," she temporized.

"I do not think you are capable of it," he replied, putting his arm about her shoulder and pulling her closer. "Oh, tonight I watched you tease and flirt with the best of them, but—"

"And I should do none of that," she interrupted. "I was not raised to be so dissimulating."

He leaned back and smiled into the dark. "I suppose it would be hard to resist at your age, especially with so many of my friends admiring you. Come on, Hannah, you're just avoiding my original request. Do you love me? Am I essential to your happiness?"

"Yes," she whispered, the word wrenched out of her, "but it's very uncomfortable, Daniel. I do not see much happiness ahead for me, no matter how much I love thee. And that is why I say no."

He was quiet a long moment. He took his arm from around her shoulder and leaned forward, isolating himself. "I suppose you are right," he agreed finally. "I have told you that I will be at sea, and you will be in a foreign land."

She nodded. "Do people in your country ever compromise?"

"Some do, I suppose. I do not. If you love me and wish to marry me, you will be an Englishwoman, living on my estate in Dorset, and I will be at sea as long as Napoleon requires it. That could be years." He spoke quietly, but with great intensity. "And better than most wives, you will know how dangerous that is."

"Thee would not give up the sea for me, but remain in England?"

"Never."

"You would not give up your country, and go to sea in my land?"

"No."

"Then I would be the one giving up everything," she said, her voice low.

"Yes, as things stand now." He reached for her hand again, and his eyes were pleading with her. "I would like to think that my love for you would be sufficient compensation for your losses."

She was silent again. He kissed her fingers. "At least consider my offer, Lady A."

"I will consider it," she agreed.

Three days later, she stood with Captain Spark's arm about her as Adam Winslow sailed for Boston on the *Elizabeth Young*. He was only going home ahead of her, she told herself, but when she finally had to say goodbye and watch him cross the gangplank to the ship, her heart failed her. She started for the gangplank, but the heavy pressure of Spark's arm on her waist kept her where she was.

"Just give me a chance, Hannah," Spark said as she strained against his arm. "You promised."

So she remained where she was, crying and waving goodbye to Adam, who blew her a kiss and held up the letter she had given to him for her parents. She had written the letter over and over, sitting in the bookroom with Daniel, trying to find the words to say that she had decided to remain a while longer in England, and that perhaps when she saw them next, she would be a married woman.

"There's no easy way to write it, my love," Spark had told her the night before when the clock struck eleven and he rose to stretch. "Just put it in an envelope."

She had chosen the best letter of the fifteen she had written and done as he said, leaving it outside Adam's door for him to find in the morning. And now he waved it back at her like a condemnation, and she wished she had made no promises to Captain Spark, as much as she loved him.

She missed Adam Winslow more than she cared to admit to herself, even as she smiled and made herself pleasant to the many female callers who brought their cards and their company to the house on Half Moon Street during the next week. They were mostly dowagers and matrons of Lady Spark's age, but some brought their own daughters in tow to meet the American heroine. They spoke of everything and nothing as they talked for hours over ratafia and tea cakes in the drawing room, admired each others' clothes, and stared Hannah up and down when they thought she wasn't looking.

Lady Spark was in her element, accepting their visits with high pleasure. "My dear, once you are safely riveted to my son, and the season begins in the spring, you will be the toast of the town!" she declared over luncheon after the morning's tumult of guests had giggled and admired their last and been shown to the door, with protestations to return soon.

"I do not see how that can be, seeing that I have not accepted his proposal," she murmured in reply, closing the door on their guests.

"My dear, you will, I am sure!" Lady Spark said. She laughed and gathered Hannah close to her. "I am not biased in any way, I assure you, but Daniel is a fine-looking man." Her face clouded suddenly. "If only his nose had not been broken in the Azores. The French have such dreadful manners." She brightened again. "But he is worth so much, too, my dear, what with all those prize ships taken in the Caribbean. Yes, you will be the jewel in next season's crown, depend upon it."

"And if I am married, why, surely Daniel will be on the blockade by spring, and I will have no right to flirt through a season in London," Hannah said.

Lady Spark would have none of it. "There is no harm in

gentlemen companions to while away the hours here until Daniel returns."

"I could never," Hannah said, shocked.

Lady Spark laughed, a tinkling sound artificial and so obviously practiced that Hannah felt a chill down her spine. "You may sing a different song when your bed is cold."

She could scarcely believe her ears. "Madam, he is your son!" she protested. "How can you speak so?"

Lady Spark only raised her high arched eyebrows higher and tittered again. "My dear, this is our society. I can see that I have my work cut out to make you fit into it. Daniel was wise to bring you here."

She left the room then, murmuring something about Madame LeTournier arriving after luncheon for another ballgown fitting. Nauseated to her soul, Hannah went to the salon, wishing herself on board the *Elizabeth Young,* arguing with Adam and pulling farther and farther from England. She drew her legs up to her chin and thought of Mama, who would no more flirt with another man than smoke a pipe or spit tobacco. And neither would I. What am I doing here? she thought to herself.

She wanted to ask Spark that question when he returned from his daily visit to the Admiralty House. He came into the salon, letters in hand from the basket by the front door, and sat down beside her. He kissed her cheek and then set the letters aside when he took a good look.

"I see mutiny on that lovely face," he said, his voice mild. He tried to take her hand, but she pulled away from him. "Dear, dear, I fear that since I left the house this morning, the wind has quite blown my sails in chains."

She said nothing, too shy to speak of what his mother had so artlessly exclaimed, because she had never been raised to talk so casually of infidelity. He moved closer and took her hand.

"Hannah, has my mother been speaking out of turn?"

She turned wide eyes upon him and the words rumbled

out of her, even as her face reddened. "Daniel, she is already encouraging me to take a lover when we are married and thee is at sea!"

"My God," he exclaimed softly. "I would prefer that you did not, of course."

"How can thee joke about such things!" she shouted, leaping from the davenport and crossing to the window, where she hugged herself and stared at the driving rain. "And it does nothing but pour in London! I am weary of small talk and ratafia makes me gag!"

He was at her side in a moment, pulling her into his amts, letting her sob out her misery against the cold comfort of his medals and buttons. She pulled away and he removed his coat, tossing it onto the floor, then drew her close again to rest against the softness of his linen shirt.

Her arms went around him finally. "I think I like thee better this way," she said and then stood back in his arms to look at his face so close to her own. "Suddenly there are too many medals and buttons, and ideas and modes of doing things. It's all getting in the way of what I feel."

He tugged her close to him again, his hand on her hair and then his forefinger running idly inside her ear. "My mother is from a generation that raised infidelity to a fine art."

She wanted him to continue his careless examination of her ear and then her face, but he was too distracting. She freed herself from his embrace. "It is more than that, Daniel," she said, wishing that she did not feel so breathless when he touched her. "The younger ladies are so ... so vapid! I do not suppose one of them has ever cooked a meal, or washed a dog."

He laughed out loud, opening his arms for her again. "I am sure you are right, Hannah! Oh, come here! That's better. And they've never dressed grisly wounds, or even made coffee for a grumpy sea captain."

She let him kiss her then, and even raised her arms to encircle his neck as he picked her up off her feet. "I would wish at times that you were taller," he murmured and then kissed her again. "Perhaps you will grow yet," he said, his voice unsteady as he set her down.

She was at the window again, staring out at the everlasting drizzle. He came up behind her and circled her in his arms. She leaned against him, secure in his arms, but still gnawed by a vague unease.

"See here, sir," she began and stepped away.

He kissed the back of her neck as she retreated. "I am coming to dread those pronouncements that begin, 'See here, sir,' " he murmured.

She turned around and then pushed him off at arm's length. "I must tell thee, Daniel, that when I am in your arms, everything is fine."

"Better and better. I like that, too," he said and smiled.

She took a deep breath and plunged ahead. "I also do not doubt that if you wanted my body this minute, I would give my virginity to you right here in your mother's salon and not care a snap what anyone thought."

"I know that," he replied softly, but made no move to touch her. "It's fairly obvious to me."

"I thank thee, then, for being more in control than I am," she continued relentlessly, pressing her hands to her blushing face. "There have been so many times I would gladly have let you make love to me."

"I know that, too. What's the matter, my heart? Won't my love, when it finally comes, be enough?"

"Suppose your mother is right," she began, pausing to choose her words carefully.

"She is not. I know that much about you," Spark said.

"Daniel, thee will be a long time on the blockade!" she burst out passionately. "And I suspect that I will greatly enjoy lovemaking." She paused, mortified at her words.

He only smiled. "I am certain you will. I also suspect that you will save it for me alone."

"You are so sure?" she murmured.

"I am so sure," he replied.

She could only sigh. "I wish I knew what to do," she said finally.

"I wish you would say yes when I propose again." he commented as he walked with her back to the window and draped his arm over her shoulder in a friendly gesture that had nothing of the lover in it. "It would only be a morning's work to have you declared a ward in chancery—I have been to my solicitors, my dearest Hannah, and so they assure me. We could be married in a few weeks after the banns." He peered around to look at her face. "Hannah, thee is a trial to me."

'Then why does thee persist?" she demanded.

"I cannot imagine life without your 'thee's' and 'thy's', and your quaint, funny ways, and the indisputable suspicion that you will love me within an inch of my sanity," he said. He laughed as she blushed again. "And the way you blush! Are you always going to do that, even when we have children, and know each other better than any couple that ever lived? I suspect you will."

She couldn't help but smile. He patted her back and took her hand, walking her to the door. "Go pack your bags, Hannah Whittier, I think it is time you saw my estate in Dorset and we kissed London goodbye. It's not doing you any good."

"But Madame LeTournier is coming by this afternoon for another fitting," she said, even as her eyes lighted up at the prospect of leaving London.

"And she can be easily dismissed by you."

"I am afraid of her!" Hannah exclaimed, her eyes wide. "She is so ... so ... French!"

Daniel laughed, grabbed her about the waist, and whirled her around in a froth of petticoats and protestations. "You, who have climbed riggings, teetered on window ledges, and told the great Wellington himself to cut his toenails? Hannah, get rid of her and pack your bags. I mean to have a yes out of you before I am too much older."

Chapter Fifteen

Getting rid of Madame LeTournier was a daunting experience, but Hannah was equal to it, even as Captain Spark had suggested. It involved a lie, informing the redoubtable modiste that the captain's favorite aunt had taken sick in Devon and required their presence at the family estate immediately. Hannah delivered it with such aplomb, and received such instant, solicitous response that she owned to considerable chagrin when Madame LeTournier curtseyed herself out of the room, closing the door quietly behind her. "See here, Hannah," she scolded herself. "Thee is becoming altogether too adept at lies. What will thee do next?"

The stumbling block to immediate removal from London proved to be Lady Spark, who would not be budged until she had blackmailed an additional two hats and two more dresses for herself from Captain Spark, in exchange for her necessary services as chaperon.

"And we will leave in the morning, son," Lady Spark ordered. "I have every intention of attending a loo party tonight ...."

"... and losing your shift and garters," he finished, snapping out the newspaper and retreating behind it. "Mama, you are a dreadful gambler. And who pays your bills when you find yourself at point non plus? It certainly isn't your older son, the esteemed head of our family. I confess to a definite uneasiness over your gaming habits, particularly since they always seem to involve me in your rescue."

Hannah made herself small on the sofa beside Daniel, wondering what her own mother would make of this conversation. She would gather me up, grab her bonnet, and run, she thought as she watched the small muscle work in Daniel's cheek as he forced himself to be polite to his mother.

"All the same, son, if you wish my presence in Dorset, and therefore Hannah's, you will come up to snuff on this one."

"Very well, Mama," Spark growled behind his newspaper. "I haul down my colors."

"Done, then!" she exclaimed. "We will leave in the morning, and not too early. I do not keep ship's hours." Her mouth turned down for a brief moment, and Hannah was struck by the resemblance between mother and son. "I do not know why you feel so strongly about that little estate, anyway, Daniel. It is nothing to our manor in Kent."

Daniel folded the paper in his lap. "It has the virtue of being entirely unencumbered with debts, madam. It is mine alone, and my dear wastrel brother cannot lay a finger on it." He nudged Hannah. "It is also well timbered, shipshape and draft-free, with a wonderful view of the ocean. I could even mention my bailiff, who would never dream of cheating me, and his wife, who makes almond cake the way I like it."

Any comments Lady Spark may have wished to express on the view or the hired help remained to herself as the butler showed in Mr. Futtrell, who nodded to the dowager, winked at Hannah, and drew himself up before the captain.

"You wished to see me, sir?" he asked.

"Oh relax, Futtrell." Daniel said, and indicated a chair opposite the sofa. "It is merely a small matter. I wish you to keep in daily contact with the Admiralty House while we are in Dorset. I want to know the moment they decide on another ship for me."

"Consider it done, sir," he said, grinning at his captain. He looked at the floor then, divided between embarrassment and pride. "And thank you for naming me your number one."

Hannah clapped her hands. "Mr. Futtrell! Such good news!"

He grinned again, looking ten years younger, and then stared down at the floor one more time. 'Trouble is, Hannah, the only other person I would want to share the news with is Mr. Lansing."

Daniel nodded to his first lieutenant. "I know how that feels, Mr. Futtrell."

"Sir, does it ever hurt less?" the lieutenant asked quietly.

"Well, I will put it to you this way," Daniel replied after a moment's reflection. "When it doesn't hurt at all, then it is time to leave the sea for good."

"I do not know why navy men have to be so morbid," Lady Spark said as she left the room.

It is something I understand perfectly, Hannah thought as she reached over to touch Futtrell's arm. He looked up at her and nodded.

"Surely thee can think of something more pleasant," she urged. "Is thee not on leave now? Does thee have a young lady?"

Futtrell leaned back in surprise, his eyes wide. "No, ma'am! I couldn't be so heartless as to actually expect a female to dangle after a seagoing man!" He glanced at Captain Spark's glowering countenance and reddened. "Beg pardon, sir, but I would not."

"First my mother, and now you," Spark said. "Futtrell, perhaps you have some urgent business elsewhere."

The lieutenant grinned. "Aye, sir!" He stood up and winked at Hannah again. "This might amuse you, Miss Whittier. I hear there is a lively betting pool at White's as to whether the little Quaker will actually succumb to a certain sea captain's proposal. Isn't that famous?"

Hannah's jaw dropped. Captain Spark groaned and slapped his forehead with the newspaper. "God damn your eyes. Mr. Futtrell," he roared, as though he stood on his quarterdeck. "Another remark like that and I'll break you right down to powder monkey!"

Futtrell was out the door before Spark got to his feet. The captain stood at the door a moment, as though gathering his forces, then turned back to Hannah, who had retreated to the window again, to stare out at the everlasting rain.

"My dear, I had heard something about that," the captain mumbled. "I had hoped to spare you the knowledge."

Hannah continued to stare out the window, seeing nothing of the rain that sheeted against the glass and spilled into the gutters. People are gambling with my name, she thought, and closed her eyes in shame.

Spark cleared his throat. "Some would think it amusing," he ventured, but there was no assurance in his voice.

"I think it infamous," she said, leaning her forehead against the cool pane of glass. "Surely thee does not approve."

He crossed the room quickly and pulled her into his arms, resting his chin on her head as he held her as close as he could. "No, I do not," he whispered into her hair. "My love, there is only one place on land where I do not feel out of place, and believe me, it is not in this damned city, with creatures who have nothing better to do than gamble and toy with a lady's good name."

She stood in his arms, her ear pressed against his heart, and listened to its steady beat until she felt calm enough to look him in the face. "Please tell me that if I marry thee, I will not have to come back here ever again." she pleaded.

He looked down at her and grinned. "I will only insist upon it if I am ever named a Lord of the Admiralty." He shuddered elaborately until she smiled. "As I do not see the eventuality of that, you may safely shake the dust of London off your shoes. Lady Amber."

While they did not leave London early enough to suit Hannah or Captain Spark, it was still too early for Lady Spark, who suffered the ill effects of last night's overindulgence at the gaming tables. "I think you are perfectly heartless!" she railed at her son as he handed her into the family carriage and closed the door firmly on her protests. He blew a kiss to Hannah through the glass and mounted his horse as the carriage sprang forward and Lady Spark moaned.

Luckily she was snoring by the time they reached London's suburbs, and Hannah had ample time for reflection. Such an odd family, she thought as she regarded the older woman, and recalled, with a pang, her own family, Mama so gentle and dignified, and Papa firm and deliberate. I wonder if they ever had any doubts about marriage to each other, she thought as she observed Captain Spark riding beside the carriage. Did they ever wonder if they were doing the right thing? Did the idea of sharing a bed with Papa ever frighten Mama? She longed more than ever for the safety of her mother's arms, and for some word of advice. I wonder if I would have the good sense to take her counsel, Hannah thought as the miles turned London into just a memory. I never did before; would I now? Have I learned anything?

These were not questions she could ask Daniel's mother, who woke up finally, straightened her hat, and complained about the damp, her head, the shabbiness of the carriage ("For all that Daniel is not head of this house, I do not know why he cannot buy another carriage and spare his poor brother, who is always under the hatches.") They stopped for luncheon not a moment too soon for Hannah.

After their meal, Captain Spark must have noticed her reluctance to continue the journey in the coach with his mother. "My dear, you could use some roses in your cheeks," he said as he pulled her up into the saddle in front of him. "Mama, I'll keep Hannah a while."

With a look of extreme ill usage on her face, Lady Spark

allowed the postilion to help her into the carriage. "If she takes ill with a putrid sore throat and dies a wasting death, then *you* must explain that to the American ambassador!"

"Mama, Hannah is healthier than a horse," Spark said, doing his best to keep the amusement from his voice. "See you at the estate!" He dug his heels into his horse and they shot ahead.

As the horse established its rhythm, Hannah sighed and settled back against the captain. "Healthier than a horse, am I?" she murmured.

"So I have observed," he replied, tightening his arms around her. "Think how handy that will be in years to come." He was silent a moment, rubbing his free hand over her arm. "I am sorry to have to subject you to my mother, but, damn, we do need a chaperon."

She sighed and he kissed her neck. "I think we Sparks do not measure up well against the Whittiers of Nantucket," he ventured.

"No, you do not," she said simply, "and I am sorry, truly I am. I fear that you do not love your relatives."

"Would you love them, in my place?" he questioned in turn. "And you have not even met my brother yet. I do not know a more worthless slug on the face of the earth than Edmund Spark, the current earl. Between Mama's recriminations and Edmund's petitions for relief from his debtors, do you have any doubts why I prefer the sea?"

She turned around to look into his arresting eyes, marveling again how fascinating they were up close. "Would your reluctance for the land keep you from me?" she asked.

He kissed her in answer, dropping the reins as the little kiss turned into a searching rediscovery of her mouth, neck, and eyes that left them both restless and the horse chewing grass by the side of the road.

"I am not the horseman for lovemaking in the saddle," the captain said as he gathered the reins again and coaxed the horse back onto the road. "I merely had to assure you that was a silly question."

"Was it?" she murmured, half to herself, as the agony of unsettled love was replaced by a distinct chill that went to her heart before she could wish it away. *I wonder what will happen when Mr. Futtrell brings you news of another ship.*

They arrived at Spark's estate too late for a good look at it in the fading autumn light. "It's always better by morning light, my love," he whispered in her ear as he reined to a stop in front of the well-lighted house. "*Early* morning light, need I add?"

"Oh, please, not before eight bells," she said, trying to keep her eyes open.

He laughed, handed her down, and dismounted with a groan. "I know *this* man's natural state is a quarterdeck, and not the back of a quadruped," he said, then picked her up and started toward the steps. "Here, Hannah, you knock on the door. My hands are full," he said.

"Not until you put me down," she said, then touched his cheek, closing her eyes when he kissed her palm and her wrist, where the pulse beat faster. "If I marry you, you can carry me over the threshold, but not now."

"Spoilsport," he said, and lowered her to her feet. He knocked and the door was opened by a handsome woman in cap and apron who held out her hands to them both.

"Captain," she said, taking his hand and Hannah's. "You've been too long away. This is Hannah Whittier?" she asked, her eyes on Hannah, her smile of welcome genuine.

"The very same. Hannah, may I introduce my housekeeper, Mrs. Paige? She raised me and I purloined her from the family estate, when I bought this place. Edmund is still smarting from that piece of impertinence, by the way, as the bailiff came with her."

In a few minutes they were in the kitchen, eating almond cake with icing so gooey that Hannah could only roll her eyes and follow one bite with another one.

"My love, I think you can see why only a few of these bring me right back up to my precruise tonnage," Spark said as he scooped up more icing with his finger, dodged Mrs. Paige's slap, and stuck his finger in his mouth. He leaned back finally and patted his flat stomach. "*Now* I am home! Mrs. Paige, how do you do?"

"Excellently well, sir," said the housekeeper, who sat next to Hannah with her hands folded in her lap. "Your mother is already in bed with a hot water bottle. She was sure you had been delayed by pirates or smugglers, so I gave her a sleeping draught."

"Bless you, Mrs. Paige," Daniel said fervently. He glanced at Hannah, who was hard put to keep her eyes open. "Lady Amber here doesn't need a sleeping draught. Did you put her in the corner room?"

"As you wished, Captain," said Mrs. Paige as she rose to her feet and picked up a candle by the kitchen door. "I believe Mr. Paige has already put her trunk in there. Come, little one, let me show you upstairs."

"I can do that," said the captain, his eyes lively.

"No, sir! You can eat another piece of cake," said Mrs. Paige firmly as she took hold of Hannah's arm and helped her up. "Plenty of time for that later. Right my dear?" Hannah nodded and smiled at Spark. "Now, remember, not too early."

She was asleep almost as soon as Mrs. Paige helped her into her nightgown and pulled back the bedcovers. She sank into the feather bed with a sigh, burped from the effects of almond cake at ten o'clock, murmured "Excuse me," and closed her eyes. She thought she recalled someone coming into her room later to stand by the bed, and then brush her cheek with his own, but she couldn't be sure. It may have been a dream. Heaven knew she was dreaming about Captain Spark more than she should, anyway. The impression that he needed a shave led her to believe it was not a nighttime fantasy, but she was too drugged with sleep to explore the matter beyond patting his face, murmuring something nonsensical that made him chuckle, and surrendering unconditionally to the mattress.

She woke to a world of sunlight and lay with her eyes closed, waiting for the sound of birds. But it was September now, and they had flown to South America, or at least New Orleans. But no, this was England, not Nantucket. The songbirds of an English summer would be in Spain, or over the Pillars of Hercules to North Africa. She opened her eyes then, wondering why she felt like she was home.

Without raising her head from the pillow, she stretched luxuriously and looked around the room, her eyes opening wider with delight. The curtains were simplest muslin and fluttered slightly in the breeze that came through the barely open window. The walls were pale blue, with no ornamentation beyond a sampler with a Bible verse. Intrigued, she raised up on her elbow to admire the severe bureau, and smiled to herself. There was no mirror on the bureau, and the room smelled suspiciously of new paint.

"Daniel, what has thee been up to?" she murmured out loud, and threw back the bedcovers. Her bare feet trod plain boards to the window and she curled up in the window seat for her first view of the ocean. Tears sprung to her eyes. The view was a powerful reminder of Nantucket, with the sea, such a deep blue that her heart flopped, peeping like an afterthought through the trees in the distance. She glanced around the sparse room again, and her heart was full to bursting. I could almost be home, she thought. Oh, I do love you, Daniel Spark.

She closed the window and climbed back in bed, amazed that it was possible to feel so good with her stomach rumbling for breakfast and her eyes still foggy from sleep. She folded her hands gently across her stomach and stared at the ceiling. "Hannah Whittier, thee is loved, truly thee is," she whispered.

Someone knocked at the door. She knew it was too firm a knock for Mrs. Paige, and she gloried in that knowledge. "Oh, please come in. Captain Spark," she said, sitting up and tucking the bedclothes demurely around her, even as she wondered if her hair was as unruly as she suspected.

He carried a tray with a teapot and two cups, and his eyes seemed even lighter against that pale blue background. He stood in the doorway, just looking at her until she put her hands to her hair.

"I know I am a fright, but thee needn't stare so," she said at last when he closed the door with his foot, his eyes still on her.

"Idiot," he said, his voice unsteady as he put the tray on the table by the bed, sat down beside her, and took her in his arms without another word. In a moment he was lying next to her, his hands in her hair, smoothing it back even as he kissed her over and over, each kiss more insistent than the one before.

She could scarcely form thoughts in her mind as she kissed him back, beyond wanting to pull back the covers and invite him under them with her. She heard his shoes hit the floor and knew he had the same idea, but the sudden sound on the bare boards brought her around. She pushed herself away from him, even as her whole body cried out for him to come closer.

"Please stop," she said.

"I don't want to."

"Stop anyway." she insisted.

"Damn," he said, and his voice was wistful as he caressed that curse into a loving epithet "Time is so short, Hannah, I hate to waste it."

He didn't move from her side, but flopped onto his stomach and turned his head to watch her. "Well, do you like your room?"

She nodded, her eyes delighted as she touched his back lightly at first, and then with a firmer gesture. He closed his eyes as she rubbed his back. 'Thank thee for this room. I felt I was home," she said finally when she stopped.

"That was my intention. I am an unscrupulous lover, Lady Amber, and don't you forget it. I'll do anything to keep you here."

"You even took out the mirror," she marveled. "How did you know?"

"Oh, it was something you said during those damnable midnight watches when you were telling me everything you knew, to keep me awake. I couldn't find a rag rug for the floor, however."

"How will I ever know what I look like?" she teased as he sat up and put on his shoes again.

He turned to her suddenly, his face more serious than she had ever seen him. "You can see yourself in my eyes, beloved," he said, his voice soft. "I will be your mirror."

"Then I will marry thee," she said.

"Done, madam!" he shouted and grabbed her up from the bed, whirling her around. "You won't go back on that?"

"I couldn't," she said and stood on tiptoe for another kiss.

He hugged her so tightly that her ribs hurt. "No, I do not suppose you could," he said. "Hannah. I love you, but God knows, this is not going to be an easy thing." He took her by the hands and held her away from him, gazing at her with a light in his eyes that set her whole body tingling.

He led her to the windowseat, sat down, and patted the space beside him. "I suppose we always come back to your list, Miss Whittier."

She smiled and touched his lips with her finger. "I do consider thy welfare above my own, or I never would have said yes."

"Then I suppose there is nothing to do but write my solicitor and plot the next course, Lady Amber, which will involve some legal thrust and parry," he said, leaning back against the window frame, never taking his eyes from her face.

She blushed. "Do not stare so, my love!" she protested.

"I cannot help myself," be confessed. "I never thought that in the middle of war and national emergency, I would find my wife." He broke his gaze finally and took her left hand in his, turning it over. "I may even have a diamond or an emerald suitable for an engagement ring."

She drew her hand away. "No, none of that," she said, her eyes wide with dismay. "We Friends do not hold with such fashion, Daniel. Nothing more than a plain gold band, if that, once we are wed."

"It's not enough for you," he protested.

"It is more than enough," she insisted, her voice firm, "just as this plain room suits me."

He smiled finally, and touched her under the chin. "I never anticipated that a wife would be so economical!" He got to his feet and stretched. "Well, at least allow me one indulgence."

"What?" she asked, her eyes merry.

"Let me have an engagement party within the week to introduce you to your neighbors."

"Well ...."

"You need to know them, considering that you will be falling back on their society when I am gone." He watched her face. "What, my love?" he asked, his voice gentle.

"Nothing," she murmured, wondering at the chill that settled around her heart with his words so casually spoken, even as the window glass warmed her back and promised a sunny day. "I suppose I am just hungry."

He nodded. "Mrs. Paige has breakfast waiting for you. Get dressed and I will join you. Then it's off to the bookroom to compose a letter to my solicitor." He paused in the open door. "Mama will come into her own here, my love. No one plans a party better. Lively now."

If Lady Spark was disappointed with her son's news of his engagement and impending marriage, the carrot of a party dangled before her eyes took away any misgivings. "It will take two heads to have everything ready by Thursday." She shook a warning finger at her son, who was finishing his coffee by the window and grinning at her. "That means Hannah is my property until this party is over! Now, go on to the bookroom and write your letters."

Hannah was composing invitations in the bookroom as soon as luncheon was over and Daniel returned from the village. He scooped her out of the chair pulled up to the desk, sat down, and pulled her onto his lap as she shrieked and made a grab to hold the inkwell as it teetered over a completed invitation.

"Thee is a sore distraction," she exclaimed as he moved the inkwell out of her reach and took the quill from her hand.

"Then pay some attention to me for a few minutes, Hannah!" he insisted, nuzzling her neck at that junction by her jaw where his lips seemed to fit so naturally. "Much better," he said after a moment. He rested his chin on her shoulder. "I mailed that letter and also spoke to my solicitor here. He said that once we have that writ of chancery, we can even be married by special license, and waive the banns."

She nodded, her eyes closed, and rested against him, wondering how it was that someone as hard and unyielding as Captain Spark on his quarterdeck could be so soft to lean upon.

"Do you suppose we can find a Quaker preacher to marry us?" he asked.

She shook her head. "Thee does not perfectly understand, Daniel. When I said I would marry thee, that also means that I am severing ties with my church. They will read me out of Meeting at home when my parents learn of this."

Her quiet words hung in the silent room. Daniel got up and set her back in the chair, sitting on the edge of the desk so he could look at her, his face serious. "I had no idea, my love. You're giving up everything you hold dear for me, aren't you?"

She nodded, unable to speak for a moment. She composed herself, but could not look at him. "Now, if thee was to become a Friend someday, then we could be welcomed into Meeting again."

He shook his head. "I do not think the Friends would have much patience with a man who deals in death." He took her hand and kissed it. "I hope I am worth all this."

"So do I," she said and picked up the quill again.

The invitations were mailed the following morning. Spark braved his mother's threats to take Hannah with him in the gig to the village to post the letters.

"I promise to return her promptly," he said as he dumped the invitations in Hannah's lap and gathered up the reins.

"You had better," Lady Spark insisted. "If we are to sit thirty at dinner tomorrow night, I need Hannah more than you do!"

"Thirty? Do I have that many friends in Dorset?" he teased. "Very well, Mama. If I had known what a lot of trouble this was going to be, we would have eloped to Scotland and married over the anvil!"

Lady Spark delivered such a stem look at her son that he shuddered elaborately when she was out of sight. "You'll need to take a look in my bedroom and tell me what you want changed," he said as they rode along. "I have an even better view of the sea, and the bed is wider."

She blushed. "Does this mean I cannot keep my little room?"

"I was thinking it would make an excellent nursery." Eyes on the narrow lane, he lifted her hand to his lips. "I do not plan to come home from sea and find you down the hall from my bed. God knows, as it is, I'll be away from you too much to suit me without having to knock on your door when the mood strikes. There would be a regular trough in the wood to your door."

Thee needn't be away from me at all, she thought as she settled against his shoulder. She looked at him to speak, but he shook his head. "I know what you're going to say," he said. "It doesn't bear thinking on, because I will not leave the sea."

The day passed quickly enough, following Lady Spark's orders as she polished silver with Mrs. Paige, arranged autumn bouquets in vases, and accepted the replies that poured back from the invitations. Who are these people, she thought as she fingered the notes with their unfamiliar names. Will they like me? Will I be too quaint for them? If, as Daniel suspects, our countries will soon be at war, will they turn their backs on me?

She gazed at the notes, a frown on her face, until Lady Spark dragged her away to another task.

It wasn't until the house was quiet and the dowager was in bed with a headache that she found solace in Daniel's arms. How is it, she thought as he held her close, that thee can kiss away my fears and leave me so shaky with love? She clung to him, knowing that the smallest gesture from him would send her over the top and into his bed without a single regard for everything she had been taught since childhood.

She spent a restless night more agitated than the one before and woke long before dawn, bleary-eyed and discontent. She sighed and tried to return to sleep, burrowing deep into the mattress and knowing that it was hopeless. She would only toss and turn, filled with desire and worry, until Daniel came into her room with tea and confidence enough for them both. She firmly resolved to be sitting in the window seat when he came in. The pleasure in his eyes on seeing her in the morning had been replaced by something much more intense now. There was a hunger in his gaze that made her gulp and hope the chancery writ would not be long in coming.

She heard a carriage on the gravel drive and got up, hurrying to the window to look out. It was the Spark carriage, and not the gig used for everyday trips into the village. As she watched out of curiosity, Mr. Paige carried out the new sea chest Daniel had bought the day before, and on which she had stenciled SPARK in large letters only last night.

"No," she said out loud. Hardly daring to breathe, she threw on her clothes, ran a comb through her curly hair tousled from a night's agitation, then hurried down the stairs without her shoes or stockings. "No," she said again, louder this time, as she ran to the open door.

Daniel, dressed in his uniform, stood by the carriage, speaking to Mr. Futtrell. He looked at her with real delight and grasped her by the shoulders, nearly lifting her off the ground.

"My love, this is too famous! Mr. Futtrell brought such news last night after you went to bed."

Futtrell, fully uniformed, tipped his tall hat to her. "We have a ship, Miss Whittier! A ship!"

She could think of nothing to say, but it did not matter. Spark was not listening or even looking at her. He spoke over her shoulder to Mrs. Paige. "When my other uniforms come from their alterations in the village, have them posted to the H.M.S. *Clarion* in Portsmouth harbor." He picked Hannah up off the ground. "My darling, it is a commerce raider of the new Falmouth class!"

"There is a party tonight," she reminded him, her voice subdued.

He set her down and grinned at her. "My orders say to report at once to oversee refitting, Hannah." He turned away, his voice impatient with command. "Mr. Futtrell, do you have any idea how she handles under all sail?"

"Surely tomorrow would be soon enough," she said, her back straight, her hands twisted tightly in front of her. He was not listening, and she repeated herself.

"I couldn't possibly wait that long, my dear," he said and nodded to the coachman, who climbed into the box.

She stood in silence for a long moment, taking in the coach ready to travel, and the sun only just now coming over the horizon. "Daniel, you were going to leave without saying goodbye, weren't you?"

"I left a note in the front hallway," he replied as he opened the carriage door. "I'll be back in a couple of weeks, when things are in order. We'll have a few days before we sail for the blockade to get married."

"You're leaving me to face a houseful of guests tonight that I do not even know?"

"You'll do fine," he said carelessly. "Come, Mr. Futtrell. There's not a moment to lose."

She began to cry, the tears sliding down her cheeks. "I did not think thee was so heartless," she gasped through her tears.

He took her arm then and pulled her close until they were chest to chest. "It's war, my dear." He kissed her hair. "Forgive me if I sound sentimental, but England sorely needs what I do best. The sooner I am back on the blockade, the sooner some other poor captain can put into port before he goes crazy with the strain." He ruffled her hair. "But I'm only going now to get the revictualing started. I'll be back before you know it." He kissed her one more time and climbed into the carriage, closing the door behind him. The coachman snapped his whip and they were off down the lane.

She was still standing barefoot on the gravel drive when the sun rose and Mrs. Paige, her eyes filled with tears of her own, came out to help her inside.

Chapter Sixteen

"Men are beasts, and my son is no exception," was one of Lady Sharp's few repeatable comments when Hannah threw herself into her before the sun was much higher and told her the bad news, choking back her tears. "Daniel only comes to go away. I would not wish him on a dog," she said as she accepted a cup of tea from Mrs. Paige and indicated that the housekeeper should join them in a council of war.

"Well, Hannah, do we cancel?" she asked, her voice crisp with decision, when the tea was drunk down to the leaves.

Hannah took her gaze from her own bare toes to regard Lady Spark with something approaching affection. There was nothing of defeat in the dowager's voice. If anything, her chin was raised higher than usual, and her lips pursed in a firmer line. It began to dawn on her that this was a woman for a crisis.

When Hannah said nothing, Lady Spark threw back the covers and hunted about for her slippers. "My dear girl, if you wish to break off your engagement to this supremely selfish man, I would not be surprised, but after all, we have prepared a wondrous amount of food, and I really can't think any other man will ever treat you better, the male sex being what it is.

Savages. I wonder why we submit so willingly to them. Well. Hannah? Are you a jellyfish or a woman?"

It was curious commentary, and Hannah smiled in spite of her misery.

"Come, come, dear girl, do you love that worthless Jack Tar or not?" Lady Spark demanded, sounding surprisingly like her absent son.

"Oh, I love him," she said, and believed it with all her heart.

Lady Spark clapped her hands and nodded in triumph to Mrs. Paige. "Excellent! To celebrate that absurdity, I say we place an additional order for more of the most expensive smuggler's champagne and make Daniel pay through the nose for his perfidy."

Hannah laughed. "He can pay dearly for more cut flowers, too! I think I actually saw a few bare spaces in the dining room."

Lady Spark embraced her for the first time. "Now you are thinking like a woman! Hannah Whittier, I believe you will be a credit to the Spark family name. Living extravagantly at the expense of men is always the best revenge! It really should be the motto on our family crest."

Hannah let herself be swept along that day by Lady Spark's curious energy. She hurried from task to task at the dowager's command, and realized late in the afternoon as she dragged herself upstairs for a quick soak in the tin tub that Lady Spark had been making sure that she had not a spare second to repine. She twisted her hair high on her head and sank into the lemon-scented tub gratefully. I will be too tired when this evening is over to do anything but drop down dead into dreamless slumber, she thought as she scrubbed herself vigorously. "Thank you, my lady," she said out loud, secure in her heart that she would have no difficulty loving her future mother-in-law, even if her own son did not.

While it was true that butterflies collided against each other in her stomach as she greeted the dinner guests, they soon settled down. No one was even slightly surprised at Daniel

Spark's absence. "We know seafarers, Miss Whittier," the vicar explained to her as he grasped her hand in welcome. "I suppose at one time or other, half the females in my parish have been where you are." He laughed and released her. "It only has come to you sooner than most! Let us blame Napoleon, but not let the beast of Corsica spoil our evening."

As she greeted the guests, she debated whether to use her Quaker "thee," and decided she would. If we are to be neighbors, they must come to know me as I am, she thought. And if I am quaint, well, what of it? Daniel does not mind, and did he not promise me that he would be my mirror? Dressed in pale gray, her unruly curls subdued with a lace cap, she moved gracefully among her guests, wishing that her own mother could see her. And whenever conversation flagged, Lady Spark slipped adroitly into the gaps and smoothed them over until everyone was full of champagne and good feeling.

With genuine regret, Hannah allowed her company to depart after tea in the parlor. She shook their hands again, promising to pay return visits, and assuring them of invitations to the wedding. When the last guest departed, she sank into a chair in the parlor and looked at Lady Spark, who sat beside her.

"I would say that went off remarkably well, considering that neither of us knew a single guest," Lady Spark commented as she kicked off her shoes. She glanced sideways at Hannah and they both dissolved into giggles.

"Oh, dear," Hannah said finally as she wiped her eyes. "Did I drink too much champagne?"

"I fervently hope so!" Lady Spark said, the militant light back in her eyes. "I don't know about you, but I could feel the pounds sterling just rolling down my throat, and it felt so good." She started to laugh again, and Hannah joined in. After another moment of glee, she patted Hannah's leg. "Well, my dear, do we stay here and wait for that sailor to return, or do we go back to London and order a half dozen new dresses?"

Hannah smiled at Lady Spark with genuine affection. "I

think I will remain here with Mrs. Paige another week or two. If he does not return by then, I will see thee in London."

"I approve, Hannah," the dowager replied. "At any rate, I will return to this godforsaken wilderness for your wedding."

"Thank thee!" Hannah rose and stretched her arms high over her head. "And now, please excuse me. Since thee has driven me like a slavemaster all day, I am tired down to my toes." She leaned forward impulsively and kissed Lady Spark.

Lady Spark returned her kiss, and touched her cheek. "I cannot credit it, but my son seems to have done something very smart in the way of wife-hunting."

"He fished me off a grate in the middle of the Atlantic," Hannah said.

"My dear, that is merely philanthropy, and not love," Lady Spark teased, and smiled at Hannah. "Now, go to bed before you drop!"

She woke in the morning with renewed optimism, and a willingness to admit that as long as England was at war with France, she would rate a pale second in Captain Sir Daniel Spark's life. It was a fact she could live with. I am nearly eighteen, she thought, and this war will not last forever. And when it is over, I will be first in his heart. I can wait in line behind Napoleon until then. Others are doing it.

Soon Daniel would return from Portsmouth, full of his new ship, distracted by plans to refit and supply, swearing at quizmasters, and leaping up from the dinner table, or whenever the wind changed direction. She had seen her brother Matthew prepare for whaling voyages, and she knew the signs. He would stew about this and that, eat his food with dogged determination, his mind miles away. When we are married, I will offer him what comfort I can, and I will swallow my fears and wave him off from our front door, hoping to God that he will return.

Marriage to a seafaring man was not a career for the faint of heart, she told herself, but I can manage. And when he is in my bed, I will make him forget the life that has chosen him, even if it is only for a few hours. She sighed and sat up, restless with thoughts of the man she would call husband soon, and who would father her children. "Oh, hurry up and get back here," she said into her pillow before returning to sleep. "I am ready for mischief."

Lady Spark endured another week in Dorset, then threw up her hands over breakfast one morning and said that she could not suffer another hour of country silence. "I would almost give a year off my life for news of a really juicy scandal," she declared as she shook her head over another of Mrs. Paige's muffins. "And too many more of those will mean boiled potatoes and vinegar water until I can fit into my clothes again!"

"I shall stay another week," Hannah said as she accepted another muffin. "Mrs. Paige and I are doing an inventory on household contents."

Lady Spark made a face. "You are so domestic already! Next you will tell me that the chickens are off their laying."

Hannah chuckled as she buttered the muffin. "Well, they are, my dear. I wish I could remember Mama's receipt for difficult poultry. Or did she just chop off their heads and fricassee them?"

She waved Lady Spark off that afternoon in a post chaise, with promises to write as soon as Daniel returned with a writ of chancery and a special license. "My dear, I will pick out the silk for your wedding dress. I will have Madame LeTournier copy the pattern of your blue walking dress. That is so simple it will be done in a day. Just name the day," was Lady Spark's final command as Hannah was closing the door. With merry eyes she blew her a kiss.

The household inventory was complete in two days, as well as a list of new wall coverings and paint. "We've been needing a change, Miss Whittier," Mrs. Paige said as she organized the lists in the bookroom that night and extinguished the lamp.

"Tomorrow, Mr. Paige and I will go into the village and see about the paint."

"Thee doesn't think it will be too severe?" she asked. "It is what I am used to."

Mrs. Paige flashed one of her rare smiles. "I do not see how any home with you in it could ever be too severe."

The house was hers the next afternoon when the Paiges left with their lists, so she let herself into Daniel's room for a look around. It was shabby and comfortable, smelling vaguely of tar. She traced the unmistakable odor to a tarry bag still filled with shot that he had dumped into a corner after one voyage or another and forgotten. She picked it up between thumb and forefinger and carried it into the hall, stopping to sniff it once and remember those desperate days and nights after the fight with the *Bergeron.*

It seems so long ago, she thought as she returned to survey the room where she would be waking up for all the mornings of her life to come. There was a telescope on a stand, conveniently positioned by an armchair next to the window. She sat down, opened the window, and trained the glass out. "Sail ho," she whispered, thinking again of those wonderful watches in the lookout of the *Dissuade,* sitting trousered and barefooted, the summer wind ruffling her head. There was nothing on the ocean now, and far in the distance, only a carriage. She closed the window again, shivering in the late September breeze. "I hope thee has another boat cloak, my dear," she said, rubbing the goose-bumps on her arms. White walls would be the thing in here, she thought, and perhaps muslin curtains with just a touch of blue, light as Daniel's eyes. He would probably object if she recovered the chair by the window; it could wait for a time when he was about to return from a voyage and would be more interested in bed than his chair. And I can sit there and watch for him.

The mattress was firm, with no give to it. We may have to discuss this mattress, she thought as she tried to bounce on the bed. She remembered Mama's generous mattress and how good it felt to crawl in bed with her and Papa when it was storming, or her childish dreams proved too vivid. Mama would plunk her between the two of them and they would go back to sleep, arms around each other and her safely tucked in the middle. "We will need a softer mattress, Daniel," she said as she straightened the bedcovers that were already stretched taut as new rope. Mama could send her quilts from home, and rag rugs. It would be as close as she could get to Nantucket.

She was sitting on the second floor landing by the stairs, dusting between the railings, when she heard the crunch of gravel in the front drive. She frowned. The Paiges must have forgotten their list, she thought as she returned to her work, humming to herself. The front door opened and she peered down the steps.

It was Captain Spark. She set down the dust cloth and brushed her hair back from her face, her heart lively with greeting. Her first instinct was to leap to her feet and hurl herself down the stairs and into his arms, but she sat where she was, relishing the rare opportunity to observe him unawares.

As she watched, the smile left her face. She folded her hands in her lap as he took off his tall hat, sighed audibly as he ran his fingers through his curly hair, and set the hat on the hall table. He picked up the mail on the silver tray, but his eyes did not seem to be seeing any of it. She leaned closer for a better glimpse of his face and held her breath at the way his mouth turned down and his whole body seemed to droop as though his cloak were too heavy for his shoulders.

He just stood there, staring at the mail, making no move to look about for her, or call her name. It was as though he did not expect to find her there. My dear, I would never leave you, she thought. She almost called to him, but there was something different about him that stopped the loving words in her throat. She could never have expressed her concern in words; it was more a feeling that something was terribly wrong.

She held her breath and waited for him to call her name. In another moment he had slung off the boat cloak to join the hat on the table, then carried the mail down the hall to the bookroom, where he closed the door behind him. A door seemed to slam in her heart, and she did not know why. She got to her feet and hurried down the stairs.

He must have heard her on the stairs, because the bookroom door opened and he stood there. His eyes brightened when he saw her, but he did not raise his arms to welcome her into them. She stood before him then put her arms around his neck and pulled him toward her in a fierce embrace. His arms went around her then, and he returned her kiss as though he could not help himself. Her fingers were in his hair then, tugging at it as he kissed her until she was breathless.

"Welcome home," she said when she could speak. She released her grip on his hair, looked into his eyes, and still did not care for what she saw there. If he was her mirror, there was no reflection this time.

"I didn't know if you would be here, not after that dreadful way I left," he said.

"Thee cannot be serious, my love," she chided. "I will never leave thee."

He sighed again, left her embrace, and leaned against the door frame. "It wasn't nice of me."

"No," she agreed, "but I am made of sterner stuff." She touched his stomach playfully and blushed when he pulled away from her teasing fingers, as though she were taking liberties not hers. "Thee knows that about me already."

"So you are made of sterner stuff? Hold that thought my dear," he said enigmatically. He inclined his head toward the front entrance. "I think I hear the Paiges. I passed them on the way home." Hannah held her breath, dreading that sound of relief in his voice, as though he did not wish to be one more minute alone with her. "They went into town to buy some paint, Daniel." She tried to smile, but it was a failed attempt.

"I ... I ... have ordered some paint for the breakfast room, parlor, and your room."

"Did you? Hannah ..." he began, and then shook his head. He was silent, as if waiting for the Paiges to hurry inside and spare him the pain of conversation with her.

"It can keep," she said softly. "Thee must be tired."

"I am," he said. "More than you know."

The Paiges came into the front hallway then, full of greetings and questions about his new commerce raider. Then Daniel and Mr. Paige were deep in discussion about the estate, and the harvest, and anything that would keep him away from her, Hannah thought as she stood in the hallway and heard her heart breaking.

Dinner was a dreadful affair, full of jovial conversation with the Paiges, whom he had invited to dine with them. "For propriety's sake," he assured her, "now that my mother has beat a retreat back to the fleshpots of London." But it was more than that, and she knew it, as he laughed and shared stories of the *Clarion,* and spoke of the coming winter on the blockade as though he looked forward to it. Mr. Paige delved deep into the conversation, but Mrs. Paige gradually dropped out, her eyes turning more and more to Hannah, a question in them.

We must talk, she thought as she pushed Mrs. Paige's delicious dinner around her plate without the energy to see it to her lips. Please, Mrs. Paige, get your husband out of here.

The housekeeper seemed to know her thoughts. "Come, husband, you may help me with the dishes tonight, since I let the scullery maid visit her sister. Hannah has many plans to share with her captain."

Daniel shook his head. "Oh, not tonight. I have a head this big from too much rum last night. Hannah, please excuse me, but I am off to bed. We can talk in the morning. Good night."

He left the table without a backward glance. She sat, stricken with anguish in the dining room, until she heard his slow footsteps on the stair and the closing of his door down the hall.

The Paiges looked at each other, then at Hannah. Mr. Paige began to gather the plates together.

Mrs. Paige came to sit beside Hannah, and leaned closer, her voice low. "My dear, I would never breathe a word if you decided to go to his room to talk to him, and neither would Mr. Paige." She grasped Hannah's hand. "What could be wrong?"

"I cannot imagine," Hannah said. "He seems like a different person." She rose slowly to her feet, as if infected with the same lethargy that had overtaken Daniel Spark. "Good night."

She went to her room, unable to face the closed door to Spark's room that seemed almost like a reproach. She sat on her bed for a long time, as if unable to remember what she should do next. Oh, yes, it is night, she thought finally. I take off my clothes, get into my nightgown, say my prayers, and get into bed.

Still she sat, helpless to do anything but dwell on dread that deepened by the moment. Only the greatest force of will compelled her to prepare for bed. It was useless to pray; her mind was a great blank that the Lord would not appreciate. She crawled between the covers and shivered there, wishing for a warming pan, wishing for her own bed at home, with its familiar lumps, wondering why she had ever imagined herself in Daniel's hard bed. Sleep seemed farther away than America. She heard the clock strike midnight and then one, before her eyes closed.

She woke toward morning to the sound of her door opening, and sat up, her heart in her throat. The room was dark, but she knew it was Daniel.

"It cannot wait until morning, Hannah," he said.

Sleep was gone in an instant. "Come here, Daniel," she said, and held out her hand to him.

"No. I will sit here in the window," he said. The curtains rustled, and then she saw him silhouetted in the faint moonlight, his face away from her, not even able to look at her in the darkness.

"May I at least join you there?" she asked, struggling and failing to keep the desperation from her voice.

"No."

The silence stretched into next week and she wanted to scream. She picked her words carefully. "My love, I really am not upset about the engagement party. Thee told me about the fortunes of war, and I do understand."

"I wish you were not so reasonable, Hannah," he burst out, loud enough to make her jump. "It would make what I have to say so much easier for both of us."

"Then don't say it," she said, leaving her bed to stand by him in the moonlight.

"Go back to bed, Hannah. You'll catch your death on this cold floor." His voice was sharp and she thought of the quarterdeck.

"Very well, but only if thee tells me plain what is the matter."

He got up then to turn his back on her and gaze out into the fading moonlight, his feet planted wide apart as though the room pitched. "I have booked passage for you on the *Bonny Jean,* bound for Boston. It sails from Portsmouth in two days."

"No."

He did not turn around at her soft-voiced protest. His own words seemed to drag out of his throat with all the slowness of a nightmare. "I tore up the writ of chancery and returned the special license. I am breaking our engagement."

"No." It was as though she could say nothing else.

"You are welcome to tell people that you broke the engagement I wouldn't for the world make you an object of anyone's derision."

"No." Her lips felt numb; she couldn't even discern a heartbeat in her breast anymore. "I love thee. We are to be married."

He turned to face her then, sat on the bed, and took her hand between his hands. "You're not hearing a thing I am saying, are you? I will not marry you. Not now, and not later."

She broke free from his grasp and covered her face with her

hands, willing herself not to cry. "I love you, Daniel Spark. I will have no other man."

He got up then and stood by her bed, looking down at her. "Of course you will, Hannah," he said, with just a trace of humor in his voice. "You're just a baby."

She leaped up again to stand next to him. "I am a woman, Daniel Spark, and thee knows it. Thee will have to do better than that." She was shouting now, but she did not care. "Thee will have to tell me plain that thee does not love me."

He took her face between his hands, and she held her breath, hoping.

"I do not love you, Hannah Whittier," he told her, saying each word distinctly, as though he spoke to a child just learning speech. "You are young, and silly, and impulsive, and a dreadful nuisance. I cannot imagine what I was thinking." His voice rose, too. "I do not love you! Is that enough?"

He released her and she stepped back, her whole body limp. She dragged herself back into bed, pulled the covers up, and turned her face to the wall.

"It is enough."

"Good night, then. I'll see to a post chaise for you in the morning."

He closed the door behind him and left her to the most acute misery she could imagine, an agony almost physical that raked against every nerve in her body like a harrow over winter stubble. It was shame, humiliation, embarrassment, regret, horror, and bitterness all rolled into one terrible blow that struck at her heart and left her bleeding from unseen wounds. She could only lie there and suffer as though from a mortal blow that struck her again and again, pulling no punches.

She lay there, her hands in tight fists, willing herself dead. In a terrible flash, she understood finally why Andrew Lease could drop a lighted match in his medicine satchel filled with gunpowder. Love gone was deadly pain, and she groaned as it bowed her to the ground. She waited for death to release her, but it did not. After a time, the pain was augmented by the most exquisite urge to flee from Daniel Spark's house, even if she had to walk all the way to Portsmouth.

She was out of bed then and in the dressing room, reaching with numb fingers for her dressing case. She only needed a few dresses, a nightgown, and a cloak for the journey. In a moment, she was dressed warmly and the dressing case was full, but not too full. She could carry it across the fields until she came to the village and the mail coach that stopped early in front of the inn.

She started to draw on her gloves, then looked around the room again and stopped to make her bed. Thee is not entirely dead to duty, Hannah Whittier, even if thee is silly and impulsive and a dreadful nuisance. Shark chum. She covered her mouth with her hand, wishing she were outside so she could throw up into the bushes and be done with it. She fought down the nausea and pulled on her gloves.

She left her door open, fearing to make any more noise than needful. She knew the stairs well enough to skip the squeaky treads. She had trouble lighting a candle in the bookroom because her hands would not stop shaking, but she finally managed to put the match to the wick. Using the tiny light, she found the pile of coins that Daniel was accumulating in a jar by the window. It would be enough for the mail coach, and he said he had already booked passage, so she need not fear that expense.

Dawn was coming as she let herself out of the house. She traveled the lane swiftly, looking back once, and then turning away as tears finally blurred her eyes. Thee cannot cry, she told herself over and over, and it became the cadence that got her across Daniel Spark's fields ripe for harvest, to the village, and onto the mail coach bound for Portsmouth.

To her inexpressible agony, Portsmouth next day was full of naval officers in uniform. To her further distress, one of them was Mr. Futtrell. The distress lasted only long enough for him to call her name in surprise. For the second time in her life, she fell into his arms, but this was different from Lisbon. Her tears wouldn't come, and she could only shiver and shake her head at his questions. She finally managed to gasp, "He told me he doesn't love me."

Mr. Futtrell stared at her, his eyes wide with disbelief, then gathered her close. "I told him it was no life for a woman," he said finally, his voice filled with remorse. "I am sorry. Hannah."

She stood in his embrace until she felt strong enough to remain on her feet by herself. "I am to sail on the *Bonny Jean.* Can you take me there?"

He took her dressing case in one hand and tucked her hand under his elbow. "I always seem to be rescuing you from docks," he said, and she was aware enough of what she owed him to manage the wan smile he was so desperate to see. "There you are, my dear. Come on. It's not much farther."

She almost gasped with relief to hear the stringent Yankee accent so like her own as Mr. Futtrell introduced her to Captain Josiah Trask from Boston. She must have looked as sick as she felt, because the captain took her right on board, barely giving her time to say goodbye to Mr. Futtrell.

"We'll sail tomorrow, Miss Whittier," Captain Trask said. "Tide'll be right then." He rubbed his jaw as he walked her along the dim companionway. "I can't say I'll be sorry to kiss this place goodbye. Here you are. If you need anything, just ask."

She dropped her dressing case and sank onto the narrow berth. The blanket smelled of ship's mold and wood, and very faintly of tar. The tears came then.

Chapter Seventeen

Hannah Whittier celebrated her eighteenth birthday at sea, wrapped in her cloak and sitting on the deck grating, watching the mountainous waves throw the *Bonny Jean* up and down its troughs. The other passengers were below, suffering through various levels of seasickness, and she knew the crew wondered at her endurance. She said nothing to enlighten them on her own late career with the Royal Navy.

She eyed the lookout several times, wondering what they would think if she climbed the rigging and sat there. It was far above the deck and away from everyone—not that her mind would be any clearer for its distance from others. Even after a month at sea, she could not put consecutive thoughts together without hearing Daniel Spark's carefully spaced words, "I do not love you." She dreaded sleep, because it only meant the words repeated endlessly, the articulation so relentless that it woke her, shivering, into a night sweat.

Hannah stared out at the gray water, deckled with white caps that marched in endless rows across the whole face of the ocean. I have learned so much since June, she thought. I can pick oakum, climb a rigging, spy for ships, help patch broken bodies, and I discovered that I love a man's touch. I have also learned that it may be entirely possible to die of heartbreak. She welcomed the idea, knowing it was far superior to living another sixty or seventy years without Daniel Spark. She bore him no ill will for his declaration. Obviously she had mistaken the depth of his feelings for her. He couldn't have been more plain in his rejection of her love.

And now she was eighteen. "Happy birthday, Hannah Whittier," she said. If she were home, she would have her birthday dinner served on the special red plate, and it would be all her favorite foods. She frowned. What was the meal she used to like so much? She could not remember. Papa would honor her by reading the Bible verses that told of Hannah, beloved wife of Elkanah, and mother of Samuel. *Beloved wife.* "Oh, God, I cannot bear it," she said, her voice loud. She looked around quickly, to be sure that no one heard, but her cry was carried away by the wind that blew toward England.

She followed her usual pattern and did not go below until dinner, which she ate in silence, or pushed around her plate, depending on whether she remembered to tell herself to eat. She must have forgotten to remind herself that night because Captain Trask shook his head at her. "Miss Whittier, you will waste away before we raise Boston, if that is the best you can do."

She managed a smile. "Oh, I am as healthy as a horse. I have it on good authority."

"Not if you continue your present course," he argued. "And we have another month at sea."

She went to her cabin then, grateful to close everyone out once more. Ordinarily she would go to sleep as soon as she could, hoping to outwit the nightmares. Sometimes it worked; other times she woke before light, her cheeks wet with tears. Tonight would be different, she told herself. She had planned a special event for her birthday.

The letter from Daniel Spark had come just before the *Bonny*

Jean prepared to tack from Portsmouth Harbor. Someone pushed it under her door as she lay in the berth, staring with dull eyes at the deck above. She recognized Daniel's precise handwriting, small and up and down from years of writing cramped log entries. She made no move to pick up the letter; several days passed before she did more than walk over it on her way to and from the main deck. When she finally retrieved the letter, she debated one entire evening whether to throw it overboard, then decided against it. That would require the effort of going on deck again, and she was weary. She tucked it in her dressing case under her clothes and out of sight. Perhaps in years distant from this one she would look at the envelope and use it as a good lesson in not making mountains out of molehills, if she really needed any reminders. She knew she would never open it. That kind of pain went beyond anything she had the stomach for.

But as each day dissolved into another one like it, her curiosity grew. She felt anger at first, rage so strong that it left her shaken, when she considered that he felt it necessary to smite her again, this time with words on paper. This emotion was followed by sorrow that he thought her so dense that she needed further explanation. As her birthday neared, she decided she would read the letter, reasoning that it was impossible to feel any worse than she already did. Perhaps if she could begin to make fun of her own folly, she would recover eventually.

She took out the much-trampled letter and placed it on her pillow, then turned away, her hands over her eyes, as she remembered his head on her pillow once. After a few minutes, she took a deep breath, sat down in the berth, and picked up the letter. The wax seal was already shattered from all the times she had trod on it. She drew out the letter and held it until the cabin grew so dark that she had to light the lamp.By the unstable tight of the swaying lamp, she opened the pages and spread them out. Her heart stopped in her breast as she stared at the salutation. "Daniel, what has thee done?" she whispered. She held the letter closer, reading out loud.

"Beloved," she began, her lips scarcely able to form the word. "If I know you as well as I think I do, you are somewhere in the middle of the Atlantic right now, and you have deliberated for some weeks on whether to read this."

She looked up from the words. Daniel, thee knows me too well. She looked back at the letter and continued. "Of course, any other woman would have thrown this overboard. Hannah, I am relying upon the fact that you are not like any other woman."

Of course I am not, she thought, a wooden smile on her lips. Any other woman would not have flung herself so trustingly at thee. Any other woman would have known better than to believe thee. Put it down to my youth.

"My conduct last night was inexcusable," she continued, and nodded in agreement, "but if it had not been dark I could not have said such hurtful things to you. You would have known I did not mean them." She paused again, feeling an odd buoyancy that bumped against the wall of pain that had formed around her heart. She pulled the letter closer to her eyes, wishing that the sea would be still for a moment so the lamp would stop swaying.

"As I went about refitting the *Clarion* in Portsmouth, you were never far from my thoughts. In fact, you consumed me. It's hard to argue with a harbor master over kegs of salt beef when all you want to do is hurry home and make ferocious love to the woman there."

"Daniel," she said out loud. Her hands started to shake and she could not read the words until she composed herself. "My dilemma is this, beloved. I began to think about your list again, especially that part that seems to be causing us such grief right now. Do I need to write it? *He will place my welfare above his own.*"

Why did I ever tell him about that? she asked herself for the thousandth time. Why did I ever think that I could list the qualities of the man I would marry? Was I so stupid once? She returned to the letter.

"Late one night, when I should have been reconciling the ship's manifest, it occurred to me that you had created, with that single, innocent stipulation, a dreadful conundrum. It is this: if you place my welfare above your own, you will marry me, because I need you so badly. But if I place your welfare above my own, I will not marry you."

"My God!" The words were torn from her lips as she leaped to her feet and threw the letter across the cabin. Just as quickly she dropped to her hands and knees to retrieve it, sitting on the deck because her legs had not the strength to help her rise.

"I belong to the most suicidal of professions, even in peacetime," she read. "You know, as few women do, how doubly dangerous it is during war. I've already outlived the normal life span of a man so long at sea. Every voyage now is like fluttering a red flag in the path of death. I cannot be so callous with your heart, my love. It is because I love you so much that I cannot marry you. I have truly placed your welfare before my own, and this, I believe, is what any woman needs."

"Then I was a fool, Daniel," she whispered. "Why can't thee be selfish, like other men?"

She dragged her eyes back to the page. "I hope you will marry someone else, Hannah," she read. "Whatever you do, and wherever the years take you, please know there was a man who loved you too much to marry you. Yours, now and always, Daniel."

Hannah sat where she was, far beyond tears. "Thee has met the only stipulation that matters," she said, staring down at the letter, "and look what it has done to us!"

The *Bonny Jean* docked in Boston's crowded harbor a month later, in the middle of a snowstorm. She allowed Captain Trask to escort her to Charleston to the house of her uncle, who stared at her as though she had risen from the dead, and then held her in a tight embrace. "My brother will be so pleased thee came to thy senses and did not remain in England," he said when he could speak. She was up most of the night, telling them the story of the *Dissuade*, the fight with the *Bergeron,* and her narrow escape from matrimony. She had not the strength to tell the whole story; that would keep for Mama's ears alone.

In the morning, in a thicker cloak, and with a footwarmer at her toes, she kissed the Whittiers goodbye and went on to Nantucket, where she arrived as night was falling. She was the first person off the ferry and had to be reminded to return and retrieve her dressing case. She smiled her thanks to the ferryman, crossed the gangplank, and found herself on firm ground again. Where I will stay, she told herself, ignoring the pain that washed over her because she was used to it now.

She thought she would remain unnoticed as she hurried through the snow toward Orange Street, but one man on horseback—was it the postmaster?—recognized her and spurred his horse ahead. When she turned onto her street, Mama was running from the front door, her arms open wide, Papa right behind. With a cry of her own, she dropped her dressing case and was swallowed up in their embrace.

She was too tired to tell the story all over again, but she did, tucked up in her own under the eaves with Mama holding her hand, and Papa seated close by on a stool. "He broke the engagement, so I came home," she concluded, looking at her father. She knew better than to look at Mama, who would know there was more, much more, to the story. Papa was content that she had come to her senses. Trust him, by the end of the month, to set forth any number of ideas on a more suitable husband, she thought as she watched the relief settle over his features.

"My little daughter has returned," he said and kissed her cheek. "Mama, let us leave her alone to sleep now." He touched her under the chin, in a familiar gesture from her childhood.

"Think how many people will want to hear this story again!"

She sighed. "Is Adam Winslow about?" she asked.

Papa shook his head. "He is in the Caribbean serving as number one on his uncle's brig." He rubbed his chin. "Whatever deficiencies Captain Spark may have as a lover, he certainly taught Adam seamanship! I think if you send Hosea a letter, he will see that Adam gets it when they return from Barbados."

"I will do it tomorrow."

Mama kissed her fingers, but did not let go of her hand. "Thee will do it when thee feels like it." She looked up at her husband. "My dear, I will be along in a moment."

He left them then, closing the door quietly. Hannah stared straight ahead until Mama took her by the chin and gently turned her face toward the light.

"I do not believe for a single instant that what thee has told us any resemblance to the actual facts," she said, her voice soft, her eyes concerned. "Adam told us how much the captain loves thee. What has happened? Can thee tell me?"

Hannah shook her head. "It can wait until morning, Mama." She down in the bed and closed her eyes. "I am not going anywhere."

When Papa left for the store in the morning to sell a little merchandise and spread the news of her return among all his customers, Mama climbed the stairs to Hannah's bedroom and refused to leave until Hannah had poured out her whole misery into her lap. Mama's fingers shook, too, as she read Daniel Spark's letter. A thoughtful look on her face, she set it aside and took herself to the window.

"Thee must write to him, Hannah. Thee must tell him …."

"Tell him what, Mama?" Hannah interrupted. "That I cannot live without him? I was willing to give up everything I hold dear for him, and it was not enough. No, Mama, I will not write to him. I will forget him."

"Can thee?" Mama asked. I do not think thee can."

"I have to," Hannah replied.

Mama looked at her for a long moment, then kissed her. "Very well, Hannah. Thee can try."

She did try, and it was a wonderful act that fooled almost everyone. Hannah made herself eat, but it all tasted the same. By sheer force of will she put on weight until her clothes fit again. While Mama was pleased by this outward sign of recovery, she was not content, and told her so one snowy day in January while they kneaded bread on the kitchen table. "Hannah, thee could almost pull off this deception but for one thing," she mentioned casually as Hannah greased the bread pans and stared out the window at the icicles that hung just above the ground.

"Thee said something?" Hannah asked, and then realized that her mother had caught her.

"Precisely, my dear. Thee hears not above one word in ten, and if thee does not go to the east window to stand all evening tonight, as thee has done since returning, I will be amazed!"

Hannah said nothing.

"Why the east window, my dear?" Mama asked. 'The view is nothing but Godspeed Wilkins' front door."

Hannah set down the bread pan. "Because it faces toward England. And if I turn a little south, then I can imagine Daniel cruising off France or Spain. I know it is cold on the blockade. I hope he is warmly dressed." Her voice was breathless, as though she disclosed too much for her own comfort. Without another word, she lifted her cloak from the hook by the back door and let herself out into the snowy afternoon. She walked to the end of the kitchen garden, ragged now, snow-covered, empty of fruit, bereft of yield. Almost like me, she thought as she stared at the empty cornstalks and listened to them crackle against each other. If thee had married me, Daniel, I would probably be carrying thy child by now. I would have taken such care of this evidence of thy love, and when thee returned from the blockade, we would have such joy.

She smiled bleakly to herself. And now I talk to cornstalks, and stare out east windows, and ignore Mama's conversation. I wish spring would come. Perhaps Hosea will want me to come to Charleston this year. I could help with the little one, and perhaps the sailmaker is still single. But this time I will travel overland to Charleston, and not by water. Never by water again. And if I am truly careful, whoever I marry will never know how much I ache inside. Only Mama will know.

It was useless to pretend to Mama now, so she dropped all her attempts. If it caused Papa pain to see her stand by the window night after night, or shake her head over food that held no interest for her, she was sorry, but it could not be helped. She worked in the kitchen in silence, and watched the icicles gradually grow shorter. Then the day came when they dripped steadily, and disappeared. Spring was here.

"Papa, I would like to go to Charleston," she announced over dinner one night when the sky was still light with spring, and the front door open to the smell of lilacs all over Nantucket. "Can thee book me passage on a mail coach?"

"Of course I can, Daughter," he said, his face lighting up with love for her, and anxiety that went deeper than concern. "You mean to visit Hosea?"

She nodded and smiled. "I think I am overdue there, and I did promise his wife that I would help with the baby."

"It seems so long ago," he said, his voice wistful.

"It is so long ago," she agreed. "But I am not dead to duty, Papa! I still should get to Charleston."

When she left the next week, Mama clung to her longer than usual as she kissed her goodbye. Hannah laughed and tried to pull away from the strength of her mother's embrace. "I will be back!"

"I do not think I will see thee soon," Mama said, and her lips trembled. "But if I do not, please know I love thee and all thy decisions. God keep thee, Hannah Whittier."

It gave her food for thought as the mail coach rolled through the spring morning toward Boston, and something to think about beside Daniel Spark for a change. I must write Papa and tell him to keep an eye on Mama, she resolved.

Boston became New York, and then New Jersey, and then Pennsylvania as April slipped into May as they traveled south. The road was terrible in places, and merely dreadful in others, necessitating frequent layovers that stretched the limits of everyone's equanimity except Hannah's. Each day was much like the next to her, she reflected as she watched the other riders so impatient over delays. I am going nowhere to see no one, really, so what is another day on the road?

Virginia bloomed with dogwood and hawthorn. She breathed deep of the scented air and felt peace settle over her for a moment. It went away quickly enough, but it was nice to know she could feel something still.

They rolled into Richmond for the noon meal, and the food was better than usual. No matter how good the food, she did not dawdle over it. A veteran of the coach by now, she was first back to the coach so she could claim a seat by the window. She looked out with interest, wishing she knew which house belonged to John Marshall, Chief Justice of the Supreme Court, and one of Papa's heroes. And was that the spire to St. John's Church, where Patrick Henry had spoken of liberty or death?

"Pardon me, Lady Amber, but is this seat taken?'

Her heart stopped, then started again. She continued to stare out the window, but she wasn't seeing anything this time. Her breath came in little gasps and she felt herself getting light in the head.

"The last time you did that you were watching a flogging, and I distinctly remember pushing your head between your knees, Hannah. I'll do it again if I have to."

"Say my name again," she said, her voice almost inaudible to her ears.

"Hannah." It was a caress.

She turned from her stare out the window to see Daniel Spark smiling down at her. He took off his hat, an elegant low-crowned beaver hat, and waited for her response.

"Pl-Please sit down," she stammered. "I know there are others, but I am sure there will be room for ...." Her voice trailed off as she stared at him.

"Excellent!" He sat next to her and tapped on the side of the coach with his walking stick. She heard the whip crack as the coach sprang forward.

Hannah half rose in her seat to look out the window. "But ... the others!" she exclaimed.

"I have paid them a ridiculous sum of money to remain behind and wait for the coach I was following you in to change horses," he explained, sounding perfectly reasonable. "They were a bit disagreeable at first, even with all that money, until I told them it was a matter of the heart." He took her hand and twined his fingers through hers, pulling her back down beside him. "Americans are so absurd."

Hannah rose in stupefied silence, looking down once to make sure that it was Daniel Spark's hand she held, and that her wits had not finally wandered away for good. "It's your hand," she mumbled. "I'd recognize it anywhere."

"Well, yes. It's attached eventually to a shoulder that really cries out to be leaned upon. Ah, excellent, my dear. Actually, if you don't mind too much impertinence so soon after lunch, I would rather put my arm around you. I seem to recall that you fit so well there. Better and better."

It required no great strength of will to slip her arm around behind him, and he smiled as she patted him to make sure he was real. "It's really me. Hannah." he insisted. "If you have any doubts ...." He kissed her then, pulling her onto his lap as the coach rolled along through some of Virginia's prettiest unappreciated scenery. One kiss led to another, and another, until she was rosy with whisker burn. He stopped finally to rub his chin. "I've been traveling some pretty terrible roads to catch up with you," he said. "That last inn ran out of hot water before I could even lather up." He touched her red cheek. "You should have told me I was hurting you." He grinned. "If I was."

She did not waste time with words, but kissed him instead until he was breathless and breathing hard. Then she held herself off from him and gently touched his face with the back of her hand. The little gesture sent tears to his eyes. "I am not going to disappear, Hannah," he managed finally.

"Thee did before," she reminded him as she arranged herself more comfortably on his lap.

"I was a damned fool," he replied, placing his hand possessively on her hip. "Your mother pointed that out to me in her letter."

"Her letter ...." Hannah began. Her eyes widened. "My mother wrote thee a letter?"

"Well, to be more specific, she sent copies of the same letter to the Blockade Fleet, the Admiralty House, my brother's estate in Kent, my home in Dorset, Mama's town house in London, and one to the Prince Regent for good measure," he said, and grinned at the startled expression she knew was on her own face. He hugged her close. "I wonder ... I must ask her someday if she sent one to Napoleon, on the odd chance that I was languishing in one of his prisons awaiting execution."

"Did you keep a copy?" Hannah asked.

"I have the one from the Blockade Fleet." He tugged off her bonnet and tossed it across the coach. "It's such a hindrance to fine kissing, Hannah. I have it on good authority that the other letters are on their way to becoming collectors' items. Lord Tichenor says he will only relinquish his to our first son who serves in the navy."

She took in that piece of news and allowed him to lean forward and rest his head against her breasts. "Hannah, she told me plainly that if I wanted to be noble and self-sacrificing, I was to do it with someone else's daughter."

"Mama wouldn't say boo to a goose," Hannah marveled, unbuttoning her pelisse so the buttons would not dig into his face as he rested against her.

"Well, she did, and so did your father, when I met them in Nantucket a month ago!" he said.

"You didn't!"

"I did! How do you think I knew where you were?"

"Was I hard to find?"

He kissed her. "You would ask such a question of the man who raised the Azores in a fog bank from the deck of a sinking ship? Of course, I did have to stop in Washington." He winced at the memory. "I would blush to call it a capital city, but Lord Erskine, our ambassador, assures me that it will improve. Hannah, those pigs in the streets really must go."

"Washington?" she asked. The mail coach was getting so warm that she removed her pelisse entirely.

"Yes, my love. Which reminds me ...." He set her carefully off his lap and rapped on the side of the coach again. It rolled to a stop and he opened the door. "Sir, perhaps you would turn this vehicle back to the District of Columbia?"

In another moment they had started back up the road they had just traveled. "Lord Erskine assured me that he could take care of any legalities concerned with our marriage, and I have a notarized letter in my pocket from your father, giving his consent to our nuptials. I think all that remains is for us to collect the documents from Lord Erskine this afternoon and present our bodies before some magistrate and say 'Yes,' or 'Hell, yes,' or maybe 'It's high time.' "

"Daniel, I love thee," she said softly.

"I know, my love, I know," he whispered as he pulled her close again. "My feelings are precisely as I expressed in that letter. I still love you too much to marry you, but it seems the entire Royal navy, my regent, and my relatives will flog me around the fleet if I cannot come up to scratch and do my duty."

"Not to mention my mother," she added. Her hands trembled as she cupped them about his face and looked deep into his eyes. "I know exactly what I am getting into. I can wait in

Dorset for the war to end, but when it does, thee must promise me to leave the sea for good."

"Done, madam," he said and turned his face to seal the promise with a kiss in each palm. "After we return to Dorset, it's back to the blockade for me. We're in for some rough years yet ...."

She put her finger to his lips and shook her head. "They will be years thee will look back on with great joy, my love. I can make that happen for thee, and thee for me."

"Done again, madam," he said as tears shone on his cheeks. "Promise me one thing, though."

"Yes?" she asked as she wiped his face with her sleeve.

"No more lists, my love. Well, nothing beyond shopping lists for trips into the village, or perhaps Christmas presents."

Her arms were around his neck then, her lips against his. "Thee won't mind if I write over and over, 'Hannah loves Daniel'?"

"Hannah," he said, and it said the world.

Conversation seemed as much an encumbrance as her bonnet and pelisse that they dispensed with it for a lengthy spell. When they finally decided that words might be better, considering that they hadn't actually married each other yet, Hannah sat up and smiled into her dear love's somewhat glazed eyes. "Tell me something, Daniel."

"Anything," he murmured as he rebuttoned her dress.

"Does thee have something against the South?"

He looked at her, a question in his eyes.

"It seems that in the company of the Royal Navy, I am doomed never to see Charleston!"

A well-known veteran of the romance writing field, **Carla Kelly** is the author of twenty-six novels and three non-fiction works, as well as numerous short stories and articles for various publications. She is the recipient of two RITA Awards from Romance Writers of America for Best Regency of the Year; two Spur Awards from Western Writers of America; a Whitney Award for Best Romance Fiction, 2011; and a Lifetime Achievement Award from Romantic Times.

Carla's interest in historical fiction is a byproduct of her lifelong interest in history. She has a BA in Latin American

History from Brigham Young University and an MA in Indian Wars History from University of Louisiana-Monroe. She's held a variety of jobs, including public relations work for major hospitals and hospices, feature writer and columnist for a North Dakota daily newspaper, and ranger in the National Park Service (her favorite job) at Fort Laramie National Historic Site and Fort Union Trading Post National Historic Site. She has worked for the North Dakota Historical Society as a contract researcher. Interest in the Napoleonic Wars at sea led to a recent series of novels about the British Channel Fleet during that conflict.

Of late, Carla has written two novels set in southeast Wyoming in 1910 that focus on her Mormon background and her interest in ranching.

You can find Carla on the Web at:

www.CarlaKellyAuthor.com.

Made in the USA
Charleston, SC
23 February 2014